THE AGE OF TREACHERY

GAVIN SCOTT

THE AGE OF TREACHERY

A DUNCAN FORRESTER MYSTERY

TITAN BOOKS

The Age of Treachery
Print edition ISBN: 9781783297801
E-book edition ISBN: 9781783297818

Published by Titan Books
A division of Titan Publishing Group Ltd
144 Southwark Street, London SE1 0UP

First edition: April 2016
10 9 8 7 6 5 4 3 2 1

A CIP catalogue record for this title is available from the British Library.

Printed and bound by CPI Group (UK) Ltd, Croydon, CR0 4YY

TO NICOLA, REBECCA, LAURA AND CHLOE

1

THREE LUMPS OF COAL

SUNDAY, 13 JANUARY 1946

The snow had been falling since noon, and Duncan Forrester brushed urgently at the stone bench to clear a space to sit down before the vertigo overcame him. The spinning sensation continued for a moment, but then silence began to seep in and he felt his heart slow.

The buildings around St. Mary the Virgin were mostly Baroque, and the snow was piling deep on their window ledges. The church and its adjoining houses shut the churchyard off from the bustle of the city, and Forrester felt as if he was in a tiny clearing in a dense, silent wood.

There were few cars in Oxford just after the war, and little fuel for them anyway, so what noise there was mostly came from footsteps in the street beyond, and even they were muffled. As the snow came down and the light leaked out of the afternoon sky, he closed his eyes and waited for the demons to slip away into the gloom.

He could not banish them; he'd tried that. He could

only let the images rise to the surface unopposed. He felt the familiar wave of nausea but he forced himself to ride it, reminding himself this was not reality: it would fade.

He felt again the peculiar gliding sensation as the knife passed through the cartilage of the sentry's throat; he smelt the youth's skin as he gripped him, and then the warmth of the blood as it poured over his fingers and the body slid down to his feet, looking up at him with mildly reproachful eyes. Forrester guessed he was about seventeen. As the sentry died Forrester could see, through the archway leading to the castle courtyard, SS guards taking the prisoners into the basement.

There were many such images. He let them unreel at their own speed.

He saw Barbara again too, that last time at Waterloo Station, and the look in her eyes that made him think of Arctic winds blowing over the ice.

He did not see the man watching him from the tall, unlit window of the vicarage, but the watcher noted the set of Forrester's shoulders and the tilt of his head, and long experience allowed him to infer the nature of the man's thoughts with some accuracy.

For a long time, both of them were motionless, separated by no more than fifty yards of snow and lichened stone.

Suddenly, from the archway that led to the street, Forrester heard the word "*vintersolstånd*" followed by laughter, and then a brief babble of Swedish before the speakers passed on. There were students from all over Europe in Oxford now, a flood pent up by the war, released by the peace. They were not the high young voices of his own university years, but deeper, more mature. Many of the British undergraduates were ex-servicemen, their education postponed by the conflict. They too poured in, thirsty for knowledge.

Duncan Forrester had graduated before the war began, and now, just months after the German surrender, he was back at Barnard College, Junior Research Fellow in Archaeology. But though he was still in his twenties, he felt bone tired, as if he were an old man.

He held out his hand and watched the snowflakes settle on it. As the heat of his body turned them to water, the drops rolled into his palm, forming a tiny pool. By the time he realised his hand was numb with cold he was calm again.

He paused a moment, savouring the calm, and went through the ritual. He was alive; he was in one piece; the war was over; he was back in Oxford; he was free to pursue his research. Images of Barbara came and went, but all they evoked now was remembered pain – and deep behind that, remembered joy, like a distant Eden.

The man in the window watched as Forrester rose to his feet, shook the snow off him, tightened the belt of his British Warm overcoat, headed back through the archway into the street, and disappeared. Only then did the watcher switch on the light inside the room, letting it spill over the empty churchyard like liquid gold. Moments later he closed the curtains, plunging the enclosure back into the afternoon half-light.

Among the crowds in the street, Forrester felt almost normal again, just one of the many going to the shops on their way home from work. Not that there was much to buy, for this was austerity Britain, a victorious nation ruined by the struggle for victory. CADBURY'S MILK CHOCOLATE IS THE BEST proclaimed a poster showing the familiar purple and gold wrapper so evocative of pre-war pleasures. Then in smaller letters below: "Unfortunately we are only allowed enough milk to make extremely small quantities of our famous product, so if you are lucky enough to get some, do save it for the children."

But Forrester, who had not seen a piece of chocolate for at least a year, knew no children to save it for. He glanced into the brightly lit interior of Woolworths, an Aladdin's cave of gaudy trinkets before the war, now full of half-empty glass counter-trays scattered with a sparse collection of wooden pegs, darning needles and penny notebooks. Outside a grocery shop a notice announced a limited supply of dried egg powder and a queue was already forming. For most of the war people had had to rely on the hated dried eggs instead of the real thing. Cakes made with egg powder had the texture of old cement; when mixed with water and fried, the powder turned into luridly yellow leather pancakes. And then, with victory, not only did fresh eggs not reappear but even dried egg powder had vanished; unavailable until Britain could borrow more money from the Americans. So women were now lining up patiently with their string bags, shivering in the cold, desperate for a product they had despised for five years.

And this was what happened when you won.

A woman darted out of the queue – which closed up immediately behind her – and ran towards Forrester. Her name was Margaret Clark, she worked at the Bodleian Library, and in his eyes she was the most desirable woman in Oxford; a thought he tried to suppress because she was also the wife of his closest friend. And though her eyes were bright with affection, he knew the affection wasn't for him – her gaze was fixed on someone on the far side of the road.

As a result of which, as she stepped off the kerb it was into the path of an oncoming bus.

Forrester shouted a useless warning as the bus swerved and sent up a spray of grey slush. The slush momentarily blinded him and when he had wiped it from his eyes the bus was gone and so was she. But to his astonishment no blood stained the snow; no crushed body lay in the road. The bus had missed her. He peered at the crowd across the road but she had vanished as if she had never been.

"Got something for you, Dr. Forrester," said Harrison, materialising at his elbow, a pipe clamped between his teeth. Forrester forced himself to concentrate.

"Delian League?"

"Oh, that," said the student, dismissively. "No, much better." Ken Harrison was a cheerful, stocky former Signals Corps lieutenant of twenty-four, who had been trying furiously to get a faulty field radio to work when he was captured at Arnhem and taken as a POW to Germany, an experience which seemed to have left no mark at all on his sunny disposition. Forrester was tutoring him in Greek history.

"Better than one of your essays?" said Forrester.

"That wouldn't be hard," said Harrison equably. Both he and Forrester were well aware that Harrison's disquisitions on the Golden Age scaled no heights of brilliance, but Harrison was as unperturbed about that as he seemed to be about all the vicissitudes life threw his way.

They passed under the worn stone archway of Barnard College, past the porter's cubbyhole with its tabby cat and ticking clock and pigeonholes full of messages, and entered the first quadrangle. The snow lay thick on the famous lawn and the Great Hall and the Lady Tower, festooned with scaffolding where builders, under the impatient supervision of Deputy Bursar Alan Norton, were slowly – very slowly – repairing the damage done when it had been an air raid warden's observation post during the war. Undergraduates and fellows hurried back to their rooms along the cloisters as the light dimmed and the afternoon turned to evening.

Forrester and Harrison scraped the snow off their feet and clumped up the narrow wooden stairs to Forrester's rooms. The air struck cold as Forrester knelt down by the fireplace and fiddled with his matches; Harrison reached into the canvas army satchel he used as a book bag, pulled out something wrapped in newspaper and gave it to his tutor. Forrester read the headline as he unwrapped the paper.

ALBANIA GOES COMMUNIST. WHO'S NEXT?

Inside were three lumps of coal.

"Where did you get these?" Forrester said, and immediately added, "Actually, better not tell me," and put the lumps on the fire. "But it's very kind of you. Thanks."

Coal was another item Forrester had not seen enough of

since he came back from the war. But Harrison had a knack for getting his hands on these things. Perhaps that was what he had learnt in the German camps.

They both kept their coats on in the frigid air as the kindling flamed up and Harrison took out his essay and began to read. By the time the flames were sending out any heat both men were far away, on the plains of Athens with the sun glinting off the marble of the Acropolis – and Forrester had, for the moment, forgotten all about Margaret Clark.

Outside, around the college, one window after another began to glow with yellow light, like the opening doors of an Advent calendar.

The fire was dying down by the time Harrison left, and Forrester took a shovel full of ashes and banked it down to preserve the coal. The warmth in the room would last until it was time to go to the Great Hall for the evening meal. Then he took Sir Arthur Evans' photographs from his desk drawer and began to look at them again. They were very bad photographs; or rather, infuriatingly imperfect for his purposes, showing small rectangles of clay, thickly inscribed with symbols and stick figures. Here and there he could make out a symbol that might be a horse's head, and another which looked like a double-bladed axe, but most were indecipherable. The script was known as "Linear B" and the tablets on which it was inscribed had been baked in the heat of the fire that had destroyed the palace of Knossos in Crete a thousand years before Athens rose to glory.

No-one had been able to decipher the tablets since Evans discovered them, and Forrester suspected that some of Sir Arthur's guesses had put his fellow archaeologists on the wrong track. What if, for example, the old man had been wrong about the significance of the symbol that looked like a double-bladed axe? What if it did not in fact signify a religious ritual, but was actually a phonetic indicator? He turned to the drawings Evans had made of other inscriptions, and wondered how accurate they really were.

"You're busy," said a voice. Forrester looked up to see Gordon Clark looking round his door. For a moment he was tempted to tell the Senior Tutor "I *am* a bit busy, actually, old chap," and turn back to the tablets, but when he saw Clark's white, strained face he hadn't the heart.

"Absolutely not," he said. "Come in and have some sherry."

"Thank you," said Clark, and closed the door. He entered the room nervously, glancing into the shadows as though expecting a hidden observer.

Forrester, pouring the sherry, realised the bottle was almost empty. He thought of dividing the liquid between both glasses and decided against it. With his back to Clark he filled his own glass with cold tea before he handed the full one to his friend.

"Your health," he said, and Clark nodded and sank back into a chair on one side of the fire. Forrester reached in with the poker and stirred it into life.

"Any progress?" said Clark, nodding towards the photographs spread out on Forrester's desk.

"I'm not at the progress stage yet," said Forrester. "I have to dig myself in much deeper before I can start digging my way out." He sipped his glass of cold tea with every appearance of appreciation. "I saw Margaret in Broad Street this afternoon. I think she'd just given up queuing for powdered eggs."

He waited for Clark to tell him that it was he, her husband, she'd been running across the road to see, but the Senior Tutor just nodded and looked into the fire. Finally he said, "Have you ever understood them, Forrester?" When Forrester did not reply, Clark said, "Women, I mean."

"Good Lord, no," said Forrester. It was not what he felt, it was not what he believed; but it was what Clark needed to hear. "But surely a married man has a better chance than most?"

"You'd think so, wouldn't you?" Clark sipped the sherry, but Forrester knew he could have given him the cold tea and the Senior Tutor wouldn't have noticed. Suddenly his friend looked up, his eyes hot with pain. "She used to love me, you know."

"I'm sure she still does," said Forrester, with a strange sinking feeling in his stomach.

"No," said Clark. "She's found someone else."

Again, Forrester decided silence was the best response. His own feelings for Margaret Clark made it almost impossible to make the right comforting remarks.

"And you know the worst part of it?" said Clark. "I feel... slighted—"

"Well, of course—"

"—by the man she's chosen." Forrester held his breath. "Do you know who it is?" Forrester shook his head. "David bloody Lyall."

"That's ridiculous," said Forrester, automatically, quick to cover his own swift stab of jealousy, but in truth he was not in the least surprised at Margaret Clark's choice. David Lyall was handsome, self-confident and stylish. He was ambitious and successful; he'd leapt ahead of several other abler candidates for the Priestley Latin Fellowship and was a serious contender for the Rotherfield Lectureship, but Forrester understood why Clark felt slighted: Lyall was also shallow, meretricious and glib; a showy scholar without real insight. But scholarship, of course, was not what Margaret had been looking for.

"I always used to look down on Italians, you know," said Clark. "All that passion and jealousy. It seemed so self-indulgent. But I tell you, Forrester, I could cheerfully strangle that little swine."

"Do him good," said Forrester, and despite himself, Clark laughed.

"Unfortunately they didn't teach us much about unarmed combat at Bletchley," said Clark. Forrester nodded. He knew enough about what had gone on at Bletchley to understand the intense intellectual strain Clark had been under for the last four years, his nerves strung out like a taut wire.

"As someone who was taught unarmed combat," said Forrester, "I can tell you I don't recommend its use in polite society."

"Not even in special circumstances?" asked Clark.

"This Lyall thing's an infatuation," said Forrester. "It'll pass."

"How do you know?"

"Because Lyall is a complete second-rater; you are a man of real worth and Margaret is an intelligent woman," replied Forrester decisively. "She'll see through him before long."

"And I should just hang about until she does?"

"I don't know," said Forrester. "I can't advise you there. All I'm saying is don't do anything precipitate."

"Like sticking a knife in his heart?"

"I think that would qualify as precipitate."

"I've got to sit at High Table with the swine."

"Ignore him. Sit at the other end. If you catch his eye regard him with cold contempt."

Clark grinned ruefully. "Cold contempt, eh?"

"Buckets of it. I'll do the same. He'll have cold contempt everywhere he turns."

Clark finished his glass and stood up. "Thank you, old chap," he said. "I had to tell somebody; I was going out of my bloody head."

Forrester stood up too. A bell began to toll. "Shall we go down?"

Clark hitched his gown around him. "Why not?" he said. "I've worked up quite an appetite."

2

RAGNARÖK

In the event, inevitably, the Master kept them hanging about in the Fellows' Chamber before they could go through to High Table. A giant with a face like a Viking axe was standing in the centre of the room as they entered, his sherry glass like a thimble in his massive fingers, the timbre of his thickly accented Norwegian voice so deep Forrester could swear his glass was ringing as he spoke.

"In the year of Our Lord, 998," the Norwegian was booming, "Sigrid the Strong-Minded was wooed by both Prince Weswolf and Harald Skull-Splitter, neither of whom pleased her. She took them to a beer hall, got them drunk and as they lay sleeping, set fire to the place, burning them both to death. After this only the boldest suitors approached her, which is what I think she intended."

There was a murmur of appreciative laughter, led by Professor Michael Winters. The Master of Barnard College was a plump man with a fringe of white hair around his egg-shaped cranium and a face which looked slightly too small for the size of his head, like a child's sketch painted on a balloon. He turned to Clark and Forrester, gesturing at the Norwegian. "This is Professor Arne Haraldson, from the University of Oslo," he said. "My star turn at the reading tonight. I trust you're coming?"

Forrester sighed inwardly. Winters' evenings of readings from the Icelandic epics were, for those unenthused by Dark Ages poetry, famously painful. But he liked the Master too much to let him down. "Of course, Master," he said. Clark had managed to edge away before he had to respond; Forrester knew that in Gordon's present state of mind an evening listening to tales of Vikings hacking one another to pieces was more than he could bear.

"What are your views on the links between Norse mythology and Nazism, Professor Haraldson?" Forrester turned and saw that the speaker was David Lyall. The question was typical of the man: designed largely to draw attention to the questioner.

Forrester saw a curious expression on Haraldson's face as he turned to Lyall – a flash of surprise that morphed swiftly into fury, as though someone he trusted was reneging, quite shamelessly, on a deal. For a moment Forrester expected the big man to reach out and grasp Lyall by the throat but instead, after a beat, he drew in a deep breath and smiled.

"There are no true links between Nazi fantasy and Norse mythology," he said at last, "whatever Hitler might have imagined."

"Adolf was pretty much convinced otherwise, though,

wasn't he?" Lyall persisted. "He had that mystic experience in a wood during the Great War, didn't he?" Lyall had an athlete's build, with a fine head and bright blue eyes. Forrester could see why Margaret Clark had been attracted to him.

"What 'mystic experience'?" said someone. The smile remained on Haraldson's face, but it was fixed now, his eyes hard.

"The future Führer described the scene very vividly," Lyall went on, apparently oblivious to Haraldson's anger. "It was on a hill above his line of trenches: a place he called Wotan's Glade. Apparently it was very cold, snow everywhere, and he used his bayonet to carve certain runes on a fallen log. He claimed it was there that Odin revealed his destiny to him."

"The future Führer was deluded," said Haraldson, "as the events of April last year demonstrated." It had been in the previous April, of course, that the Führer had shot himself in his Berlin bunker, and the Thousand Year Reich had come to a premature end.

"And those of us who study literature would very much prefer that those delusions should be forgotten," said Roland Bitteridge. His voice was high-pitched and unattractive, like a triangle being played after a great bell had been struck. "These fantasies have nothing to do with serious study, Dr. Lyall, as you must know."

"I couldn't say," replied Lyall. "It's not my field." He was speaking to Bitteridge, but Forrester felt, for some reason, that the remarks were still addressed to Haraldson.

The Master intervened swiftly to set the conversation in another direction.

"I have one disappointment for you this evening, I'm afraid." He paused and cleared his throat apologetically. "Professor Tolkien isn't coming." There were polite murmurs of regret from around the room. Tolkien had begun the tradition of readings from the sagas at Oxford, forming with C.S. Lewis a group known as the Coalbiters, after an Icelandic phrase referring to those who sat so close to the blazing hearth on winter evenings that they seemed to be eating the fire.

"He was supposed to be here," the Master went on, "but he's moving house and everything seems to have got into a tremendous muddle. Some manuscript he's mislaid."

"Another *Hobbit*?" Tolkien's children's book, written in the thirties, had just been republished and Forrester had seen its distinctive green and white dust jacket in Blackwell's bookshop that afternoon.

"Oh, something much bigger," said Bitteridge. "He's been trying to finish it for years – but you know what he's like. Jack Lewis will pip him at the post if he's not careful."

"I don't follow you."

"Jack's writing his own fairy stories. Dwarves and nymphs and fauns and that kind of thing. I suspect Tollers thinks it's pretty meretricious stuff, and it probably is."

"They're both looting the sagas, aren't they?" said Forrester.

"Of course," said Bitteridge. "But C.S. is writing his stuff on behalf of the Christians, and Tolkien doesn't approve of that. Can't say I blame him."

"At any rate," said a voice somewhere behind them, "it's better than writing on behalf of the Devil, isn't it?" Forrester turned to see who had spoken, but the face was lost in the crowd.

At last they went through to the Hall, built when Henry VII was on the throne, and were seated at High Table, looking down at the undergraduates watching impatiently as the food approached. The silverware sparkled in the light of the candles and the shadows they cast flickered against the great hammer beams supporting the roof. Forrester hoped the sheer familiarity of the scene gave Gordon Clark the comfort it always gave him.

Bitteridge was placed next to Haraldson, and they were deep in conversation, Forrester noted, with the Norwegian nodding vigorously as he shovelled food into his mouth. He would have looked even more at home, Forrester thought, if he'd been chewing on a leg of wild boar. Bitteridge, by contrast, merely ferried fastidiously tiny forkfuls from the plate to his thin lips.

He looked down the table towards Gordon Clark and cursed under his breath as he saw that the Senior Tutor was sitting opposite David Lyall. But of course as no-one knew about Lyall's affair with Clark's wife, no-one had thought to separate them. Forrester forced himself to listen to the languid Foreign Office man seated beside him. His name was Charles Calthrop, he had attended the college in the early thirties, been recruited into the Foreign Office when it was dominated by the appeasers and was now speaking airily of the growing Soviet domination of Eastern Europe. "Oh yes," he was saying. "Albania declared a People's Republic two days ago. It'll be the same in Hungary within the month. And then we should all look out for the Russian army marching towards us with snow on their boots."

"Is that a serious possibility?" asked Forrester.

"Of course it is," said Calthrop. "If they can't get the local communist parties to do it for them. Italy could go red any day. Look at what's happening in Greece. The fact is, if we want to keep the Russians from taking over, the Americans are our only hope."

"I don't see why you're afraid of Russia," said the man on the opposite side of the table. "Stalin saved this country during the war." The remark came from Alan Norton, X-ray crystallographer and deputy bursar, responsible for repairs to damage done to the college fabric during the late hostilities. "Hitler would be living in Buckingham Palace today if it hadn't been for the Soviets."

Calthrop favoured him with a long, amused glance.

"I can't say anything about hypothetical accommodation arrangements for the Führer," he said, "but I have to tell you that Stalin is a truly bad man."

"And you make that statement on what basis?" asked Norton.

"Meeting him," said Calthrop, mildly. "I was close enough to him at Yalta to be aware of an aura of... how shall I put this? An aura of pure evil."

Before Norton could rebut this shameless piece of one-upmanship, the balding, sandy-haired German beside him spoke up. "My own view is that the Russians have swallowed as much of Europe as their Slavic stomachs can digest."

The German's name was Peter Dorfmann, and it was rumoured that he was being groomed for power when the occupying forces set up the new, democratic Germany. Forrester wasn't clear exactly how he'd managed to remain a respected academic in the Third Reich without either joining the party or falling foul of it, but apparently he had. "Besides," said Dorfmann, "I do not believe the Russians have any desire to fight the Americans."

"The Americans," said Norton contemptuously, "are the occupying power in Europe these days. They've turned us into one big aircraft carrier."

"You're not suggesting we could have won the war without them, are you?" remarked Lyall from across the table. "I mean, were you out in the streets on D-Day saying 'Yanks go home'?"

Forrester saw Clark glance up as Lyall spoke and shot him a look that warned him to stay out of this dispute, but Norton was in full spate. "The Americans were pursuing their own interests when they finally deigned to come into the war, and that's what they'll go on doing," he said. "Anyone who thinks otherwise is naive."

"Naivety," said Lyall, as if savouring the word. "It's a wonderful word for clubbing your opponents over the head,

Alan. Much used in Party circles, I believe?"

"I'm not a member of the party," snapped Norton, "as you very well know."

"You might give that impression, though, to our guests," said Lyall, like a picador enraging a bull. There had been plenty of speculation that Norton was a communist fellow traveller.

At which point Gordon Clark could no longer resist. "I'm sure our guests don't expect to hear fellows quizzing each other about their political affiliations, Lyall," he said. "After all, this is a bastion of learning, not an inquisitorial chamber." It was a splendid stroke: Clark had neatly defined Lyall's baiting of Norton as boorish and crass. For a moment the younger man was at a loss. Then he smiled warmly at Clark.

"I'm so sorry, Gordon," he said. "I'd forgotten how delicate your sensibilities are." He looked around the table. "Dr. Clark is Senior Tutor," he said as if in explanation. "I think dealing with undergraduates takes a great toll on his nervous system." He looked again at Clark with apparent solicitude. "I promise to keep the conversation innocuous from now on," he said, and turned back to Dorfmann.

Clark was silent for a moment; Forrester could see that his friend was boiling with fury at Lyall's revenge, which, true to form, neatly combined truth with slander. Clark was indeed highly strung not because of the demands of being Senior Tutor but due to the toll his war work had taken on him. It was impossible to establish the distinction, but Forrester knew Clark was too angry to let the gibe pass.

"It's not blandness one seeks at High Table, Lyall," he said. "It's – how shall I put it? – *incisiveness*. Something I have to constantly remind my undergraduates: there's no point in speaking for the sake of being heard, however amusing one finds the sound of one's own voice."

The Master intervened before Lyall could hit back. "I'd be very grateful for your opinion of the claret, Roland," he said to Bitteridge. "We've just opened a new bin and I'm wondering if we left it too long." Winters turned to ensure everyone else was part of this new conversation. "Roland is not just a great English scholar," he said, "but he also has one of the great noses."

There was general laughter and Bitteridge looked enormously pleased at the compliment. "Well," he said, considering the claret judiciously, "I think, Master, you are to be congratulated."

And the conversation moved onto safer ground. Forrester felt himself start to breathe again. He'd been afraid, for a moment, that his friend would throw himself across the table and knock Lyall backwards out of his chair. God knows, he'd been tempted to do it himself, and it wasn't *his* wife that Lyall was making love to.

By the time those who had agreed to attend the Icelandic reading crunched through the snow across the inner quadrangle to the Master's Lodge, clouds were scudding across the moon. As well as Haraldson, Calthrop and Dorfmann there was a mix of Barnard Fellows, and wives and dons from other colleges. David Lyall, Forrester noted with relief, had decided to absent himself.

Inside the Lodge, a minstrels' gallery ran around the upper part of the large drawing room and carved beams like those in the Hall ran across the high ceiling. There were gently worn Turkish rugs on the floor and a crackling fire in the grate. Lady Hilary, the Master's wife, was supervising two tall young men as they shifted furniture for the new arrivals. Lady Hilary was a tall, slightly awkward woman who Forrester suspected was not quite comfortable in her skin. He liked her, but he was not sure she liked herself.

"I want you to meet Hakon and Oskar," said Lady Hilary, introducing her two assistants. "The Master specially asked them to join us this evening because they're from Iceland."

"And children in Iceland learn the sagas at their mother's knee," said the Master genially. "In the absence of Professor Tolkien they will gently correct us if we get our Old Norse pronunciation wrong."

Hakon and Oskar shook their heads. "No, no, we are engineers," said Hakon. "It is many years since we read the sagas. But as this is our last night in England, we offer to do our best." Haraldson said a few words to the boys in Norwegian and they laughed. With Lyall gone, he seemed to have regained his good humour.

"You understand it is because of the ancestors of these young men that the Eddas and the sagas exist," he said to the rest of the company. "The stories and poems were first created in Norway and other parts of Scandinavia, but they were not written down. When Norwegians went in search of new land—"

"Rather like the settlers in the American west," said the Master.

"Very much like that," said Haraldson. "They took the sagas with them to their new home in Iceland. When they became literate, they wrote them down, which is how the sagas survived."

"In short," said the Master to the Icelanders, "your ancestors preserved Viking culture when it would otherwise have been lost." He turned to his wife. "And everything is perfectly arranged, my dear. Thank you." As the audience settled itself, he addressed the room. "The work we're going to read tonight, the 'Völuspá', is one of the most important poems in the canon. Hakon, Oskar, Professor Haraldson and I will take it in turns to do the reading from the minstrels' gallery. The acoustics are splendid and when I've turned the lights down to help you, imagine you're listening to genuine Norse bards declaiming from the depths of time."

Then he ushered the readers through a small door that led to the stairs. Moments later tiny reading lights came on up there and they heard his voice again, speaking from the shadows of the gallery above. As he had promised, the acoustics were perfect, and it sounded to Forrester, as it always did, as if the readers were right beside him.

"In the passage you're about to hear," said Winters, "Odin, chief of the gods, bids a certain wise-woman to rise from the grave. She then tells him of the creation of the world, the beginning of years, the origin of the dwarfs. She describes the final destruction of the gods in which fire and flood overwhelm heaven and earth, using a phrase '*ragna rök*', meaning 'the fate of the gods', which has become synonymous with the German word '*Götterdämmerung*'."

"A subject about which we Germans know all too much," said Dorfmann wryly. Calthrop frowned, and the reading began.

"I saw there wading through rivers wild," declaimed Haraldson, sounding like a Viking chief booming down a fjord.

> *Treacherous men and murderers too,*
> *And workers of ill with the wives of men;*
> *There Nithhogg sucked the blood of the slain,*
> *And the wolf tore men; would you know yet more?*

"The phrase 'Would you know yet more?' is uttered by the wise-woman," said the Master. "She is asking Odin if he really wants to hear what is about to befall."

> *The giantess old in Ironwood sat,*
> *In the east, and bore the brood of Fenrir;*
> *Among these one in monster's guise*
> *Was soon to steal the sun from the sky.*

There was a rustle of pages as Haraldson handed the book on to the next reader.

There feeds he full on the flesh of the dead,
And the home of the gods he reddens with gore;
Dark grows the sun, and in summer soon
Come mighty storms: would you know yet more?

On a hill there sat, and smote on his harp,
Eggther the joyous, the giants' warder;
Above him the cock in the bird-wood crowed,
Fair and red did Fjalar stand.

Again the reader changed, but by then the audience was scarcely noticing: through the magic of the incantatory words, combined with the darkness and the firelight, they found themselves transported back to a world where gods roamed the earth and dwarves delved in its depths.

Involuntarily, Forrester's thoughts went back to what Lyall had said about the Nazi obsession with Norse mythology, and the role the sinister, Nordic-obsessed Thule Society had played in Adolf Hitler's rise to power. But he knew all this was a perversion of the ancient beliefs: the product of warped minds, with no connection to reality. Except when you listened to a Viking saga being recited in the darkness.

Then to the gods crowed Gollinkambi,
He wakes the heroes in Othin's hall;
And beneath the earth does another crow,
The rust-red bird at the bars of Hel.

Now Garm howls loud before Gnipahellir,
The fetters will burst, and the wolf run free;
Much do I know, and more can see
Of the fate of the gods, the mighty in fight.

A new reader began: one of the young Icelanders.

Brothers shall fight and fell each other,
And sisters' sons shall kinship stain;
Hard is it on earth, with mighty whoredom;
Axe-time, sword-time, shields are sundered,
Wind-time, wolf-time, ere the world falls;
Nor ever shall men each other spare.

He paused – and as he paused there was a sharp sound of glass breaking from somewhere outside the Lodge. Lady Hilary looked up, puzzled, then walked over to the window, pulled aside the curtain and peered out. Forrester heard her sharply indrawn breath.

"Michael," Lady Hilary called up to the gallery. "I'm so sorry to interrupt, but something strange has happened outside. I think you should come and look." Her voice was oddly flat, as if she couldn't quite put strong emotions into words. Moments later Forrester and the other guests were all crowded around the window, peering out into the quadrangle. The only light came from the moon, still partially obscured by clouds, but against the whiteness of the snow it was perfectly clear what Lady Hilary was looking at.

Below a broken window on the second floor a body lay spread-eagled in the snow.

3

OPERATION TORCH

They ran out across the untouched whiteness of the quadrangle, the light from the windows of the Lodge behind them – and stopped a few feet from the body of David Lyall, as he lay amidst a halo of broken glass in the otherwise untouched snow, staring sightlessly towards the Lodge.

"My God," said Peter Dorfmann. "The poor fellow."

Forrester came forward then, and as he knelt beside the body to check there was no pulse, he saw the puncture wound between the second and third ribs. He looked up at the window from which Lyall had fallen and knew, with a sinking feeling, exactly whose window it was.

"Isn't that Clark's set?" asked the Master, his gaze following Forrester's. No-one replied. "Perhaps I'd better go and see if he's there." He began to walk towards the cloisters, then paused and turned to Forrester. "Would you mind calling the police?"

"I don't think anybody should go up there yet—" said Forrester, but Winters had already disappeared.

"I suppose we'd all better move back," said Calthrop. "We're rather messing up the evidence." It was all too true; half a dozen sets of footprints had trampled the snow into a slushy mass around the body.

"We can't just leave him there," said Lady Hilary.

"I'm afraid we have to," said Forrester. "It's too late to do anything to help him now." Suddenly the Master's wife was sobbing in his arms.

"That poor young man," she said, again and again. "That poor young man."

Bitteridge stared at the scene as if it had been designed to give him personal offence. "This is appalling," he said. "Absolutely appalling."

The two Icelanders stared, white-faced. Arne Haraldson was frowning, as if trying to solve a particularly difficult crossword puzzle. The remaining guests milled about, wondering what to do next.

The Master's head appeared through the broken window of Gordon Clark's room, and Forrester noted blood dripping from his hand where he had cut himself on the glass.

"There's no sign of Clark," he called down. "Does anyone know where he might be?"

"He's probably at home," said Forrester. "He only uses his set for tutoring."

"Very well," said the Master, and disappeared inside again.

"To think it should have happened now," said Lady Hilary, "when we were all just sitting there, reading. It's too horrible." Forrester took her back into the Lodge and handed her over to the wife of a don from Magdalen. Then he went to the Master's telephone and dialled 999. As he gave the details he felt the nausea return; but this time it was not a response to his own memories, but to the conviction that his friend Gordon Clark had committed an act for which he would eventually be tried, convicted and hanged.

Forrester heard the clanging bells of the police car from far away, which did not surprise him: he was familiar with the peculiar acoustics of snowy landscapes; there had been times when his life depended on it. The rest of the party, remaining in the Lodge on the Master's instructions, were sitting around the drawing room in a state of shock; even those with drinks in their hands simply held them, not raising them to their lips. As Forrester watched them he was willing Clark to keep moving, to take a train, get to a Channel port and onto a ferry, to get out of the country as soon as he could.

It was while he was thinking this that he noted Arne Haraldson was no longer present and then, glancing out into the quad, saw him disappearing into a stairway.

Seconds later there was a flash of torchlight in the upper floor.

Almost without thought Forrester slipped out of the drawing room and opened the front door. Bells still clanging, the police car was turning into the driveway, its headlight illuminating the bushes. Forrester melted into the shrubbery even as the car pulled up outside the front door.

As he did so he remembered Lyall taunting Haraldson with his references to Nazis and the occult – and

Haraldson's look of fury in response.

But Haraldson had been in the room with him when Lyall had died: Forrester had been listening to him. It was impossible that he had had anything to do with Lyall's death.

From the front of the Lodge, Forrester slid into the passageway that separated it from the chapel and found himself in the cloisters below the damaged Lady Tower. He hurried along them until he reached the wooden stairs on which he could still see traces of the snow from Haraldson's boots.

At the top of the stairs a single forty-watt bulb dangled from the ceiling of the corridor, leaving most of it in shadow. Then his eyes became accustomed to the dark and he could see a pale glow of light emerging from the open door of one of the rooms. Keeping his back against the wall he edged up the stairs and along the landing towards the open door of David Lyall's rooms.

The light came from under the body lying face down on the floor, feet towards Forrester, dark head pointing towards the window. It came from a torch, trapped under the man's chest. Below, in the quadrangle, he heard the Master speaking to the police. As Forrester knelt down he saw that his impression the victim's hair was dark had been wrong: the hair had been darkened by blood, in copious quantities, running from Haraldson's blond head.

Forrester's eyes flickered around the room. What had Haraldson been doing here? And who had wanted to stop him? Not Lyall, obviously: Lyall was already dead. The books on the shelves seemed to have been disarranged, and one or two drawers were open. He looked at the shelves: English classics, some Russian novelists; nothing unexpected.

He stood back for a moment, contemplating the room as a whole, glanced at the ceiling; the plaster seemed to be intact. He knelt down again beside the Norwegian and as he examined the floorboards, felt a pair of massive hands clasp themselves around his throat.

"*Du jævla drittsekk!*" said Haraldson – and began to throttle him. For a moment Forrester was too startled by the realisation that Haraldson wasn't dead to do anything to defend himself, and when he grasped the man's wrists and began to tear them away from him he found it was impossible: the Norwegian had the strength of a berserker.

"It's me, Forrester," he croaked, but the other man's eyes were wild and Forrester was certain his words had had no effect.

Then, as the flow of oxygen to Forrester's brain was beginning to diminish and his vision was beginning to dim a voice said, "What the bloody hell is going on here?" and someone dragged them apart. As Forrester staggered to his feet, he realised his rescuer was a police constable. Another man wearing a raincoat stood in the doorway, silhouetted against the light from the hall, watching them.

For once, the police had arrived in the nick of time. "What's all this about, then?" said the man in the raincoat.

Forrester massaged his bruised throat. He could still feel the imprint of Haraldson's iron fingers.

"It's alright, officer," he said. "It was a misunderstanding. Somebody hit this gentleman, I found him lying here and he thought it must have been me who attacked him. My name's Duncan Forrester. I'm a tutor here – I was with the party that found the body. And you are?"

"Detective Inspector Alec Barber," said the man in the raincoat. "Oxford Constabulary." He had a pale, weary face and the lid of his left eye drooped oddly. "Is this true?" he said to Haraldson.

"*Hvor er jeg? Hvem er du jævler?*" said the Norwegian.

"Can't he speak English?" said Barber.

"Perfectly well," said Forrester. "I think it's the blow to the head. He needs medical attention."

"*Hva gjør jeg her?*" said Haraldson. "*Jeg har en forelesning til å gi ved Oslo universitet i en halv times tid!*"

"What's he on about?"

"That he has to give a lecture in Oslo in half an hour's time," said Forrester.

"Ask the doctor to step up here," Barber said to the constable. "Tell him we've got a live one." He straightened up and looked around the room in a leisurely way, almost as if he was alone. Then he turned to Forrester.

"So what were you doing up here, Mr. Forrester?"

"*Dr.* Forrester, not that it's important, just for the record," said Forrester, lightly. "I saw a torch go on in Lyall's room and came up here to find out who it was."

"And you hit this gentleman because?"

"I didn't hit him," said Forrester impatiently. "As I said, I came up here and found him. I thought he was dead. That's why I was still in the room when you arrived."

"I see," said Barber noncommittally, and turned to

Haraldson. "Who do *you* say hit you then, sir?" he asked.

"*Likevel er det ax-tid, sverd-tid, vind-time, ulv-time*," said Haraldson. "*Når skjermene er sundered og verden faller ned i avgrunnen. Vil du likevel vite mer?*"

"What?" said Barber.

"I think he's quoting from the Icelandic sagas," said Forrester. "Wolf time and sword time and axe time, that sort of thing. The end of the world. It's from the saga he was reciting before David Lyall was killed."

"*Noen slo meg med dette*," said Haraldson.

"What's he saying now?"

"Somebody hit me with that," translated Forrester, as Haraldson pointed at the torch, which had rolled under Lyall's desk during the struggle.

"Somebody's been searching the place," said Barber, bending down to examine the torch. "Was it you?"

"No. It must have been Haraldson – or whoever attacked him."

"Hmmm," said Barber. "Well, I'd like to have a talk with you about that."

An old man with a pronounced tremor appeared in the doorway. "Ah, Dr. Hopkins," said the inspector, pointing to Haraldson. "Would you take a look at this gentleman's head?" He smiled thinly at Forrester. "This'll be a nice change for him," he said. "He usually only gets to look at people after they're dead."

Then he stood up and looked Forrester full in the face. "As for you, sir," he said, "I think we need to have that little chat, don't you?"

4

MEETING IN A RUINED CITY

But Barber's "little chat" with Forrester was unexpectedly postponed. Haraldson, his head bandaged and still muttering incomprehensibly in Norwegian, was taken to the Churchill Hospital, but the police kept nearly everyone else well beyond midnight, despite Winters' pleas to allow them to go home. Forrester was not surprised: as the police forces of occupied countries and totalitarian states alike had long known, human beings are at a low ebb in the early hours of the morning and less able to resist questioning. Normally British policemen did not have the opportunity to take advantage of this fact, but with Lyall's body outside in the quadrangle and all the witnesses assembled, Detective Inspector Barber had the perfect excuse.

"But by definition all these people are innocent," protested the Master. "They were all in this room when the murder happened. What possible reason can you have for interrogating them now?"

"*Questioning* them, sir," corrected Barber, courteously

enough. "While their memories are still fresh."

"They are exhausted, in a state of shock and eager to go home," said Winters.

"It will not be long now, sir," said Barber. "Provided no-one delays me."

There was a pause, and the Master turned away. Oddly enough Forrester was one of those allowed to leave earliest, because after the encounter in Lyall's rooms, Barber had made a mark beside Forrester's name and the sergeant in charge of drawing up the schedule of interviewees assumed that he had already been questioned. Forrester knew that the respite was temporary, but he was grateful for it; the calm he had found in the churchyard that afternoon was beginning to dissipate. He returned to his rooms, went to bed and prepared to spend several uncomfortable hours tossing and turning as the events of the night replayed themselves in his mind. Instead he fell into a sound sleep from which he was awakened by his scout, Nesbit, who pointed out that unless he got a move on his chances of catching the train he needed for his appointment with the Empire Council for Archaeology in London were now very slim.

But Forrester was fast; the last few years had given him plenty of opportunities to prove that. After cramming his papers into a very shabby briefcase and sprinting through Oxford as fast as he had through the streets of Bordeaux when the Vichy police were pursuing him, he caught his train and threw himself into one of the dirty, crowded, unheated carriages just as it lurched arthritically away from the platform. He squeezed into the last available seat opposite a clergyman doing his best to suppress his unchristian resentment of the intruder, and began hauling documents from the briefcase to prepare for his meeting. As the train groaned and wheezed its way through snow-covered fields, past leaden streams and leafless woods, Forrester focused on what he needed to say to convince the ECA to approve and fund his expedition to Crete.

For some months during the war Forrester had been part of the Special Operations Executive Group in German-occupied Crete, under the command of Patrick Leigh Fermor. Leigh Fermor was a showman, a daredevil, a born partisan; and he had seen in Forrester a fellow spirit – the very man to help him crown his extraordinary military career by kidnapping one of the German generals in command of Crete and taking him to Egypt by submarine.

It was Forrester who had led the Cretan guerrillas in the diversionary raid that made the kidnapping possible; who had scrambled over the bony spine of the island with the Jäger patrol in pursuit to lead them away from the real action. Who had encouraged the Cretan guerrillas to scatter while he himself lured the Germans after him into the Gorge of Acharius.

And it was in the Gorge of Acharius that he found the cave.

The Germans had found the cave not long after him, of course – they were good. But they weren't sure whether he was there or not, and as they entered he had forced himself into the cleft at the back, fighting his horror of confined spaces, wriggling backwards until, far beneath the earth, the passage brought him to the chamber.

It was an almost spherical space, and in the centre was an irregularly shaped rock. And as Forrester ran his hands over it he realised he had found his own personal Rosetta Stone.

Moments later, the Jäger patrol in the cave above him heard a noise from the cliffs on the other side of the gorge and raced out to investigate. Forrester waited for them to come back, but they did not, and when darkness finally fell he had emerged and headed down to the coast to join up with Leigh Fermor and the kidnapped German general.

Not long after, he left Crete in a Greek caïque and eventually made his way to Cairo. He had never seen the cave again, but he knew it was there, waiting for him.

Which was why he was going to see the Empire Council for Archaeology.

He looked down at his shoes to make sure they looked moderately respectable, and was relieved to see they were at least clean. The broken and re-mended shoelaces slightly marred the effect, but it couldn't be helped – unless he came across one of the increasing numbers of ex-servicemen who were appearing on the London streets with trays of laces and boxes of matches.

Then, just when he was feeling confident he was ready for the fray, the train began a series of doleful, unexplained stops, first in the middle of empty fields and then in the dispiriting fringes of West London. Unconsciously, he began grinding his teeth.

"Well," said the clergyman, "if our new Socialist government decides to nationalise the railways the Great Western will deserve everything that's coming to them."

Forrester glanced up from his papers. "There are in fact times when the railway services between Oxford and London," said the clergyman, "put me in mind of the more lurid passages in the Book of Revelation."

Forrester found himself smiling, realising that the man was trying to help, and answering in the same vein. "I wouldn't be surprised," he said, "if the Beast with Seven Heads isn't the chairman of the board."

"Certainly the sandwiches on sale at the Oxford Station café could easily have been made by the Great Whore of Babylon," said the clergyman. As if stung by the gibe, the train started again, wheezily.

"Haven't I seen you in my churchyard? Just yesterday, I think. I was considering asking you to come in out of the cold – except it's not much warmer inside these days."

"Yesterday?" said Forrester, and then remembered. "Yesterday I was best left alone."

"Ah," said the clergyman. "My name is Glastonbury, by the way. Vicar of St. Mary the Virgin."

"Duncan Forrester. Barnard."

A concerned look came over Glastonbury's face.

"I was so sorry to read about your loss," he said, and when Forrester stared at him blankly he held up a copy of that morning's *Oxford Mail*. Forrester felt as if he'd been kicked in the stomach; since the moment he'd woken he'd not given a thought to Lyall's death. Suddenly it all came rushing back: the Icelandic readings, the body in the snow, Haraldson, Barber – and the probability that the murderer was one of his closest friends.

"I'm so sorry," said Glastonbury. "I didn't mean to upset you. It's just that I knew your Master before the war. I feel for the poor man with this happening right on his doorstep, so to speak."

"Yes, it's a rotten business," said Forrester. "How did you know Professor Winters?"

"I used to edit a little magazine, and he wrote for it sometimes."

"Really? On the sagas?"

"Not really. We dealt with cultural subjects, very high-minded. Whither Western Civilisation, that kind of thing."

"Whither indeed," said Forrester.

"Yes," said Glastonbury, "whither indeed."

Glastonbury looked out of the window again. "My goodness, we actually seem to be arriving."

Forrester peered into a solid mass of thick yellow fog augmented by plumes of steam from waiting engines. Paddington Station echoed with the clang of carriage doors and dropped steamer trunks, while incomprehensible voices boomed from invisible loudspeakers high above in the rafters as Forrester stuffed his papers back into his briefcase.

Glastonbury got to his feet and began pulling his case down from the rack. "Do drop in to the church the next time you're nearby. If I'm not there, feel free to knock on the vicarage door. Depending on the time of day, there may be some very bad sherry available."

"Thank you," said Forrester with a grin. "I may well take you up on that attractive offer." And then, even before the train had come to a stop, he was on the platform, moving as fast as the crowd would allow.

The fog inside the vast canopy of the railway station, illuminated fitfully by overhead lights, muffled Forrester's footsteps and blanketed the murmur of the throng, lending the whole place an air of vast conspiracy. Porters' trolleys piled high with crates and suitcases rattled past him as he wove his way through the crowds, hoping that, hours before, Clark had fled through here on his way out of the country.

As Forrester left the train in London, in Oxford, about a mile from the college, Arne Haraldson was waking up in Ward Three of the Churchill Hospital. He had been brought in the night before by the police and carefully examined by a junior doctor who had been on duty for thirty-six hours, written up careful notes, put them in his briefcase and unwittingly carried them home with him.

As a result there was no-one with Arne Haraldson when his eyes first opened, and he was able to conceal his return to consciousness from both the patient in the bed next to him and the nursing staff. He woke in a curious state in which he seemed to drift between everyday reality and the mythic world of Ragnarök. He was conscious he was on the track of something deeply important and unable to remember exactly what it was. The faces of Duncan Forrester, the Master, Inspector Barber and David Lyall floated in and out of his mind, and he lay there, trying to fit them together. Forrester in particular puzzled him. Why had he been fighting him? What had he got against him?

His head hurt abominably, and he sometimes closed his eyes and went back to sleep before a thought had been fully formulated. Beneath the covers, the fingers of his large, powerful hands began to flex; and when he drifted off it was into a sleep perfumed by the metallic smell of blood.

Forrester took the Underground to Russell Square and then walked swiftly to the offices of the ECA in a tall, gloomy house in Bloomsbury, not far from the British Museum. He was twelve minutes late for his appointment but the twelve minutes, as is so often the way, dissolved into a sea of time as he sat waiting with the other supplicants outside the room in which the Advisory Committee were conducting their interviews. Who exactly the Committee was supposed to be advising Forrester did not know and suspected he would never find out.

He went over his papers again, surreptitiously eyeing his fellow applicants. A thin, weedy man balanced a small cork model of the Acropolis on his knees and stared unseeing into the middle distance. A large, hearty man tore little pieces off his copy of *The Times*, twisted them into tiny cones and thrust them systematically into the pockets of his tweed suit. A scholar bearing an uncanny likeness to the late Dr. Goebbels filled page after page of a cheap notebook with paragraphs of writing in purple ink. One after another they disappeared behind the green baize door that led to the committee room, and did not re-emerge.

When it was his turn and Forrester passed through the baize door, the suspicion that his quest was in vain turned to certainty. There were three men behind the long table and one woman. The woman glared at him the moment he walked in. She was about fifty, angular and angry. Forrester knew the anger had nothing to do with him; it was just he had been caught in its beam. Her name was Miss Henslowe. Beside her sat a tall man and beside *him* was a personage so old Forrester would not have been surprised to learn he had actually lived among the ancient Greeks. The chairman wore an expression of infinite sadness, which deepened steadily as Forrester described the Gorge of Acharius, the cave, and the hieroglyph-covered stone, which he was certain held the key to the mystery of Linear B.

Secretly, he had hoped that the dramatic circumstances of his discovery would help his case, but it was clear the committee disapproved of anything that smacked of derring-do, and kidnapping a German general was hardly the sort of thing they expected from a respectable archaeologist.

Instead he concentrated on the potential significance of the inscriptions, the problems Evans had encountered with Linear B, and what riches deciphering them would uncover, but there was no response. The tall man made copious notes, the old man doodled, the chairman shook his head sadly and Miss Henslowe kept up her unrelenting glare. In the end they told him they'd let him know, but warned him of the "extreme" restraints the Treasury had just put on them, of the "draconian" limitations on the use of foreign currency, and of the "deeply uncertain" political situation in Greece. He made his last bid for their attention as he approached the small door through which, it turned out, the candidates were expected to depart.

"What I'd like you to think about is this," he said. "Crete was the bridge between ancient Egypt and the beginning of civilisation in Europe. The key to our understanding of Minoan culture lies in deciphering the surviving texts; and I believe the expedition I propose could be a major step forward in helping us achieve that."

"Thank you," said the chairman. "We'll let you know."

Moments later Forrester was outside again in the fog. The British Museum was closed, most of its collection still hidden in disused stretches of the London Underground. Taking his life in his hands he stepped into the murk that obscured Tottenham Court Road (most of its shops still boarded up) and passed into the narrow alley leading into Rathbone Place, his footsteps sounding almost metallic in the strange yellow gloom. He drank a half pint of tasteless beer in the Wheatsheaf and failed to see anybody he knew. He had occasionally seen Dylan Thomas there, when home on leave, complaining about the boredom he suffered writing film scripts for the Ministry of Information. Once he'd seen Orwell wagging his finger at J.B. Priestley, doubtless rebuking him for excessive cheerfulness, but today there was nobody except a few BBC radio producers arguing about whether the advent of the Light Programme spelt the end of civilisation as they knew it.

Unable – after his unsatisfactory meeting with the committee – to face the prospect of an immediate return to Oxford, Forrester left the pub, pulled the belt of his British Warm tighter to keep out the cold, and began walking south through the fog-shrouded ruins. *So might a Goth or Vandal have made his way through the smoking wreck of fallen Rome*, he thought. But then, he reminded himself, the British Empire was still intact. So far.

Ruins befitted Soho; its seedy charm was perfectly suited to heaps of blackened bricks and weed-grown basements open to the sky for the first time since the reign of Queen Anne. Even the hand-written offers from tarts in newsagents' windows looked more interesting in the context of fallen church spires. The phrase "Love Among the Ruins" came to his mind, and with it the memory of walking here with Barbara.

He had met her at a club off Denmark Street and it wasn't her beauty that first struck him, but her voice. He had turned his head as he heard her speak, and though he could never for the life of him remember what she had been saying, it was as though the sound itself came from somewhere he had always longed to be – or perhaps not longed to be, but believed existed, just out of sight, beyond the drab banality of the real world. The word *melodious* was appropriate, but it didn't quite capture it; it was as if he was hearing an echo of a melody from the dawn of time, when the world itself was pure and unspoilt. As soon as he caught her eye she smiled at him without hesitation or self-consciousness and moments later he was laughing till his eyes watered at her description of the elderly general she drove around the countryside making snap inspections of the Home Guard.

Most of the people around Barbara Lytton seemed to come from the same sort of background as she did: country houses; large, interconnected families; good schools; skiing holidays at Gstaad. In other circumstances this would have set his teeth on edge, but he felt as comfortable in her presence as if he had not been born in a two-up-two-down terrace house on Hessle Road or seen his father boarding the trawlers on Hull docks. Among Barbara's many gifts was one for inclusion.

And when, that weekend, he found himself among the party she had assembled at Cranbourne, the country house in a wooded Kentish valley that was her family home, she made him feel as if he had been in such places all his life. When they climbed to the folly and looked down the ride towards the house and she told him how she'd hidden there as a child and read *The Golden Age*, it almost seemed as if he had been there with her instead of playing among the broken fish crates beside the River Humber.

Even when she persuaded him to tell her about his father's life on the trawlers and the cleaning jobs his mother had taken on after her husband was drowned, there seemed to be no gap between them: it was as if he had been living the other half of her life for her, just as she had been living the other half of his. His love for his own parents did not prevent him falling for hers. He delighted in doing conversational battle with her father as much as her father enjoyed jousting with him. He felt no resentment at the generations of privilege that had given the Lyttons the life they led but he made no bones about his determination that after the war things would change, and what they enjoyed now would one day be available to the millions, not the few.

Sir Phillip Lytton told him the millions were simply incapable of appreciating it, and Forrester told him he was talking through his hat. Lady Elspeth Lytton told him on the terrace one day that her husband looked forward to his debates with Forrester almost as much as Barbara looked forward to his visits. And she teased him for being so obsessed with social justice. Social justice was always something just out of reach, she said. Men got far too carried away trying to grasp it, as they got carried away with most things. All that really mattered in life was having a good seat on a horse. And some decent hounds. And a fox to chase, added Barbara. Of course, said her mother. Everybody needed a fox to chase. Shortly after that conversation Forrester had been parachuted into Sardinia.

When he was posted 'Missing Believed Dead' Barbara had wangled her way into the SOE and been sent to France. By the time he returned safely to England, she'd been caught and shot by the Gestapo.

A numbness had enveloped Forrester's soul when he heard the news, and in the years since had lessened only enough to allow slightly unreal infatuations with other women, of whom Margaret Clark was one. In his soul he did not believe this state of being would ever change. So he concentrated on going to Crete, finding his cave again and losing himself in a world that had been gone for four thousand years.

* * *

At this same instant Arne Haraldson – still in his Oxford hospital bed – was finding that his head had cleared sufficiently to allow him to take note of the comings and goings of all the staff, so that he could begin to make plans for the moment when he could slip out without being observed.

He had realised that the chances of him being able to do this were greatly increased by the fact that he was in some kind of administrative no-man's land, with each shift convinced the other was responsible for him. Now all he had to decide was the optimum time for his move. As the short winter day began to wane, he knew that time was coming closer.

As Forrester reached Whitehall he saw that the sandbags had gone but many of the windows were still boarded up. He remembered the hurried night-time summonses to map-filled offices along this street during the war; the clipped orders about this or that mission; the hair-raising drives through the blackout to various military airfields on the outskirts of the city; the all-too-brief flights over occupied territory – followed by the "Mind how you go" from the drop-masters as he stepped into the void.

"Mind how you go."

He was smiling at the absurd memory when he saw Calthrop emerge from the Foreign Office with Peter Dorfmann – and felt an odd prickle of unease. There was no reason why a Foreign Office official should not be speaking with a German academic on a visit to Britain. If Dorfmann was being groomed for political power in the new Germany, it made sense that Calthrop was in communication with him. But Forrester was aware that neither of them had appeared to know each other the night before, either before going in to High Table, during the dinner itself, or afterwards in the Lodge. In fact, he was certain they hadn't even spoken. Had he failed to notice them speaking? Or had they avoided alerting anyone to the fact that they were acquainted? It was odd. *And irrelevant*, he told himself. The facts of what had happened the night before were all too obvious, however much he wanted it to be otherwise. His friend had killed the academic rival who had stolen his wife.

Before either Calthrop or Dorfmann could notice him he had slipped into the passageway leading to Old Scotland Yard and made his way down to the Embankment. The stone of the balustrade was clammy under his hand as he looked out through the fog; invisible barges hooted mournfully from the river. Clark had taken another man's life and ruined his own. Bloody idiot! A train whistled as it passed over Hungerford Bridge. Forrester knew he ought to be heading back to Oxford. Reluctantly, he began to walk towards the nearest Underground station.

5

FENCING MATCH

There was a note from Margaret Clark waiting for him in his rooms, asking him to telephone her. Involuntarily he found himself holding the note close to his face, breathing in the scent, and then damned himself for his weakness, screwed up the page and dropped it in the wastebasket. Then he went down to the Porter's Lodge, called her and agreed to meet by Magdalen Bridge in half an hour.

It was dark by the time he got to the river and she was already waiting for him, wearing a pale mackintosh and headscarf, pacing up and down, her breath producing little clouds in the cold. Harassed, distraught, without make-up, she was still effortlessly capable of making his heart stand still. She wasted no time on preliminaries as they walked down to the towpath beside the black water.

"They've taken him in for questioning," she said. Forrester's heart sank: he realised he'd been assuming all along that Clark had managed to get away.

"Where did they find him?"

She seemed surprised. "Why, here, of course. At home."

"He didn't try to leave the country?"

"Of course not. Why should he?"

Forrester paused to consider this, but before he could speak she had taken his hands. She had never taken his hands before. Hers were pleasingly cold, the flesh soft; he could feel the delicate bones beneath. "You know, don't you?" she said. "About David and me. He told you, didn't he?"

"Yes."

"You must promise me you won't tell the police." Forrester stared at her. She went on quickly. "It would look so bad. As if he had a motive."

"He did have a motive," said Forrester.

"Yes, but there's no reason for the police to know that. They might jump to the wrong conclusion."

Forrester's eyes narrowed. "You don't believe he did it," he said.

She looked at him, astonished. "Of course he didn't. Can you imagine Gordon stabbing someone?"

Forrester could imagine it perfectly well. "The murder happened in his rooms," he said. "Lyall fell out of *his* window. We all saw the body."

"He didn't kill him," said Margaret Clark firmly.

"How can you be certain?"

"Because when David was killed, Gordon was at home with me."

Forrester blinked. "That's what you've told the police?"

"It's the truth."

"Do the police accept that?"

"They might not if they knew about David and me," she said. "That's why you mustn't tell them."

They were passing a hotel now, and its lights flickered on the dark water. Forrester stared at them, almost hypnotised, and it was several minutes before he spoke. "You're asking me to withhold evidence."

"But it's evidence Gordon gave you himself. You wouldn't know unless he'd told you."

"I'm not sure what difference that makes."

"You can't just go passing on confidences."

"Except in a murder enquiry," said Forrester.

She stopped; a lamp in the trees illuminated her flushed face, her bright eyes. "Gordon's your friend," she said. "What's more important, following the rules or saving his life?"

"They'll find out from somebody else."

"They may do, they may not. I'm asking you to promise me they won't find it out from you."

After a moment Forrester said, "Was he really at home with you when Lyall was killed?" He watched her closely as he put the question to her, saw the brief movement of her pupils as they darted away from him before she replied.

"Of course," she said. "You don't think I'm a liar, do you?"

"You're asking me to be one," said Forrester. "To the police."

"For Gordon's sake," she said.

She took his hands again, pulling him closer. Forrester felt weak with desire, weak with the effort of hiding it. "Listen," she said. "I've been a total bitch to that man. He didn't deserve what I did. I'm bitterly ashamed. But if he hangs because of it, I'll never forgive myself. Please help him, Duncan. Please." Her wide, desperate eyes were cornflower blue. Her lips were just inches from his; all he wanted was to kiss them. When he spoke it was as much as anything to stop himself doing just that.

"Alright," he said. "I won't mention what Gordon told me."

"Thank you," she breathed, and her lips touched his cheek. "Thank you, Duncan."

Almost before he knew it she had released his hand and melted away into the darkness, leaving him feeling like a man who has just sprung into the air off a diving board only to realise that the pool beneath him is empty.

Forrester dined in the hall that night, but spoke to no-one; very few Fellows were present and none of them seemed to have anything to say to one another. The undergraduates eyed them curiously, and whispered among themselves, but none of them dared ask any questions. After an indifferent meal and some indifferent port, Forrester retired early and fell swiftly asleep.

As Forrester slept, Arne Haraldson checked that there was no night nurse in the ward, and rose from his bed. Again, he paused, checked that all the other patients were sleeping, and walked quietly to the dispensary, closing the door gently behind him.

When he emerged, ten minutes later, only his eyes were visible beneath the bandages which swathed his face. In his hand he was carrying a surgical scalpel.

Nurse Elizabeth Tremain returned to the ward just as the man emerged from the dispensary, and as she pushed the heavy swing door back and stood there blinking while her eyes became accustomed to the darkness, she was unaware that he was standing behind her, hidden by the door. Unaware on one level – but some intuition told her there was something wrong, and she was about to turn round and come face to face with him when the patient in the left-hand bed at the far end of the ward cried out.

Without further thought Nurse Tremain strode down towards him between the beds, and as she did so the man with the bandaged face stepped out of the ward before the swing doors had even closed.

When he reached the ground floor the only obstacle between him and the outer door was the porter, who was seated reading that day's copy of the *Oxford Mail*, in which David Lyall's murder was fully reported. Hearing a footstep in the hall he looked up and saw – nothing.

The bandaged man was already outside in the night. The time was approximately 2.30 a.m.

In his rooms, Forrester had been alternating between sleep and wakefulness, disturbed by the usual dreams. Suddenly – he reckoned later it was just after 3.00 a.m. – he found himself sitting upright, sweat pouring from his forehead. He sat there for some time, and knew sleep would not readily return. Finally, he got dressed, put on his overcoat and walked out into the night.

Snow lay thick on the ground and it was oddly soothing to walk through the cloisters and across the quadrangles of the college while everyone slept. There was an innocence about a community asleep that made Forrester feel oddly protective towards both the students and his fellow dons. And even, somehow, to the generations of scholars who had lain and dreamt there since the Middle Ages. When he came to the Lady Tower he stopped and looked up, hoping to see the stars; but there were no stars tonight, just the silhouette of the scaffolding Norton had put up for the repair work. The cloud cover was thick over the Oxford Valley that night, and Forrester knew it was going to snow again.

What he did not know was that Haraldson was standing directly behind him, in the shadow of the tower, and the scalpel he had taken from the Churchill Hospital was just inches from Forrester's jugular vein.

Haraldson was significantly taller than Forrester, and the scalpel was raised in his right hand so that it would sweep down diagonally, connecting with Forrester's neck just below his right ear. Behind the bandages, the dark eyes glittered in the reflected light of the snow as Forrester stared up at the boarded up window of Gordon Clark's room, asking himself what had really happened there.

Had he turned back towards the Lady Tower, the sight of Haraldson's bandaged face would probably have been the last thing he saw; but as it was, not knowing the significance of what he was doing, he stepped out onto the lawn and walked across the snow to the place where David Lyall's body had lain. He then stood there, contemplating the spot, for a long moment. Behind him, Haraldson watched intently and then padded silently along the cloisters and up the stairs to David Lyall's rooms, where he pushed the bandages away from his eyes and resumed the search he had begun the night before.

Detective Inspector Barber appeared in Forrester's rooms early that morning and stood at the window with his back to him, his drooping eye studying the quadrangle as Forrester struggled into his clothes. "History," said Barber, almost to himself. "History oozing out of every pore."

Dons and undergraduates went back and forth across the snow, their gowns flapping behind them. Forrester knew Barber had positioned himself so that he was silhouetted against the window and the light would fall on Forrester when he began to question him. So before Barber could begin Forrester came and stood beside him, looking out at the same view.

"I find the view very soothing," he said. "Puts things into perspective, looking out there. Do sit down." And he pulled a hard chair behind the desk out for himself and gestured for Barber to take the comfortable one in front of it.

Which put him in the precise spot Barber had intended to take.

Forrester had been interrogated by professionals and knew the advantages of keeping the light out of your eyes as they probed. So did Barber, clearly, who accepted this small defeat gracefully and sank into the chair. "So, this assault on Professor Haraldson," he said. "What was all that about?"

"I have no idea," said Forrester without rancour. "As I told you at the time I had nothing to do with it."

"And yet I found you struggling with him. Violently struggling."

"You saw yourself he was concussed and confused. He struck out blindly and I was trying to calm him. I imagine if you've talked to him since he'll have clarified what happened."

"I visited him yesterday. He intimated that he had seen a light on in Dr. Lyall's room, and went to investigate. He was struck from behind."

"And you believe him?"

Barber ignored the question. "You and Dr. Clark were close," he stated, paused briefly to allow Forrester to demur if he so wished, and then went on, "Did he tell you why he killed David Lyall?"

"I've no reason to believe he did kill Dr. Lyall," said Forrester, levelly.

"You have some reason to doubt he was the perpetrator?"

"It's not a question of 'reason to doubt'," said Forrester. "It just never occurred to me that he had anything to do with it."

"Despite the fact that the murder occurred in his rooms? And that you were there when the body fell from his window?"

"It may have been the window of his college rooms, but I understand he was at home when Lyall was killed."

"Oh, yes?" said Barber swiftly. "Who told you that?"

Forrester caught himself in time.

"The Master," he said. "The Master went up to Clark's rooms and called down from the window that he wasn't there and must therefore be at home." Barber looked quizzically at him and then glanced at his notebook.

"Actually I believe the Master simply announced that the room was empty and it was you who told him Clark must be at home."

"I stand corrected," said Forrester, apparently graciously conceding a point of no importance. Barber looked at him sharply.

"This is a murder enquiry, sir," he said. "Your friendship with Dr. Clark does not give you license to obstruct our enquiries. I should warn you there is a crime known as 'accessory to murder'. I'm sure I need hardly point out that a charge to that effect would hardly be good for your standing in this university." It was a shrewd blow. Forrester knew he had to regain the initiative.

"I hardly think making the assumption that Dr. Clark was at home would give grounds for accusing me of either obstructing the police or being an accessory to murder, Inspector," he said. "It may or may not have been a false assumption but it was a perfectly natural one. Unlike yourself, I am not, after all, a professional investigator."

Barber opened his mouth to reply but Forrester went on quickly.

"Let me be clear," he said, "Gordon was – is – my friend; but if he killed Lyall he has to face justice and I'm not going to do anything to stand in the way of it. It's just that I find it hard to believe he committed this crime, a belief to which I think I'm entitled. Is that fair enough?"

He said this looking straight back at Barber, inviting him to question his good faith. Barber clearly decided his best move was to capitalise on this moment of intimacy. "But surely, sir, all appearances suggest your friend stabbed Dr. Lyall in a fit of jealous rage." Forrester's stomach sank: so they already knew about Margaret and Lyall.

"Jealous rage?" he temporised.

"Didn't he have reason to be jealous?" said Barber. So they were coming to the crunch at last.

"What reason?" said Forrester.

"I would have thought you would have known that perfectly well, sir," said Barber.

"I'm sorry, I'm not following you."

"Are you telling me you were unaware of any reason for Gordon Clark to be jealous of David Lyall?"

And there it was, the trap door in the floor, held politely open for him to step into. He saw Margaret Clark's face in the lamplight, looking up at him, her lips slightly open. He thought of Barber's threat if he did not co-operate. He made his decision. "Yes, that's exactly what I'm telling you."

"I see," said Barber, and let the silence gather. "I have to say I'm a little disappointed in you, Dr. Forrester."

Forrester said nothing. He had played his cards and he would accept the consequences.

Barber moved in for the kill. "You're not going to tell me you're unaware of the Rotherfield Lectureship?"

Forrester's mouth fell open. The Rotherfield Lectureship?

"Yes, I know about it, of course. But what does that have to do with—"

Barber stabbed the air with his forefinger.

"Are you saying you were unaware of the fact that although Dr. Clark believed himself best qualified to get it, the recommendation was that it should be awarded to Dr. Lyall?"

Forrester stared at him, relief welling up in him. Academic jealousy! The man had been talking about academic jealousy. Which meant he, Forrester, was back on firm ground.

"Yes, that's exactly what I'm saying. I had no idea about who was going to get the Rotherfield. I did know both men were in the running, but I didn't know Lyall had been awarded it. I'm pretty sure Gordon Clark didn't either, because he didn't mention it to me. Who told you about this?"

"That's really none of your business, sir," said Barber. But Forrester knew he had the upper hand again, because Barber had expected him to know.

Why had he expected him to know? For the moment it didn't matter: Barber's blunder allowed Forrester to be honest and co-operative and to move away from any discussion of Margaret Clark's love life.

"Listen, Inspector. I think someone has misled you. It may well be that Lyall was going to be awarded the Rotherfield rather than Gordon Clark, but it was not public knowledge and I'm as certain as I can be that Gordon hadn't heard because, as you imply, he would almost certainly have confided in me. It may seem to be a motive to you, but

I think you're probably quite mistaken."

"So what *was* the motive, then?" said Barber, as though completely at sea, and Forrester was almost tempted to supply one until he caught himself in time. "There wasn't one!" he said. "Gordon didn't do it."

"So who did?" asked Barber.

"I have no idea," said Forrester.

"Come, come," said Barber. "You're a Fellow of this college; you've been associated with it since 1936, you were present at High Table when the altercation broke out between Clark and the victim, you were one of those who found the body. And you're trying to tell me you have no idea what was going on?"

"The date 1936 is correct," said Forrester. "But I joined up in 1940 and only came back to Oxford this year. There's plenty about what goes on in this college I simply don't know." He stood up. "I'm sorry," he said, "I have a tutorial to give. If you need to continue this, can we do it at another time?"

There was a beat, and Barber apparently came to a decision and stood up too. "I look forward to doing just that," he said, picked up his hat, and left the room.

Forrester heaved a long, silent sigh of relief and went back to the window to watch the detective disappear across the quad, leaving a trail of footprints in the snow.

6

DISCUSSION BY AN UNLIT FIRE

Forrester conducted his tutorial and several more afterwards with half his mind on ancient history and the other half on Gordon Clark. Part of him hated suppressing evidence which pointed to his friend's guilt; part of him hated the fact that he had jumped to the conclusion that his friend was guilty.

And yet what other explanation was there? Clark had hated Lyall, with good reason; their antagonism had reached boiling point at High Table, and Lyall had been killed in Clark's rooms. If he were in Barber's shoes, Forrester had to admit, he too would have reached the same conclusion. By mid-afternoon Forrester's unease had reached a point where he knew he had to speak to his friend direct. The police had released him after questioning and no arrest warrant had yet been issued. Minutes later Forrester was bicycling through Oxford to Clark's house.

It was late afternoon and the winter darkness had already arrived, but none of the lights were on. Margaret was at her job at the Bodleian Library, and when Forrester entered he found Gordon sitting in an armchair in the front room staring into an empty grate. His only acknowledgement as Forrester came in was a slight tilt of the head.

"This is a bit of a nuisance, isn't it?" said Forrester, as lightly as he could.

"A bloody nuisance," said Clark listlessly.

And then they sat in silence for a while.

"The police interviewed me this morning," said Forrester.

Clark looked up sharply.

"At Margaret's request I didn't pass on anything you and I spoke about the other day."

"Margaret's request?"

"She asked to see me last night. She begged me not to reveal anything about her and Lyall."

"And you agreed?"

"I did."

Clark considered this for a moment. "I'm sorry," he said. "She shouldn't have put you in that position."

"Perhaps not," replied Forrester. "But she did and I agreed. So."

There was a pause.

"Thank you," said Clark. Then he grinned a death's-head grin. "But you know they don't even need that as a motive? They think I killed him because he was going to get the Rotherfield Lectureship."

"Yes, they told me. That was a bit of a facer. I'd no idea Lyall had been given it."

"The irony is I probably bloody well would have wanted to strangle him if I'd known, but I didn't."

"It's absurd he was preferred over you," said Forrester. "Who was behind that?"

Clark shrugged. "I have to say in my present situation the question isn't uppermost in my mind." He turned urgently to Forrester. "But I want to be absolutely clear about one thing: I did not kill David Lyall. I know what I said to you about wanting to – but it wasn't the literal truth or anything like it. I was furious with him, I was furious with Margaret; but I couldn't kill anybody over such a thing. I just… couldn't. Do you believe that?" He turned towards the cheerless fireplace. "I did not kill David Lyall," he repeated.

Forrester paused. "Good," he said at last. "I'm glad to hear that." He shivered slightly in the cold of the room. "So what the hell *did* happen?"

"If you're asking me how come he was in my rooms and who stabbed him and threw him through the window, I haven't a clue," said Clark. "I went home after that bloody awful High Table and had a blistering row with Margaret, drank half a bottle of whisky and went to bed. I knew nothing about what had happened until the police came knocking at the door."

Forrester sat there, allowing this new version of events to sink in. Despite everything he had heard and seen, he was certain that his friend was telling the truth. "You didn't speak to Lyall after High Table?"

"No."

"Did you see him?"

"No."

"You didn't see him with Alan Norton, for example?"

"Alan Norton?"

"Remember the row he had with Norton at High Table?"

"I'd completely forgotten it."

"About Norton being a fellow traveller."

"Good God, it'd completely gone out of my head. But surely that wouldn't have been enough for Norton to murder him?"

"Who knows?" said Forrester.

"Did you suggest that to the police?"

"No. I didn't want to appear to be trying to protect you. There's plenty of other people who can tell them about Lyall's row with Norton."

"But could Norton really have done it?"

"I don't know. He was certainly angry. Did you see him at all, after High Table?"

"No. As I said, I came straight home."

"Alright," said Forrester. "Let's try another tack. Have you any idea how Lyall came to be in your rooms?"

"None."

"You hadn't asked to meet him to discuss Margaret?"

"I had not," said Clark. Then a surprised expression came over his face and he leaned towards Forrester. "Listen, I made a mistake just now about Norton; the fact is I did see him after High Table. He was walking away down the South Cloister."

"Which leads to your stairs."

"Among other places."

"Like Lyall's rooms."

"Yes. But Norton couldn't have—"

"Perhaps not, but if *you* didn't kill Lyall, Gordon, someone else must have."

"But surely not Norton."

"Alright. Here's another thing you should know: Haraldson was in Lyall's room that night."

"What? The Norwegian?"

"I found him there myself, knocked out cold."

"Good God. So could he have—"

"I don't think so," said Forrester. "This was after the murder and I know he was in the Lodge reading an Icelandic saga to the rest of us when Lyall was killed."

"Hmm. He looked like the sort of chap who'd demolish anybody who got in his way. But what was he doing in Lyall's rooms?"

"God knows."

"Do you think whoever bashed him also killed Lyall?"

"Possibly," said Forrester. "Of course the police might say it was you."

"How could it have been? For one thing Haraldson's about a foot taller than I am."

"You could have been standing on something."

"Hardly."

"Nevertheless that's what the police will probably claim. They seem fairly determined you did it."

"I'm in a mess, aren't I?" said Clark.

"Have you called your solicitor?"

"Not yet."

"I think you should do that."

"He was my father's man. He must be about seventy-five."

"Ask him to recommend someone younger."

"I shouldn't need a lawyer! I'm innocent."

Forrester was about to answer this objection when the doorbell rang. Forrester went to answer it – and found Inspector Barber and a sergeant on the doorstep. Barber gave Forrester a hard look before pushing past him into the house. By the time Forrester had followed him in the detective was already speaking to Gordon.

"Gordon Alistair Clark, I have here a warrant for your arrest for the murder of David Patrick Lyall of Barnard College, Oxford, on the night of January 13th. You are free to remain silent but anything you say may be taken down and used in evidence against you."

Clark fought to retain his composure.

"I did not do it," he said at last. "My wife has told you I was at home with her."

"Unfortunately," said Barber, "it seems that alibi is false. We have two witnesses who testify that at the time of the murder your wife was seen in another place entirely. If you want to pack one or two things, sir, we have a police car waiting outside."

Clark looked at Forrester – but there was nothing either of them could think of to say.

7

A PLAN OF CAMPAIGN

Margaret Clark came home just after the police had gone and when Forrester told her what Barber had said she became wildly hysterical, repeating over and over again that she had been at home with Clark when she said she was. Inwardly furious, knowing she needed someone with her and determined not to be that person, Forrester had taken her address book and practically forced her to give him the name of a woman colleague who could come round; he also called her doctor and asked for him to bring a sedative.

While he was waiting for the doctor he called Clark's solicitor and arranged to see him, and when Margaret's friend from the Bodleian arrived he left at once, cycling furiously through the snowy streets, oblivious now to their calm and beauty.

Clark's solicitor's offices were in a picturesquely twisted, half-timbered building and Clark's solicitor seemed to have been designed to match. He was an elderly man who spent most of the time while Forrester was speaking to him nervously twisting a pipe cleaner into the shape of a cat, and at the end of the recital had nothing to say except, "Oh dear, oh dear." With tact and persistence Forrester requested that a younger member of the practice take over the case, and then sat down with him. But it was still awkward: the proffered candidate, Peter Nestleton, was certainly younger, but also stolid and unimaginative.

On the other hand he seemed competent and concerned. As Forrester listened to him he remembered that competence was all that was required of Clark's solicitor; the key to saving his friend would be the defence counsel he engaged, and that could wait for later. But as he watched Nestleton set off for the police station Forrester did not feel any lifting of his spirits. He knew the appropriate people would soon be doing all the appropriate things to comply with the demands of the system. He also felt it very probable that however thorough and conscientious they were, in the end Gordon Clark would hang for a crime he did not commit.

Ken Harrison was waiting for him when he got back to his rooms and for a moment Forrester stood looking at him, trying to remember what the hell he was supposed to be tutoring him about. Then, apologising for his distraction, he asked him to read his essay out loud. Instead, Harrison brought out a hip flask.

"I hope this isn't too much of a cheek, but it's a single malt – and you look as if you need it." Harrison handed him the flask and as he tipped it back Forrester felt the peaty liquid spread its warmth in the pit of his stomach.

"Yes," he said. "Good idea, Harrison. Thank you."

"I was very sorry to hear about Dr. Clark," said Harrison, settling himself into the chair on the other side of the fireplace.

"You know he's been arrested?"

"The college is buzzing with it."

Forrester drank more whisky. "I believe he's innocent," he said.

Harrison nodded. "He's always seemed a pretty good stick to me. But things look rather black for him just now, don't they?" Forrester handed him back the flask and Harrison returned it to his pocket. "Who do you think did it then, Dr. Forrester?"

Forrester looked at him sharply. Harrison had drawn his attention to a simple truth: the only certain way of keeping Gordon Clark from the gallows was to find who *had* killed David Lyall.

"I have no idea," he replied. "But I intend to find out." The words came out without thinking, but as he spoke he knew that was exactly what he had to do.

"Good for you," said Harrison. "And – I hope it doesn't sound presumptuous – I'd like to do anything I can to help."

"You?" said Forrester.

"Well, I'm sure you know lots of people who'd be more use—"

"No, no, that's not what I meant. But I can't ask you to do that. I'm supposed to be tutoring you in ancient history.

And you're supposed to be studying for a degree."

"I can do both. Anyway, this afternoon you're obviously preoccupied with this. Why don't we just talk about it and leave the Greeks for next week?"

Forrester considered this.

"This isn't just an excuse to get out of reading your essay, is it?"

"No," replied Harrison, equably. "I've written it." He took out the pages. "I'll leave it behind; you can read it when I've gone. Or I can read it to you now – I really don't mind."

"No," said Forrester. "I'll take you up on your offer. Actually, it'll be quite a relief to talk."

And as he said the words Forrester knew that it would be, because Harrison was exactly the sort of stolid, unflappable comrade you would want to have in the proverbial foxhole. Forrester had been in plenty of proverbial foxholes during the past five years, and the truth was he had rarely had someone with him who had Harrison's oddly comforting qualities. No matter that the man was technically his student – he knew he needed him. "Tell me what you want to know," he said.

"What would be most useful for me," said Harrison, "would be if you just told me what happened that night as if I knew nothing. I've only heard bits and pieces anyway; but pretend I know nothing." So Forrester did, only leaving out, because of his promise to Margaret Clark, the Senior Tutor's revelation about his wife's affair with David Lyall.

During the narrative Harrison puffed gently on his pipe and when it was over he found that it had gone out and required the usual ritual cleaning, refilling and relighting. During this he said, "What about the wife?"

"You mean, did she kill David Lyall?"

"Yes."

"Why would she do that?"

"I saw them together, once. Well, more than once, actually."

"Together?"

"On the riverbank. There was something about the way they stood – well, I suspected they were… close."

Forrester thought about this. If even Harrison had been aware of something going on between Margaret and Lyall, it wasn't going to be long before the police found out.

"So why should she kill him?" he temporised.

"Lovers' quarrel? Crime of passion? I don't know but that's the sort of thing that has to be considered, isn't it?"

Forrester thought about this – and realised it gave him an opportunity to get something out into the open without breaking a confidence.

"Surely if they were having an affair," he said, "the person who's most likely to have done the killing would be Clark himself?"

"But you don't think he did, so I'm discounting that," replied Harrison. That didn't get them much further, but Forrester felt obscurely gratified by Harrison's confidence.

"And there's another thing," said Harrison. "You've told me the police have witnesses proving she wasn't at home when she said she was. Could *she* have been up at the college?"

Forrester felt a cold shiver as Harrison spoke; it was an image he didn't want to contemplate. Had Margaret been there, waiting for Lyall with a knife, in Clark's own rooms?

"Well, I don't know where the witnesses who said she wasn't at home actually said she was," he replied carefully. "But if she killed Lyall in Gordon's college rooms she was deliberately setting him up as the guilty party. Are you saying she'd let her husband hang for a murder she'd committed?"

"I don't know how she felt about her husband," replied Harrison reasonably. "If she was having an affair with Lyall I'm guessing that there were at least some problems with the marriage."

Forrester thought about this. "She tried to give him an alibi," he said.

"It was an alibi for her too."

"I hadn't thought of that," said Forrester, because he hadn't. He got up and began to walk about the room. "Alright, let's note that possibility. I'm not discounting it, we shouldn't discount it, but I somehow don't believe it. Knowing both of them, I can't really give it credence. Let's talk about some other options."

"Well, what about Dr. Norton? According to you, Lyall was fairly beastly to him at High Table and Norton wasn't at the saga reading. He had motive and opportunity. Why haven't the police arrested him?"

"I don't know. I'm assuming he has an alibi."

"We should check that out."

"How do you mean, 'check it out'?"

"Get him into conversation, find out what he told the

police about where he was. Would that be practical for you? Just in casual conversation? I could try but it might seem a bit awkward coming from an undergraduate as opposed to one of his colleagues."

"No, it's a good idea. And there's no reason why I shouldn't ask him."

"There were an awful lot of people in the Lodge that night," said Harrison regretfully. "But if I understand you rightly it wasn't physically possible for any of them to have done it, right?"

"Not really," said Forrester. "And as I was in the same room with them I'm afraid I'm part of their alibi."

"What about this chap Haraldson? The one you found knocked out in Lyall's rooms? Do you think he told the police the truth? About going up there because he saw somebody poking about? I mean, there's no proof of that, is there? Barber only has his word for it."

"True," said Forrester. "And in fact I'm somewhat doubtful about his story."

"Why's that?"

"Because he was lying on top of the torch."

"The torch that was supposed to have hit him?"

"Exactly. It doesn't prove he wasn't hit with the torch, but it seems odd."

"But Haraldson was definitely in the Master's Lodge with you when Lyall was killed?"

"He was up in the minstrels' gallery, reading an Icelandic saga."

"And there were a couple of Icelanders there too?"

"Yes. Engineering students. Hakon and Oskar something."

"And some German chap?"

"Peter Dorfmann. Apparently one of the 'Good Germans'. But he wasn't one of the readers – he was down in the main room with me and the others."

"Any relationship between him and Lyall?"

"None that I know of. Dorfmann knows Charles Calthrop, though – the Foreign Office chap who was also at High Table. I saw them together in Whitehall yesterday."

"What about Calthrop? Did he have anything to do with Lyall?"

"He talked to him; perfectly civilised conversation about the state of Europe, that kind of thing. I've no reason to think they'd ever met before last night."

Harrison was silent for a while.

"I take it there's no doubt Lyall definitely fell from Clark's window?"

"Not really – there were no footprints in the snow leading to the spot where he was lying, so he couldn't have walked there. The only way he could have got there was through that window. And there was broken glass all around him."

"Alright," said Harrison. "Shall we draw up a plan of attack, then?"

Forrester smiled wryly. "It has the right military ring to it," he said. Harrison grinned.

"I suppose we both thought we were done with that sort of rot on VE Day."

"I certainly did," said Forrester, "but you're right. If I'm going to do anything for Gordon I'd better get organised.

But I *am* very reluctant to draw you away from your studies. This isn't your affair."

"Unless I choose to *make* it my affair," said Harrison. "And in effect, I have."

Forrester looked at him: solid, optimistic, the pipe clamped determinedly between his teeth – and felt he was extremely glad to have Harrison on his side. "Thank you," he said. "I appreciate that very much."

He picked up a notepad and began to write as Harrison, for the umpteenth time, tried to get his pipe alight again.

8

THE MASTER'S PORT

Forrester took the Master aside before High Table that evening and asked if he could speak to him afterwards. When the meal was over he accompanied him to the Lodge. Once inside, Winters seated him by the fire and offered him some port.

As the rich, dark wine ran over his tongue, Forrester felt a sense of ease that had long eluded him. The fire crackled in the hearth and its light gilded the spines of the books on the shelves lining the room. There was a fine Shiraz prayer rug in the space between the two chairs and its dusty pink fibres glowed gently as if with an inner light.

But it was more than that. Professor Michael Winters was a profoundly reassuring presence: massive, comfortable in himself, at ease with the world. Forrester remembered that Winters' father had been a general in the first war; he could imagine him sitting by a fire in some French chateau, talking confidentially to Field Marshal Haig about the next big push. He wondered if Winters' interest in the Viking sagas was his oblique response to his father's military valour.

Forrester's father had been in the first war too, of course; as a private. He'd survived it too, only to come back to the almost equally dangerous life of a North Sea trawlerman. His anger at the incompetence of the generals never abated; nor did his bitterness about the incompetence of the peace that followed. But Forrester had had enough of bitterness; he found refuge in Winters' comfortable view of the world.

"So, my dear Forrester, what can I do for you?" asked the Master, when they had savoured the port.

"I believe Gordon Clark is innocent, Master," he said, "and I'm doing my best to find evidence to prove it."

"I applaud you," said Winters. "Dr. Clark is your friend and deserves every effort you can make on his behalf. As Plautus said, '*Is est amicus, qui in re dubia te juvat, ubi re est opus.*'"

"He is a true friend…" said Forrester, touched, "who, under doubtful circumstances…"

"Aids in deed, where deeds are necessary," the Master finished. "As you are doing for Gordon. Needless to say I'll do anything I can to help you." Then he paused, weighing his words. "I ought to make it clear, though, Forrester, that I myself don't share your view. I simply can't see any other explanation for the facts as we know them."

"I understand that, Master," said Forrester. "And I appreciate you giving me your support anyway. Here's what I want to ask you: the police initially told me they believed there was bad blood between Gordon and Lyall because

Lyall had been awarded the Rotherfield Lectureship when Gordon believed he'd get it. Now Gordon has told me he didn't know that had happened. I certainly hadn't heard of it. Did he know?"

The Master thought for a moment.

"I can't answer that with any certainty. I know *I* didn't tell him. I don't believe the official letters have gone out yet. The decision wasn't mine, of course: it was made by the Special Lectureships Committee. It's conceivable someone on that committee let the information slip, but who knows? Tell me, if you believe Gordon didn't do it, who do you think did?"

Forrester sipped his port.

"Well, Alan Norton has to be a candidate," he said carefully. "Everyone heard the row between him and Gordon that night."

"Indeed they did," replied the Master. "Lyall deliberately provoked Norton and Norton is a very prickly character. I'm assuming he must have some sort of alibi which has satisfied the police?"

"I'm trying to find out about that, but I was wondering if you could tell me anything more about Peter Dorfmann. Apart from the fact that he's some sort of German politician I don't know anything about him."

"I think of him more as a scholar than a politician," replied the Master. "He was in the Literature Department of Berlin University, specialising in the Enlightenment – Goethe and so on. Managed to keep his head down during the war, which means he's eligible as a candidate in the next elections. Social Democrat, I believe."

"Why is he here?"

"As part of some programme run by the Foreign Office to make sure the new German politicians understand what democracy's all about. He wanted to visit some Oxford contacts and I offered to put him up at the college. As it turns out not a gesture that did much good for the image of British academia."

Forrester nodded. If the Foreign Office was involved with the democratisation programme in Germany that explained why Dorfmann and Calthrop had been together in Whitehall the afternoon after the murder.

"But surely Dorfmann is out of the picture anyway?" asked Winters. "You yourself were in this room with him when Lyall was killed."

"I was," said Forrester, "which I agree makes it unlikely for him to have slipped out, gone up to Clark's room and killed David Lyall." The Master smiled.

"He would have had to be pretty fast on his feet to do that and get back inside the Lodge without anyone noticing. Even if one could come up with a reason for him to do so."

"Exactly," said Forrester. "And I suppose the same thing applies to everyone in the minstrels' gallery."

"I'm afraid my days as an athlete are long past, Forrester," said Winters, smiling, "and as for the others up there during the reading, I can assure you none of them left his seat until Lady Hilary looked out of the window and raised the alarm."

"I know," said Forrester ruefully. "Otherwise I'd have

taken a closer look at them, particularly Haraldson. You know I found him unconscious in Lyall's rooms?"

"Yes, that was very odd. Did he explain what he was doing there?"

"No. But I have a suspicion he was looking for something. Someone had certainly been searching the place."

"What on earth for?"

"I'm afraid I have no idea," said Forrester.

Winters brooded on this for a moment. "I don't know Haraldson well, but I've never heard a word against him. He fought with British forces during the Norway campaign in 1940 and was evacuated with our chaps when we pulled out. I think he was wounded. He's a very distinguished scholar, as you know. And of course he was beside me in the minstrels' gallery until Lyall's body was found. Whatever he was doing in Lyall's rooms after the murder, I can vouch for his whereabouts beforehand. And I'm pleased to say he's sufficiently recovered from his injuries to get in a little research at the Bodleian before he returns home."

"Good," said Forrester, and stood up. "Thank you, Master. I simply wanted to let you know what I was up to and ask for your blessing on the enterprise. If anything does occur to you that might help me, I'd really appreciate it."

"Of course," said Winters. "And I think what you're doing is splendid. If I was ever in trouble I'd want to have a friend like you on the case."

"I only wish I had more confidence I'm going about it the right way," he said.

"I'm sure you are," said the Master. "And if you do

find yourself uncertain about a course of action, feel free to come back and consult."

As Forrester reached the front door of the Lodge, Lady Hilary came down the stairs and put a hand on his arm. "I just wanted to thank you," she said, "for being so supportive on that dreadful night."

Forrester gave her a reassuring smile. "I thought you held up pretty well," he said. "We were all in shock."

"You comforted me," said Lady Hilary, "and I appreciate it."

"I'm glad," said Forrester. "How are you feeling now?" Forrester's own assessment was that she was still in shock, her face pale, with blotches of high colour.

"Much better, thank you, Duncan," she said. "Much better."

And with that she saw him out.

9

CONVERSATION IN A WAITING ROOM

Forrester spotted Haraldson easily among the crowd leaving the Bodleian Library because he towered above the rest of the departing readers, but Haraldson was not pleased to see him.

"I am on my way to the station," he said. "I return to Norway tonight."

"What time's your train?" asked Forrester.

"It leaves within the hour."

"I'll walk with you to the station. I have a few questions about what happened the night Lyall died."

"I've answered many, many questions from the police while I was in the hospital," said Haraldson, "and my head is still sore. I do not really want to talk about this any more."

"I quite understand," said Forrester. "It's just that I'm afraid an innocent man may go to the gallows unless I can dig up some more information."

"But I have no more information," replied the Norwegian. "So I cannot be of any help to you." Haraldson's stride was long and Forrester had to walk swiftly to keep up with him.

"What were you looking for in Lyall's room when I found you that night?" he asked.

"I was looking for nothing: I saw someone up there, went up to find out who it was, and was hit on the back of the head by a torch."

"You were lying on top of it."

"What?"

"The torch you claim you were attacked with was underneath you. How could it have got there if it had been used to hit you on the back of the head?"

"I have no idea."

"I think the police would be interested in the fact."

"The police must already know it."

"In fact they don't. I regret that I didn't make myself clear enough to them when they arrived. I've been thinking I ought to go back and make sure they do understand that your claim about how you had been injured was demonstrably false."

"You should do what you think is best," said Haraldson.

"If I do that, and the police feel they need to question you again," said Forrester, "it may interfere with your travel plans. You may not be able to make your boat."

"What's that to you?" demanded the Norwegian. Forrester stopped and Haraldson stopped beside him.

"I've no desire to cause you inconvenience," he said, "but I would like you to help me. I think there are things you're not telling me about your relationship with David Lyall and if you're prepared to open up to me I'm prepared to postpone any revision of my statement to the police until after you've returned to Norway."

Haraldson looked at him steadily and studied his watch for a moment. "If we walk rapidly without any further talking I believe we can reach the station with perhaps fifteen minutes to spare before my train. During that fifteen minutes, in return for the promise you have offered, I will tell you what I know about David Lyall. Do you agree?"

Forrester agreed.

They reached the station with twenty minutes to spare and rattled in vain at the doors of the refreshment room with its glass dome of yesterday's sandwiches curling gently in anticipation of tomorrow's customers. Finally they took refuge in the second-class waiting room, where the gas fire remained unlit and the wind rattled the windows. Posters advertising Sanatogen Nerve Tonic and Iron Jelloids made their muted appeals in the feeble light of forty-watt bulbs, swaying gently in the draughts. A thick carpet of cigarette stubs covered the scarred linoleum floor.

"So," said Forrester. "How did you know Lyall?"

"My injuries after the Norway campaign were such that I could not fight again," said Haraldson, "but I offered my services to give guidance to the Special Operations Executive when they were sending men into Norway for operations behind the lines."

An express roared through without stopping and the windows rattled angrily in response. "I met Lyall in February 1943 when I briefed him before he was sent into Norway."

"Sabotage mission?"

"Yes."

"Was it a success?"

"I never found out. I have the impression it was not, but as you'll be aware information like that was not widely available."

"Of course."

"Lyall got back eventually, but I did not keep in touch with him. In fact, I had no contact with him between November 1943 and September of last year."

"And what happened in September?"

"He wrote to me at the University of Oslo, where I now work, asking if I intended to visit England in the near future. As it happened I had several matters to attend to here, and I told him I'd be coming in January. He then invited me to Oxford, saying he had something to show me which he thought might be of interest to me."

"What was it?"

"An Old Norse manuscript."

"A manuscript?"

"Or part of a manuscript; it wasn't clear. He said it contained—" A train began shunting a row of freight cars back and forth outside, and Forrester did not hear the next words.

"He said it contained what?"

Haraldson, for the first time, looked sheepish. Then he said, "I have no interest in these speculations, except academic interest. I do not subscribe to such outlandish notions."

Forrester narrowed his eyes. "What outlandish notions?"

"The mythology of my people is just that, mythology. It has nothing to do with the supernatural." And suddenly

Forrester remembered Lyall's words before High Table on the night he had died.

"You're talking about the occult," he said. "Lyall told you this manuscript he had spoke about—"

"I have no desire to reach through to other worlds!" said Haraldson with sudden intensity. "I am interested only in the history and literature of my people. That was why I wanted to see the manuscript, not for any other reason. I knew from the first that all his talk of encryption was nonsense."

"Encryption? Encryption of what?"

"Runes are runes. Nothing is hidden within them. They are not symbols for summoning anything."

Forrester felt something move inside his mind, as if two tectonic plates were sliding past one another.

"But that's what Lyall told you? He told you something was hidden within the manuscript? Some sort of spell for conjuring diabolical—"

"There is no link," said Haraldson decisively, "between the old gods of my people and whatever being rules the Judeo-Christian Hell. I am a Norse scholar, that is all." As Forrester watched him, he did not believe the disclaimer for a second. He knew in his bones that it was Lyall's promise of occult knowledge in some ancient Norse document that had drawn Haraldson to Oxford, like a moth to the flame, whatever he said to deny it.

"Did Lyall explain more when you arrived in Oxford? About what was in the manuscript?"

"There was no opportunity," said Haraldson. "We exchanged greetings before High Table and arranged to meet the next day. But before that could happen, he was killed."

"So you went up to his room to see if you could find the manuscript for yourself?"

"I did."

"And?"

"I was attacked before I found it. Not, as you have already deduced, by the torch, which I had picked up from Lyall's desk to use in my search, but by some other, I think considerably heavier object."

"I see. And you decided not to confide this to the police?"

"I did not believe it was relevant. Also, I did not wish to become involved in the investigation. Lyall's murder has nothing to do with me."

"How can you say that? He offered to show you a valuable document—"

"There is no proof it was valuable—"

"And he was killed before he could do so. My friend is accused of murdering him in a jealous rage. Your evidence suggests another possibility."

"I don't think so. The manuscript may have been of scholarly interest, but I doubt it had much monetary value. And as for its occult significance, you can forget it. I am certain now it was a figment of David Lyall's imagination."

"Nevertheless the police should know about the manuscript."

"You have a point. When I misled them on the subject I didn't of course anticipate your friend being arrested."

"But he has been," said Forrester. "Which rather changes things."

"True."

"So what are you going to do about it?"

Haraldson considered for a moment. There was a mournful hooting outside and a train wheezed regretfully alongside the platform. Haraldson picked up his suitcase and opened the waiting-room door. Whistles blew and carriage doors slammed and the station loudspeaker gave its usual incomprehensible announcements. Forrester grasped Haraldson's arm.

"What are you going to do?"

"I will write from Norway," said Haraldson. "I will write to the police and send them a copy of the letter Lyall sent me. They will be able to draw their own conclusions."

"I think you should go to see them now," said Forrester.

"No," said the Norwegian. "I can foresee endless complications. When I am back home, I will deal with it."

Forrester realised he was not going to get any further. Haraldson extricated himself from his grip, crossed the platform and stepped into a carriage.

"The train now departing Platform Three..." said the loudspeaker. Forrester held onto the carriage door.

"Listen," he said. "An innocent man may hang unless you do what you have promised."

"He may hang even if I do," said Haraldson. "Because I don't believe there's any connection between the manuscript and Lyall's murder."

The whistle blew and the train began to move. Haraldson pulled the door to. "Nevertheless I will write," he said. "And I hope you save your friend."

And with that, Forrester was engulfed in a blast of steam from the engine, and the train began to wheeze out of the station. He stood on the platform for a long time, watching its lights disappear into the distance.

10

X-RAY CRYSTALLOGRAPHY

Forrester made an appointment to see Inspector Barber the next day. He knew perfectly well that his threat to convince the police that Haraldson had been lying and thus prevent his departure was a hollow one, but what he hadn't expected was the force of Barber's disappointment when he told him why he had come.

"I had hoped you were going to assist us, Dr. Forrester," said Barber, "not supply us with red herrings." As he spoke he drew a fish on his blotter, and then another. "Or stories of black magic."

"I would have thought the fact that David Lyall had a valuable Norse manuscript which has since disappeared was highly relevant," said Forrester. "Unless you're discounting all possible suspects except Dr. Clark. Surely you're not doing that?"

"We are of course keeping an open mind," said Barber, "but unlike you, we come to the case with open eyes."

"Which is why I thought you would be interested in new evidence," said Forrester.

"At present, Dr. Forrester, it's not evidence, it's hearsay," said Barber. "We have only your word that this is what Haraldson said, and he, conveniently, is not here to corroborate it."

Forrester stood up. "I'm sorry you doubt my word," he said stiffly, "but Haraldson has promised to write to you enclosing Lyall's letter to him, referring to the manuscript, as soon as he gets back to Oslo. You should have it within two or three days."

"I'll read it with interest," said Barber, remaining seated.

"But there's no reason not to do something straight away," said Forrester. "For example you could start investigating people who might have wanted to get their hands on that document."

"Is that your advice, sir? On how we should conduct our investigation?"

"It's not advice," said Forrester. "Surely it's obvious that's what has to be done?"

"Obvious, eh? The kind of thing the plodding constabulary would probably miss, but which the clever Oxford don would see at once?"

"That's not what I'm saying at all—"

"I do respect your attempts to help your friend, Dr. Forrester," said Barber. "I do expect you to pass on any information you may have regarding the case. *Any* information, that is, whether helpful to Dr. Clark or not. But I do not wish to be told how to do my job. Is that understood?"

Forrester forced himself to take a deep breath. "Of course, Inspector," he said, opening the door. "I'm sure we have every reason to feel complete confidence in you."

And he walked out.

Forrester was still grinding his teeth in suppressed fury as he climbed the stairs to the laboratory where Alan Norton conducted his experiments. It was a long, low room with dark wooden floors and arrays of equipment, which vaguely reminded him of a darkroom. A young blonde woman was inserting a tiny square of glass into one of these objects. The fit was tight – in fact Forrester was tempted to wonder if the glass was supposed to go into that particular slot at all, but the young woman thrust it home with great determination and there was no audible crack.

"Dr. Norton isn't here," she said in answer to his enquiry. "But he should be back shortly." Her voice was high pitched and oddly grating. Forrester knew she wanted him to go away but felt a strange compulsion to stay there in order to irritate her. He felt as if there were great reserves of irritation beneath the surface of her personality, just waiting to be released. He watched her for a moment.

"That looks interesting," said Forrester. "What is it?" The young woman looked at him with piercing blue eyes as if deciding whether to attack him with whatever object came to hand, and then, with an effort of will, smiled icily.

"X-ray crystallography."

"And what is that?"

"The science of determining the arrangement of atoms within a crystal from the manner in which X-rays are deflected *by* the crystal," she said. "It involves scattering X-rays from a single, very pure crystal to produce a pattern on a screen behind it."

"I see," said Forrester. "And the object is…?"

"Obviously to discover the architecture of proteins," she said. "I'm supposed to be working with Professor Hodgkin on the structure of penicillin, but she's assigned me to help Dr. Norton with Gramicidin C."

"Your supervisor is Dorothy Hodgkin?" said Forrester. He remembered Dorothy from his undergraduate years, a brilliant, voluble woman passionate about pacifism and correcting social injustice. She had married a charming, serially unfaithful communist named Thomas Hodgkin, but this had not prevented her becoming the lover of her scientific mentor, the brilliant J.D. Bernal, who was also married. And also a communist. Not surprisingly, the private lives of all three were complex and full of drama. "Working with Professor Hodgkin must be fascinating, Miss…"

"Roberts," said the young woman. "Margaret Roberts." Now Forrester remembered her name too: she was a leading light in the Oxford Conservative Association, and had been active in trying to prevent Oxford electing a Labour MP in the 1945 election. He wondered how she felt about the bohemian left-wing enthusiasm that seemed to grip the Department of Chemistry, and could not resist asking her. "Listening to uncongenial opinions keeps me sharp," she said, "and somebody has to defend Mr. Churchill."

"You don't think his time has passed?" said Forrester. "You don't think he's ancient history now?"

She met his gaze with shining eyes. "If Mr. Churchill were in charge of British foreign policy today instead of Mr. Ernest Bevin," she said, "we wouldn't have Stalin breathing down our necks."

"Have you tried to convince Alan Norton of this?" asked Forrester, imagining the encounter. Margaret Roberts looked at him with contempt.

"I wouldn't waste my time," she replied. "Dr. Norton believes we would all be much better off if the Russians were in charge." And she turned back to inserting a second glass plate into a second dangerously small-looking aperture.

At which point the door opened and Norton came in, removing his shabby raincoat and hanging it on a hat stand. He checked the preparations the woman had made before guiding Forrester down to the far end of the lab.

"I see you're harbouring a rabid Conservative in your midst," said Forrester. Norton's mouth twitched.

"Grocer's daughter from Grantham," he said. "Utterly provincial petit bourgeois."

"Well qualified for the firing squad come the revolution," said Forrester.

"If you've come here to be facetious," said Norton, "you can go away again."

"Sorry," said Forrester. "I came here to talk about what happened to Lyall."

"Clark should get a medal for doing away with the bastard," remarked Norton, selecting a slide. "He's rid the world of a very nasty piece of work."

"He says he didn't do it. I believe him."

"He would say that, wouldn't he? And as his friend you'd naturally believe him."

"And of course he wasn't the only one to have a furious row with Lyall that night."

Norton met his gaze steadily.

"No. Clark backed me up when Lyall tried to denounce me for my political beliefs. Lyall switched his attack to Clark, and Clark gave as good as he got."

"What I mean is," persisted Forrester, "you were as angry with Lyall at High Table as Clark was."

"Not angry enough to stab him to death, though, Forrester. And the murder did happen in Clark's rooms, not mine."

"Look, I'm not accusing you," said Forrester. "I'm just trying to prevent them hanging an innocent man."

"Fair enough," said Norton. "But I'm not offering to step up to the gallows instead."

"I'm assuming you've already given the police an alibi," said Forrester.

"I have," said Norton. Forrester held his tongue, extending the silence just long enough for it to seem odd if Norton did not elaborate. At last Norton said, "I came straight here after High Table. The young lady from Grantham was putting in a few extra hours too, and we talked about what she was doing."

"Well," said Forrester, "if a leading light of the Oxford Conservative Association is providing your alibi, you have nothing to worry about, do you?" He spoke lightly, but he resolved to check with Margaret Roberts that she had indeed seen Norton back at the lab that night.

"If you want to look beyond Clark," said Norton, "there were a number of dodgy characters at High Table that night, weren't there?"

"How do you mean, dodgy characters?"

"Well, I know nothing about Dorfmann except that he got through the war in a prominent German university without ever offending the Nazis, which is quite a feat – but I do know Charles Calthrop is an untrustworthy bastard."

"The Foreign Office man? What do you mean?"

"I had some run-ins with him during the war," said Norton bitterly. "He had the cheek to question my loyalty; I sent him away with a flea in his ear. I've watched his career ever since. Pays to know your enemies."

Forrester thought of his brief glimpse of Calthrop and Dorfmann in conversation in Whitehall.

"What's he doing now, as far as you know?"

"I've heard he's building up an anti-Soviet spy network," said Norton. "Typical, isn't it? No sooner is one war over than these ex-public schoolboys want to start another."

"I share your concern," said Forrester. "But I can't see why Calthrop would have wanted to kill David Lyall, even if it had been physically possible, which I don't think it was. Can you suggest a motive?"

"No," said Norton. "But you asked for information and I'm giving it to you." Forrester thought about the information Norton had given him, trying to see how it might possibly be of use to his friend.

"Did Lyall have anything to do with intelligence?" he said at last, clutching at straws.

"Not as far as I know," replied Norton. "He was in the commandos during the war. In Scandinavia, I believe. I gather it was a cock-up, but that doesn't surprise me."

Margaret Roberts called from the far end of the lab.

"We're ready to begin, Dr. Norton," she said. "Whenever you are."

"I'll be there in a minute," said Norton, and leant closer to Forrester. "What about jealous husbands?" Forrester froze. But Norton went on, "I've heard Lyall was a bit of a ladies' man." Inwardly, Forrester sighed with relief.

"Really? Do you have any names?"

"No," said Norton. "The only woman I associate with Lyall happens to be single."

"Who's she?"

"Alice Hayley. At Lady Margaret Hall."

"Were they still a couple? Or had he thrown her over?"

"No idea. I just know they were going out together for a while. If you want to talk to her the easiest place to find her is the Borringer."

"Where?"

"The experimental drama place. Where that peacock fellow is."

"I'm sorry, what peacock fellow?"

"The one in the purple suit," said Norton, and Forrester knew immediately who he was talking about.

11

DRAMA KING

The man in the purple suit was in evidence the moment Forrester walked into the Borringer Theatre. He was more conventionally dressed today, but his early Oxford appearance in the purple suit, sporting a large ruby ring and wearing a gold shirt, had established an image on which Kenneth Tynan had capitalised ever since. His object, he'd told anybody who'd listen, was to become "the first post-war myth". He was on the editorial board of the *Cherwell*, he was the star turn at the Oxford Union, and the plays he put on were guaranteed to be controversial whether or not they were any good.

A London critic had described his performance in *Hamlet* as "quite dreadful", and Tynan had immediately written back: "My performance in *Hamlet* was not 'quite dreadful' as you claimed – it was in fact slightly less than mediocre." There were rumours that when he graduated the critic would be sacked and Tynan would be given his job. Now Forrester watched as, through clouds of cigarette smoke, Tynan addressed the cast of his latest production.

"This morning my beloved tutor, the saintly C.S. Lewis, has helped me rediscover Milton and to celebrate I retired to my rooms and listened to Noël Coward's blissful recording of 'Sigh No More' during which I wept copiously. But, Alice, I know your performance will move me more than either of those experiences. Your lines, please."

A dark-haired, full-bosomed young woman wearing a jute sack – which Forrester assumed was her costume – came centre-stage and began to speak.

"I opened my heart to find which part of me demands your love," she declaimed. "I found it, like a dark crystal at the core of my being. A fragile crystal, radiating the dark light of pain. A crystal that longs to be crushed under your heel even as you fall under its hypnotic spell. When I learned you had been with her I knew that on the day when you cease to love me, I will cease to exist."

Forrester saw Tynan mouthing the words as she spoke: it was clear the lines were his own. But Alice Hayley projected them with such passion that Forrester was prepared to believe they came from the heart. He waited until Tynan called a halt and drew the woman aside as the other actors helped themselves to tea and biscuits.

"I gather you knew David Lyall," he said.

"Who told you that?"

"Is it true?"

"We were lovers for three months." Without warning, tears began to run down her cheeks. Forrester, surprised at how quickly she had taken him into her confidence, took her by the arm and guided her to a chair at the far end of the hall.

"Twelfth Night is a time of madness," Tynan was announcing by the tea urn. "A pointless, idiot festival and a time for doing unreasonable and mysterious things."

"I'm sorry," said Forrester. "This must be very painful." She shook her head.

"No, it's alright," she said, blowing her nose with touching determination. "Actually it's a relief to be able to talk to somebody. I thought nobody knew about us, so there's been no-one to—" and tears overcame her again. When she had them under control she said, "I hated him, actually. He was a bastard and he deserved to die." And then she began sobbing again and Forrester found himself putting an arm around her, the jute sack prickly against his skin.

"It's alright," he said meaninglessly. "It's alright."

At last she was in control of herself again and looked him straight in the eyes. Despite the streaked make-up and her ridiculous costume, she was beautiful. Her jet-black hair was cut in stylish bangs, her lips full and red.

"You think that I killed him, don't you?" she said.

Forrester was taken aback. "No, no," he said. "It never occurred to me. I'm trying to find out more because the police think it was a friend of mine who did it and I don't believe them."

"You're a friend of Gordon Clark?"

"Yes."

"It was his wife that David left me for," she said.

Forrester suppressed a gasp. Her gaze still held his.

"If I'd had a knife when I found out I'd have stabbed him in the heart. Right through the heart."

"What in fact did you do?" asked Forrester.

"Went to my rooms, stopped up the draughts, turned on the gas fire, and didn't light it," she said. "But there wasn't enough money in the meter." Forrester couldn't help smiling, and she smiled back, though hers was a wry grimace. "Silly, isn't it? If I'd had a shilling in my purse that night I wouldn't be here. By the time I'd found somebody to borrow one off I decided to get drunk instead. And then Ken came and offered me a part in his play."

"Good for him," said Forrester.

"It's a good part," said Alice Hayley. "Though I don't really understand half of what I'm saying."

"Well, you don't give that impression," said Forrester.

"Thank you. Another good thing about it – it gives me an alibi. I was here with everybody the night David was killed."

"Ah."

"Sorry."

"No, no. I'm very glad it wasn't you. But I'm wondering if you can tell me anything that might help me find out who *did* do it."

"Could it have been one of the Norwegians?"

"Norwegians?" asked Forrester, surprised.

"Well, Swedes, Finns, Danes, I'm not sure. But David used to go drinking with them; I sometimes met him at the Eagle and Child. He'd been there during the war, you know.

Scandinavia, I mean, not the Eagle and Child."

"I gather the Scandinavian mission went badly. Did he talk about what happened there?"

"Not much. I got the impression someone had betrayed him to the Germans."

"What? You mean he was captured?" Forrester knew what had happened to British commandos captured by the Germans: their deaths were either swift and brutal or agonisingly protracted.

"No, I don't think so. I think he escaped, got home through Sweden. People helped him."

"Interesting."

"Didn't make him any less of a bastard, though."

Forrester looked at her, and wished he'd met her before Lyall had.

"Was there any mention of anything he'd found there?" he said. "Like… a manuscript? Something valuable?"

She shook her head. "Sorry. I think one of the people who'd helped him was some kind of aristocrat, though."

"He didn't mention anything to do with… the occult, did he?"

She looked at him, puzzled. "Never," she said. "He always regarded that kind of thing as complete nonsense."

"Never mentioned some hidden knowledge he'd gathered during the war? Anything to do with Norse mythology?"

"No, he didn't," she said.

"Darlings," called Tynan from the other end of the room. "Time to get back to work. But before we do I wish to recite a clerihew I have just invented. It is about Edward Gibbon. It goes like this:

> Edward Gibbon,
> Wrote ad lib on,
> The bloody mystery,
> Of later Roman history.

There were catcalls and scattered applause. Tynan clapped his hands. "That's it, my dears, on with the show."

12

DARK WATER

Forrester went for a walk when he left the theatre, crossing Folly Bridge and descending to the towpath by the Head of the River inn, with its balconies overlooking the water and the barges bobbing in the current below. Trees overhung the path here, cutting out what little sunlight was permeating through the leaden clouds; it looked as if it was going to snow again.

A commando in Norway, betrayed to the Germans. An ambitious, philandering academic in Oxford. A body, lying in the snow beneath Gordon Clark's window. All incarnations of David Lyall, who had tempted a hot-tempered Norwegian academic with a juicy morsel of ancient literature, which may or may not have included incantations for raising the Devil, who had tormented a prickly colleague as a fellow traveller, cuckolded at least one husband, seduced at least one wife, abandoned at least one lover. Did all or any of them hate him enough to kill him? Were all or any of them—

Suddenly Forrester felt that he was not alone; experienced the prickling of that sixth sense that had served him so well and so often. He shrank back against the trunk of a tree, shutting off at least one avenue of attack, peering out into the gloom with eyes alert to any hint of movement, ears straining for any scrap of sound.

Neither came. Forrester stood there, feeling the rough bark under his palms, letting his eyes become accustomed to the semi-darkness. He tuned out the distant rumble of the buses on the Abingdon Road, the shouts of the barge men and women by the moorings near the pub, the noise of dogs barking; he finally eliminated the noise of his own breath, poised to hear the breathing of the other.

Because he was certain there was another presence, and a hostile one. It was absurd, in one way: he was just a few hundred yards away from a road busy with traffic, and a towpath used by dozens of people. And yet, a sudden rush, the swift downward trajectory of a blade, and his body could be sliding down the bank into the dark waters of the river, drifting away with the current.

The bushes crackled suddenly to his right, and as he'd been taught he launched himself in that direction because any assailant would assume he'd dive away and the blow, if it was coming, would be ill-directed. And then he was slipping sideways in a patch of mud, all balance gone, and as he hit the ground an electric bolt of pain shot up his arm from the elbow and he knew that this was the moment when he would know who had killed David Lyall – immediately before he too met the same fate. Unless...

He rolled sideways out of the trees, rising in one swift movement to face his attacker – and seeing nothing except the shadow of someone crashing through the undergrowth in the opposite direction. He hurled himself to the end of the path that led around the trees but by the time he got to Christ Church Meadow its only occupant was an elderly woman walking her dog.

For a moment he stood, panting, looking this way and that, adrenalin coursing through him; and then retraced his steps to the Head of the River.

Half an hour later he was in the Eagle and Child pub, where he had arranged to meet Harrison. When he got there the younger man was already surrounded by an excited crowd of Scandinavians, arguing furiously. He was clearly in his element, enjoying the beer, enjoying the company; Forrester could see why he had survived the German POW camps so well and knew he was damn lucky to have Harrison on his side.

As he approached the bar, Harrison jerked his head, indicating a quiet corner on the far side of the room where they could talk later. Forrester ordered a pint of Burton and slid into a dark wooden settle on the far side of the fire, disturbing a slight man with greying hair dozing in the shadows.

"Sorry," said Forrester, and then recognised him. "Professor Tolkien?"

Tolkien nodded warily and Forrester introduced himself.

"I had expected to see you at the saga reading at Barnard the other evening."

"Ah, yes," said Tolkien. "I would have been there, but I'd mislaid Rohan."

"Rohan?"

"Not a real place. Part of something I'm writing. But I found it in the end. Dreadful business. What happened that night, I mean, not my manuscript. I'm always muddling them."

"Listen, Professor, could I talk to you about that? I'm a friend of Gordon Clark. I believe he's innocent and I'm trying to find out what really happened."

"Well if ever someone needed someone who believed in him, it's Dr. Clark. But I'm not sure how *I* can help."

"It's about Arne Haraldson," said Forrester. "You know about his visit?"

"Yes, Bitteridge told me."

"Well, he's gone back to Norway now, but before he did he told me that Lyall had promised to show him some kind of manuscript, possibly a Norse saga." Tolkien sat up straighter. "I was wondering," Forrester went on, "if Lyall ever mentioned to you that he had such a manuscript?" Tolkien's piercing blue eyes glinted with the sort of enthusiasm his fictional dwarves showed for gold.

"He did not," he said. "Needless to say I would have been very interested to hear about such a thing. Do you know which saga it was?"

"No, I'm not even sure it *was* a saga – that's just a guess. But perhaps you could tell me – are there certain Norse works that are particularly sought after?"

Tolkien smiled gently. "We are talking about a violent and bloodthirsty people," he said. "Unfortunate things often happened to their literary productions. For example, we would love to get our hands on the *Færeyinga* sagas, the story of the conquest of the Faroe Islands, which dates from about 1200; we know of the manuscript's existence only from references in other sagas. We'd also love to find the original version of the *Karlamagnús* saga. And during the thirties your own Master made his name with his brilliant reconstruction of the lost books of the *Heimskringla* – the volumes referred to by Snorri Sturluson."

"The *Heimskringla*?"

"Stories of the Norwegian kings. There's a particularly dramatic passage about the sacking of Konungahella, which has survived. I often recite it to my students."

Tolkien's eyes were sparkling now; it was almost as if he could see the flashing swords and the burning timbers as he spoke and Forrester knew that given half a chance the scholar would launch into a recitation. Indeed, in other circumstances he'd have delighted in the experience, but now came the most delicate area.

"One odd thing Haraldson told me was that Lyall had claimed there was some supernatural significance to the manuscript."

"In that it dealt with gods and monsters?"

"No," said Forrester. "In that it contained satanic incantations. Does that sound probable?" A shadow crossed Tolkien's face.

"Foolish people have sometimes tried to pervert the

beliefs of the Nordic peoples. It was a fad in the thirties among certain fanatics, not just in Germany but also in Scandinavia itself."

"You mean the Nazis?"

"And their like, yes."

"But if Lyall had come across such a manuscript, perhaps while he was in Scandinavia during the war, you'd have been a natural person for him to have discussed it with?"

"Either myself or Winters, of course."

"The Master didn't mention it, so I assume he didn't ask him. Which is strange, because Norse literature wasn't Lyall's field, so he'd have had to consult somebody."

"Perhaps he wanted to keep the discovery to himself?"

"Then why tell Haraldson about it?"

"True enough. But Haraldson never saw it?"

"No. He searched Lyall's rooms and was attacked before he found anything."

"What a pity. So the manuscript has gone missing."

"And the question is," said Forrester, "who took it?"

"Missing Norse manuscript?" said a voice. "I'd search Tollers' pockets first. He's probably copying it wholesale into the saga of Bingo Baggins."

A large, plump, cheerful man wreathed in pipe smoke squeezed onto the settle with two pints and thrust one at Tolkien. "After all, he has to find some way to finish it."

"Thank you, Jack," said Tolkien. "It's always stimulating to be accused of plagiarism." But he spoke without heat and clinked his mug against the other man's. "And it's not Bingo now, it's Frodo. More heroic."

"Much more," said Clive Lewis. "Is the end in sight?"

"Not even a glimmer," said Tolkien sadly. "You pushed me so hard in 1944 I got the hobbits right into Mordor; but as a result I was so exhausted everything ground to a halt, where it remains. Perhaps I'll go back to the beginning and start afresh."

"Don't you dare," said Lewis vehemently. "You've done it far too often and all you get is another half-finished draft."

"Not all of us write as easily as you do," said Tolkien without rancour.

"Ease of composition is not your problem, Tollers," said Lewis. "Your problem is thinking you have to get every detail right before you can go on. But you don't have to do that – you should just fix the details up when the book's finished. Stop wasting time on all those maps and charts and phases of the moon." He turned to Forrester. "I've caught him spending an entire morning calculating what direction the wind ought to be blowing during a battle!"

"I want people to believe it," said Tolkien, "and that means it's got to be real."

"It's not real," said Lewis, "it's a story. And nobody will either believe or disbelieve it if they never get to read it. So do Bingo or Frodo or whoever he is a favour and finish it before I beat you to it with Narnia."

"Ah, Narnia," said Tolkien with a hint of reproach, and fell silent. Sensing a sudden tension between the two men, Forrester decided this was the perfect moment to make his excuses, thank him for his help and go across to join Harrison. The Scandinavians had gone.

"Sorry to ask you to wait," said Harrison, "but I was still working on them."

"It was a profitable diversion," said Forrester. "I'll tell you about it later. But were they any use, your Norsemen? Had any of them met Lyall?"

"Not only had they met him," said Harrison, "but he'd been asking them to help him translate bits of medieval Norse."

"How very odd," said Forrester. "Why?"

"How do you mean, odd?" asked Harrison. "What's odd about it? They were Norwegians."

"He was asking *students* about the Norse sagas," said Forrester, "when he could have consulted J.R.R. Tolkien, sitting right there by the fire. Or Michael Winters, for that matter, in his own college!"

Harrison took a thoughtful pull at his pint.

"I hadn't thought of that," he said.

"Did any of them report anything in these translations that referred to Satanism?"

"Satanism?"

"Apparently Lyall tried to increase Haraldson's interest in the manuscript by hinting it held some kind of clue to communicating with the Devil."

"Well I never," said Harrison. "No, none of them mentioned anything about that."

"Alright, then," said Forrester, "so let's concentrate on laying out a timeline."

"Absolutely," said Harrison and opened his notepad.

"Lyall goes on a mission to Norway in 1943," said

Forrester as Harrison wrote. "The mission's betrayed, he goes on the run, eventually escapes with the help of some kind of aristocrat. Did he tell any of the students about that, by the way?"

"None of them mentioned it."

"Interesting. Perhaps it was a painful memory. Anyway, he gets back home and ultimately returns to Oxford, where he begins talking to people about an Old Norse manuscript he'd picked up."

"Hang on," said Harrison. "He didn't tell any of those Scandinavians that he had a manuscript. He just asked about specific lines of Old Norse. I got the impression they were typewritten."

"Typewritten?" said Forrester. "So probably not what the actual Norsemen wrote, but let's assume they were copied from something they did actually leave behind. And the only person he informs about the manuscript is Arne Haraldson in Oslo, to whom he promises to show it when he comes to visit. Now why would he do that? What's special about Haraldson?"

"Perhaps he wanted to consult him about it before publishing it?"

"In which case why not go to Winters or Tolkien? And anyway, it wasn't Lyall's field; publishing it would have done him no academic good whatsoever."

"Might he have wanted to *sell* the manuscript to Haraldson?" said Harrison. "Because of the occult material it contained?"

"Possibly. I just spoke to Professor Tolkien about that.

We know the Nazis were obsessed with Norse mythology and the occult. What I hadn't realised until he mentioned it was that there were certain people in Scandinavia before the war with the same unhealthy enthusiasm."

"And Haraldson could have been one of them?"

"That's what I'm beginning to suspect."

"Where is he now?"

"On a boat back to Norway, as far as I know," said Forrester. "Unless…" and suddenly the encounter on the riverbank came vividly back.

"What?"

"Nothing, I was just speculating. And we mustn't get carried away with Haraldson: there's another possible motive we mustn't forget."

"What's that?" said Harrison.

"The fact that Lyall was betrayed during that mission," said Forrester. "Somebody sold him out to the Germans – presumably a Norwegian. And of course, some of those students you were just talking to were Norwegian."

"Good Lord," said Harrison, "I hadn't thought of that."

"What if Lyall had some piece of information that might lead him to identify the chap who informed on him? And that person realised it and did away with him before he could speak out?"

"That's a pretty powerful motive," said Harrison. "If it's true."

"It's just speculation," said Forrester. "But now you've got to know these chaps, you might want to keep in touch with them, see if any of them thinks that one of the others has something in his past he wants to keep dark."

"Will do," said Harrison.

"But be careful," said Forrester. "You don't want to provoke somebody into doing to you what he did to Lyall."

"No, indeed," said Harrison with a grin. "I'll avoid it at all costs. But in the meantime, tell me how you got on with Dr. Norton. Do you still think he's a possible suspect?"

"He made no bones about being glad Lyall was dead – but he trotted out a pretty good alibi. He'd been working with a student in the lab – somebody called Margaret Roberts. If you get a chance you might check with her whether he's telling the truth."

"Consider it done," said Harrison.

"He also suggested I had a closer look at Dorfmann, because he was suspicious about how he kept his university job without joining the Nazi Party, and Calthrop, because he's setting up an anti-Soviet spy network."

"Is he now?"

"And he urged me to consider any number of jealous husbands who might be harbouring grudges."

"A positive avalanche of suspects."

"Plus, he directed me to Alice Hayley, one of the long list of women Lyall was taking to bed. Her I've spoken to."

"And do you think she might have done him in?"

"No, not really. But she was the one who told me about the Scandinavian students, which is why I got you to come here."

Harrison speared a pickled onion from the jar on the counter and looked at it thoughtfully. "Would I be being unduly suspicious if I pointed out that Norton seems to have gone out of his way to provide you with a large number of other people to think about apart from himself?"

"He did indeed," said Forrester. "Though that was perfectly consistent with helping me clear Gordon Clark."

"I suppose so. What about this Dorfmann chap? Even if he was a bit of a Nazi I can't quite see why that would have led him to want to do away with David Lyall. I mean, he wasn't in Norway when Lyall was on the run there, was he?"

"I've no reason to suppose so. As far as I know he never left Berlin. He was at the university there."

"And why would Calthrop have had anything against Lyall?" asked Harrison. "Low though my opinion of the Foreign Office might be, and lower still of the intelligence community, I wouldn't have said that stabbing Oxford dons and chucking them out of windows was their normal M.O., would you?"

"No," said Forrester. "But remember I did see Calthrop and Dorfmann in deep conversation in Whitehall while I was in London."

"Well that's not so surprising if Dorfmann is being groomed for political power in the new Germany. He's exactly the sort of person Calthrop would want to cultivate."

"It may be something to do with this spy network Norton claims Calthrop's setting up."

"Do you mean the conversation with Dorfmann might have had something to do with that, or that Lyall's death might have?"

"Either. Both. I'm not sure, it just came into my head."

"Well, one never knows with these cloak and dagger operations," said Harrison. "It's such a murky business. But it could be a profitable angle for us, couldn't it? All the police seem interested in is an academic rivalry, which points the finger firmly at Dr. Clark. If we want to widen the range of suspects we've got to widen the range of possible motives."

"I can't see the police being very impressed at being told one of the guests at High Table that night had something to do with the intelligence service. After all, that's probably a given in Oxford."

"True enough," said Harrison. "We'd need more than that. Something that links Lyall to either Calthrop or Dorfmann. Do you know anybody in the intelligence racket?"

"'Fraid not," said Forrester, and then realised this wasn't quite true. "Well, possibly," he said. "Ex-intelligence, anyway. And nobody, I think, is really ex-intelligence, are they?"

When the pub closed they walked back towards the college together, and Forrester decided he had an obligation to tell Harrison what had happened by Folly Bridge that afternoon.

"I hesitate because it's probably my imagination," he said. "But if somebody is thinking of putting a spoke in our investigation, you might be a target too."

"I'll watch my back," said Harrison. He grinned, but suddenly the silent, darkened streets and alleys felt different to Forrester. A man known to both of them had died, violently, less than seventy-two hours before. If Forrester was right, whoever had done it was still at large – and he and Harrison were their chief danger.

Both of them knew, after the last five years, that someone who has killed once finds it much easier to kill again.

Suddenly, it seemed their footsteps on the frosty pavements echoed more loudly than before; the shadows in the entranceways were deeper. Forrester glanced up at the scaffolding on the buildings under repair – and there were plenty of buildings under repair this winter – and wondered what was concealed behind the ice-crusted tarpaulins. And when he bade Harrison good night and climbed the stairs to his rooms, he asked himself if there was someone waiting for him around the next turn of the staircase.

Or in the hallway outside his door.

Once inside he shut the door and locked it after him. Then he went to pour himself a sherry and remembered, too late, that he had given the last of it to Gordon Clark on the night David Lyall had died.

He laughed, softly, pulled the curtains and went to bed.

13

THE BIG BOARD

Forrester made the call early the next morning. The secretary to the Foreign Manager of *The Sunday Times* had asked no questions after Forrester had explained his wartime connection, and set up an appointment for that day. He knew it was a tenuous lead, but it was also the best route he could think of into the world of intelligence.

When the London train finally got him into Paddington, he took the Circle Line to King's Cross and headed south down the bleak wasteland of Gray's Inn Road to the offices of *The Sunday Times*. After a few minutes' wait he was ushered up to the vast newsroom on the second floor, echoing with clacking typewriters and teeming with journalists, sub editors and copy boys, before being conducted to an office grandly labelled "Foreign Manager, Kemsley Newspapers". When he went inside he understood why Fleming had not proposed they meet in the pub across the road.

The desk behind which the former naval officer sat in his wood-panelled office looked for all the world like the control centre for some vast spy network. Not only were there four British Post Office telephones in different colours, several sets of red, green and white General Electric light boards and two Marconi intercoms, but on the wall behind him was a huge map of the world, with tiny flashing lights embedded in cities from Anchorage to Addis Ababa.

"Just journalists," said Fleming, waving a hand airily at the map, "but one has to keep tabs on them." The air of self deprecation on his bony, handsome, slightly querulous-looking face didn't deceive Forrester for a moment: he knew how much Fleming had enjoyed all the trappings and excitement of Naval Intelligence during the war, and it was clear that despite the loss of the Royal Navy uniform which had suited him so well, he was trying to recreate it here. There was always something of the overgrown schoolboy about Ian Fleming.

"It's all for show," said Fleming modestly. "Convinces Kemsley he's getting his money's worth from me."

Lord Kemsley had hired Fleming to help bolster the image of a newspaper group which had not come out of the war with a high reputation. Just months before the invasion of Poland its somewhat impressionable owner had blotted his copybook with the British government by rushing off to Germany to interview Hitler, and then compounded the offence by publishing intelligence which turned out to come from the top-secret Ultra programme. Now he wanted to make the paper respectable again – and had hired the well-connected Fleming as part of that process.

Grandson of a financier, son of an MP, old Etonian,

friend of Noël Coward, Fleming had failed to find any role beyond that of playboy until the war came along; once it had begun he came into his own, dreaming up grand schemes for British intelligence and even giving unsolicited advice to the Americans on how to create their own spy organisation. Forrester had met him several times at SOE training courses in various requisitioned country houses and then, memorably, in a wrecked chateau in France after the D-Day landings. Many people regarded the man as an arrogant snob, but Forrester had a somewhat perverse liking for him, sensing the insecurity behind the insouciant façade.

Beyond his slightly ambivalent job at *The Sunday Times* (what did a Foreign Manager *really* do?) Forrester had heard rumours that Fleming had another, even more unorthodox newspaper connection in the form of a risky affair with Ann Charteris, wife of Viscount Rothermere, the owner of the *Daily Mail*, and one of Fleming's closest friends.

Their sexual congress was rumoured to be somewhat outré, and it was said that between bouts of activity they would exchange notes on how their respective papers could better compete, even as Fleming insisted on his continuing affection for Ann's husband. It was, in short, a relationship replete with danger. But despite that, or perhaps because of it, Fleming delighted in gossip and was fascinated to hear an extra titbit about the Barnard murder.

"Calthrop was there that night?" he said, when Forrester told him. "He must hate that. He's such a careful man, is Calthrop."

"I've been told he's setting up an anti-Soviet spy network."

Fleming raised a highly bred eyebrow. "You're not supposed to know that. Who told you?"

"It's common gossip in Oxford," said Forrester, avoiding a direct answer. "Might he have been there because of Lyall?"

"You mean, to recruit him?"

"Or to investigate him?"

"It's possible, but he most likely came to talk to your Master."

"Winters?"

Fleming checked to make sure the door was closed.

"You remember Mycroft Holmes?" he asked, unexpectedly.

"Well, I remember reading about him in Sherlock Holmes stories," replied Forrester. "Big fat chap, wasn't he, and even cleverer than his brother?"

"*Éminence grise* of British intelligence," said Fleming. "Just like Michael Winters during the late hostilities. I'm sure Calthrop was there to ask Winters' advice about setting up the new op against the Soviets."

Forrester paused, surprised. Somehow, he'd never thought to ask what the Master had been doing, apart from being Master, during the war.

"He never mentioned it," said Forrester. "Winters, I mean. I didn't even know he'd been involved with intelligence."

"Well, he's not the sort of chap to go talking about these things, but he was very highly regarded. And of course he's very sound on communism. Calthrop may have even been asking him whether he'd be prepared to be the head boy."

"What, of the counter-intelligence operation?"

"Why not? A natural step up from being Master of an Oxford college."

Forrester considered this. "I've always just thought of Winters as an academic," he said. "This puts him in a new light."

Fleming glanced at his Rolex. "Look, can we continue this in my car? I've promised Ann I'd drop by for drinks at Warwick House. You can join me, if you like. She usually has an interesting crowd."

Minutes later Fleming was pulling his modest Morris Oxford out of its parking spot beside Kemsley's blue Rolls Royce and he and Forrester were gliding through the almost car-free city towards Green Park. Forrester said, "There was a German there that night named Peter Dorfmann, did you ever hear anything about him?"

"Professor of German Literature at Berlin University," replied Fleming, shifting gears smoothly.

"How did he manage to hold a job like that and avoid getting involved with the Nazis?"

"Low cunning, I imagine."

"It can't have been easy, keeping them at arm's length in a prominent position like that."

They were turning into Bond Street now, and Forrester noted that Sotheby's was in business again, as was Cartier's. No posters were asking people to save Fabergé eggs for the children.

"Was a German literature professor a prominent position during the war?" asked Fleming. "I mean, I can easily imagine this fellow pontificating away in the literature department without *der Führer*'s beady eye ever fastening on him."

"Don't forget *der Führer* was an author," said Forrester.

Fleming laughed. "What a dreadful thought: having to deliver solemn lectures on *Mein Kampf*."

"And Goebbels was a book lover."

"He was indeed," said Fleming. "He used to burn one before bedtime every night." He pulled the Morris neatly into a parking space opposite Warwick House. One positive outcome of the Luftwaffe's depredations: there were plenty of parking spaces in London these days.

Newly refurbished, Warwick House rose magnificently out of the surrounding ruins, and from the upper drawing room there were magnificent views over the snowy expanse of Green Park, with Buckingham Palace visible through the winter trees.

As he looked around the room it seemed to Forrester that Fleming's mistress was using her husband's money and her own formidable energies to recreate the salons of the 1930s. The place was thick with writers, artists, Tory politicians and the kind of aristocrats once described as being distinguished by "their intricate family relationships and curious nicknames".

But the centre of attention was Lady Rothermere herself, with flashing eyes and thick, dark hair, and managing, despite the opulence of her surroundings, to give an impression of bohemian recklessness. She embraced Fleming and waved her champagne glass welcomingly towards Forrester.

"Have you heard what *Time* magazine says about me?"

she asked. "Peter, show them the article." Peter Quennell, recently foisted on the editor of the *Daily Mail* by Ann as a book critic with a salary a thousand pounds more than that of the previous incumbent, obediently brought out the cutting.

"'In a beautiful new red straw hat,'" he read. "'Brought from Paris by her friend the Duchess of Westminster, the vituperative Ann, Lady Rothermere—'"

"What nonsense," interrupted Ann.

"Perfectly true," said Fleming.

"'The vituperative Ann, Lady Rothermere, 32,'" continued Quennell, "'is forcing her gloomy new husband, Lord Rothermere, 47, to pay more attention to his newspaper interests. As for him, his daily trips to the office are becoming more and more irksome, and he longs to get away from the job to travel, study, read. But his wife's enthusiasm for the paper is preventing him.'"

"All nonsense," said Ann, "but it's nice to know the people of the New World are kept informed about what sort of hat I wear."

"What else should we tell them?" asked Fleming mischievously. "I'm sure there are details that would fascinate them even more than your taste in headgear…" and as Fleming and Ann drifted away together Forrester accepted a champagne glass from a waiter and let his eye roam around the room, which seemed to him a kind of bubble floating above the surface of austerity Britain.

"Hello, you," said a voice behind him, and when he turned his fingers felt numb around the glass as he found himself looking into the eyes of Barbara Lytton.

But he knew perfectly well that Barbara was three years dead, and with him now only in his dreams. So what was she doing here, smiling up at him, looking like a schoolgirl again? "You don't recognise me, do you?" said the girl. He did not. "It's me, Gillian."

"Good God," said Forrester.

"No braces," said the girl. "Not so many spots. Well, not any, actually, I hope. And no pigtails."

"Gilly," said Forrester, feeling as though the floor was tilting away beneath him. She smiled again at him, a little wistfully.

"It's been a long time," she said, "since you were at our house."

"Yes," said Forrester and then for what seemed to him like an eternity, could not speak. At last he said: "I did come to see your parents, actually, on my next leave after… But you were away at school." He took her hand, and suddenly found it hard to speak. "I'm so sorry," he said.

The girl looked away. "Yes, it was pretty awful," she said. "I'm not sure Mummy and Daddy have ever got over it, really." She met his eyes again. "I try to fill the gap, but it's no use."

"You look so like her," he said.

"So they say," she replied. "Lot to live up to."

"No," said Forrester. "That's not the way to think about it. You've just got to be you."

"Thank you," she said. There was a pause. Then she said: "You must miss her."

"I do," said Forrester. And could not continue.

"Listen, why don't you come down to Cranbourne some time? I know Mummy and Daddy would be glad to see you again."

"I'd have thought I brought back some painful memories."

"But some good ones too," said the girl. "And we don't want her to just… vanish. Do you understand?"

"Of course," said Forrester.

"Then you'll come?"

"Yes, I'll come," he said. She smiled as if he'd just given her a great gift.

"That's wonderful, thank you." Forrester watched her disappear into the crowd, as if he was watching Barbara that last time at Waterloo Station.

Then there was a hand on his arm. "Captain F as I live and breathe!" said a voice from six inches above his head, and Forrester looked up to see Major Archibald MacLean. The red hair was tinged with grey now, but the jutting cheekbones still stood out like the rocks of some highland crag.

"MacLean!" said Forrester, with genuine pleasure. "What are you doing here?"

"Picking up gossip," said MacLean. "And women, when I can get them. That was a nice wee piece giving you the glad eye there."

"Barbara Lytton's sister."

"Ah," said MacLean, his voice softening. He knew the story.

"Bit of a shock seeing her, actually," said Forrester.

"It would be," said MacLean, and taking Forrester's

empty glass, placed it on the tray carried by a passing waiter, took a fresh one and handed it to Forrester before guiding him into a less crowded part of the room.

"I gather you've been making enquiries about Peter Dorfmann," he said.

"How did you know that?"

"You don't imagine anything you tell Ian Fleming stays private for very long, do you? That man is incapable of keeping anything to himself for more than five minutes. But it's good that he told me, because it seems to me we might be able to give each other a wee bit of help."

"How do you mean? What have you got to do with Dorfmann?"

"I'm at the War Ministry," he said. "Keeping an eye on the Control Commission."

Forrester looked at him in surprise. "Running Germany?"

"Well, trying to make sense out of the shambles," said MacLean. "And as I think you know Dorfmann is one of the laddies the Allies have decided to raise to great heights. When I say 'the Allies' I mean the Americans, of course."

"Ah."

"And you know how much reliance I tend to place on their judgment."

"You were always prejudiced."

"I was. I am. As far as I'm concerned all they bring to international politics is naivety and apple pie. Good souls, most of them. But not very canny, you know? Anyway I personally think we could be letting ourselves in for a lot of trouble if we let Herr Dorfmann loose on the new Germany."

"To be honest his politics don't particularly concern me. The reason I'm interested in him is because he was there the night David Lyall was killed. Have you heard about that?"

"I have, oddly enough."

"Well I want to know if Dorfmann had anything to do with it."

"So perhaps our interests run together."

"In what way?"

"I'd like to know more about him too."

"Well, if you're involved with the Allied Control Commission you're in the perfect position to find out anything you want, aren't you?" said Forrester. "I mean, the whole country's at your feet."

"I'm not in as good a position as you'd imagine," said MacLean. "The Yanks have given Dorfmann a clean bill of health and it would be very undiplomatic right now for me or any of our chaps to go second-guessing them. You, on the other hand, trying to get your friend off a murder charge, have a perfectly good non-official motivation for digging around in Dorfmann's past. If I get you over there would you be up for spending a day or two asking around?"

"Has he gone back already?"

"This morning."

Forrester shook his head with rueful admiration.

"Nothing ever changes, does it?" he said wryly. "How many times during the war did you take me aside in some bar and say there was a wee job it would be a great favour to you if I could do, and there was no question but that the whole thing would be wrapped up before the weekend? And forty-eight hours later I'd find myself pounding through some pine forest with a Jäger battalion on my tail?"

"Plenty of times," said MacLean, "and you loved every minute of it."

"You poor deluded fool!"

"And you were very good at it, Duncan, one of the best, if not *the* best," said MacLean, "and don't let anyone tell you otherwise."

Forrester remembered how skilfully MacLean had been able to deploy tiny drops of flattery to make the wheels of his complex machines turn.

"But this isn't anything like that," he went on reassuringly, "it's a complete doddle, just a day or two chatting to people about some obscure academic. And there'll be nobody after you – after all, we won the war, and as you say, we're in charge. And I'll get you a book of chits; you can get pretty much anything for the right bit of paper in Germany these days, you know."

"Why do I find your words strangely un-reassuring?" asked Forrester.

"Because you haven't finished that drink, Duncan," said MacLean. "Get it down you and you'll see just how lucky you were to have run into me again."

Forrester did as he was told. The champagne was good and for a moment he let himself enjoy the feeling of the alcohol going to his head.

"I can't go till the weekend," he said. "I've got tutorials to give and essays to mark."

"I'll have you fixed up with a flight from Northolt tomorrow night," said MacLean decisively. "And what's more – this time it'll actually be able to put you down on the ground in Germany."

Forrester finished his drink.

"I won't have to jump out with a parachute?"

"No," said MacLean. "Not unless you really want to."

14

HEAVY WATER

Forrester had no idea how long the journey back to Oxford took, because he was in a world when Barbara had still been alive and their future still lay before them. As the train rattled through the snow-bound countryside he walked with her again in the woods above Cranbourne, the sunlight slanting down between the leaves onto their faces. He had been alive then; he wasn't sure he had really been since.

When the train finally reached Oxford and he trudged unseeing across the greasy wood of the platform and out into the grubby snow of the streets, a hundred yards from Barnard, Harrison pounced on him in a state of high excitement.

"You up for a meeting?" he asked.

"With whom?"

"Ollie Sepalla – one of the Norwegians from the Eagle and Child. Seems he knows what happened to Lyall when his mission went up the spout."

"And he'll talk about it?"

"He's dead keen to. He'll come to your rooms if you like."

"Wheel him in," said Forrester.

Half an hour later Ollie Sepalla was sitting beside Forrester's tiny fire looking at him with large, earnest eyes. In his early twenties, fresh-faced, eager, he seemed to epitomise uncomplicated honesty. "This was happening near my village," he said. "The commandos were coming ashore in our fjord."

"What had they come to do?" asked Forrester.

"You know about heavy water?" asked Sepalla.

"I do," said Forrester. "It's water with a higher proportion of some isotope than normal, isn't it?"

"Yes," said Sepalla. "The Germans believed that they could use it to control the fission process and make an atomic bomb."

"They were making the heavy water up in Norway, weren't they?" said Harrison. "Didn't our chaps go in and blow up the plant?"

"Several expeditions tried," said Sepalla, "and Captain Lyall's was one of them. But they were betrayed before they could do anything at all."

"Betrayed by whom?"

"By a farmer. It was unfortunate: they had been told to contact a certain farmer near my village, Lenvik, and they went to that farm, but it had a new owner – the first man, the original contact, had died. They told the new man where they had hidden their boat and he promised to come to them that night. But instead he called the police, who told the Germans."

"What happened?"

"The Germans sent a gunboat into the fjord, trapping them. Captain Lyall and the other commandos fired at the gunboat and then when it was clear they could not escape tried to ram it. The Germans fired every gun they had and there was a great explosion on the British boat. The water was full of bodies and the Germans believed that everyone was killed."

"But Lyall survived?" said Forrester.

"There are some small islands in the fjord," said Sepalla. "Apparently Captain Lyall reached one of those islands – it was just a rock really – and stayed on the edge of it, keeping himself mainly underwater, until the Germans gave up searching and went away. That night he swam from the island to the village."

"I'm surprised the Germans gave up the search so easily," said Forrester, who knew something of the thoroughness of German occupation forces.

"Their boat was damaged and had to return to their base," said Sepalla. "Garrison troops were sent up by road, but it was a few hours before they arrived. It was during that time Captain Lyall arrived at our village."

"Where there would have been tremendous danger for anyone sheltering him," said Forrester.

"Yes, it was a risk, although at the time none of us knew that the farmer was a collaborator – that only came out afterwards. But anyway, my people got Lyall out of the village and into the countryside as fast as possible. When the Germans arrived and searched the houses he was gone and there was no sign he had been there."

"Where did he go?"

"His plan was to get over the mountains into Sweden," said Sepalla. "He could ski and we gave him some equipment and directions to a shepherd's house some distance away. Captain Lyall stayed with him for a few hours, and then set off for the mountains on his skis. In fact he set off just in time: the Germans searched the shepherd's house only hours after he had left – but luckily the shepherd had removed all traces of his visitor."

"And Lyall had a straight run to Sweden?"

"No," said Sepalla. "This we did not know for a very long time, but on his way up into the mountains he was caught in a storm."

Harrison and Forrester looked at each other. It was all too easy to picture the scene.

"He lost his skis and became snowblind. He wandered for a very long time before he was found near Bjornsfjord."

"Found by whom?"

"The Grevinne Sophie Arnfeldt-Laurvig," said Ollie Sepalla.

"Could you spell that?" asked Harrison, and as he wrote the name down Sepalla explained.

"There are not so many nobles in Norway," he said. "Most of them disappeared in the male line during the sixteenth century. But there are still many who descend in the female line, and the Grevinne is one of them. I think the title is like your 'countess'."

Harrison was clearly taken by the romance of it all. "Did she have a castle?"

"Well, a fortified dwelling overlooking Bjornsfjord. The family is very ancient."

"And this countess sheltered Lyall till he could get away?"

"She did."

"Did the Germans ever find out?"

"I do not believe so."

"And she survived the war?"

"As far as I know, she is still there."

There was silence in the room for a moment as Forrester and Harrison digested the information.

"Listen," said Forrester. "You know we're trying to find out if anyone other than Dr. Clark might have been responsible for Lyall's murder. Is it possible that any of the Scandinavian students here in Oxford might have had some motivation to do away with him, perhaps stemming from this betrayal? Perhaps trying to cover it up?"

Sepalla shrugged. "That I cannot say, but I think it not so likely. Within a few months it was discovered that the farmer had told the Germans about the commandos, and he is now in jail. I am proud of what my family did – it was my father who gave Captain Lyall the skis he used to escape. None of the other students here come from that part of Norway so they couldn't have had anything to do with that betrayal."

Forrester looked thoughtfully at Sepalla and decided he was telling the truth. Indeed, if he had had anything to hide, there was no reason for him to have come forward like this at all; he would have just kept quiet. Then another question occurred to him.

"I gather Lyall discussed a manuscript with you. Something with Old Norse words in it. What did he tell you about it?"

"He said he had seen it, during the war," replied Sepalla. "He remembered some of it and was curious about certain words."

"He didn't show it to you, then?"

"No."

"Did he say where he'd seen it?"

"No," said Sepalla.

"Could it have been at the Grevinne's?"

"It is possible. He certainly did not see it in our village and I am sure the shepherd who sheltered him had no medieval manuscripts – he was a very simple man."

"Did he seem fearful about this manuscript in any way? As if someone might be after it?"

"No," said Sepalla. "He was just curious about some of the old-fashioned words it contained."

"Magical words?"

"Please repeat that?"

"Were any of the things he asked you to translate… incantations, or spells?"

"What kind of spells?"

"For summoning… dark forces."

"You mean the Devil?"

"Or Odin, or Wotan, whatever."

Sepalla's brow creased. "There were incantations, yes. But who was being summoned, what they were for… that was not clear."

"I see. Thank you."

There was a silence as Forrester tried to think if there was a question he should be asking, something that was staring him in the face, but his mind was a blank. Finally he said, "Thank you for telling us this, Ollie. I don't know yet how it can help my friend, but I really appreciate it."

"You are very welcome," said Sepalla.

And minutes later he had disappeared into the night. Forrester looked at Harrison.

"Well done," he said. "That promises to be immensely useful."

"All part of the service," said Harrison modestly, but obviously pleased at Forrester's praise. "But what do you make of it?"

"Well, if Ollie's telling the truth, the idea that Lyall was killed because he might reveal who betrayed him has to be ruled out."

"*If* he was speaking the truth?" said Harrison. "You didn't believe him?"

"Think about it," said Forrester. "Even if what he said was word-for-word truth, it might not be the whole truth."

"How do you mean?" said Harrison.

"Well, what if the farmer who's now in jail had an accomplice? What if that accomplice was Ollie himself? And nobody knew except Lyall, who comes across Ollie here in Oxford and threatens to denounce him. Or perhaps doesn't threaten – is simply seen by Ollie as a threat to be removed."

"Good Lord," said Harrison. "I hadn't thought of that. He seemed such an above-board sort of chap."

"I agree," said Forrester. "And I'm not saying I think he had anything to do with Lyall's death. All I am saying is that the possibility still remains."

"How would we ever get to the bottom of something like that – I mean, something that happened three years ago in a village in Norway?"

"Hard to say," said Forrester. "But I've already been asked to go to Berlin to make enquiries about Peter Dorfmann, and that gets me halfway there."

And he told Harrison about MacLean's surprising offer. Harrison looked at him, puzzled.

"There's something fishy about that," he said.

"MacLean's offer?"

"Yes. I can understand the rationale he offered for sending you, but it seems just that – a rationale. Do you know what I mean?"

Forrester considered. Harrison had a point: he'd been so absorbed by his encounter with Gillian and his memories of Barbara that he hadn't really analysed MacLean's proposal. And of course, when he thought about it, Archie usually had several agendas he kept to himself whenever he sent Forrester on a mission. It was his standard operating procedure.

"I know what you mean," he said to Harrison at last. "And you're probably right. But frankly I'm not going to worry about that. If it gives me a chance to find out something about Dorfmann which at least muddies the waters for the police and makes the case against Gordon less conclusive, that's progress as far as I'm concerned."

"Point taken," said Harrison. "By the way, I checked

with Margaret Roberts about Norton's alibi and she confirmed it. She's a slightly alarming woman, isn't she? Triumph of the Will and all that. She nearly had me joining the Oxford Conservative Association."

"I'm surprised she and Norton haven't come to blows. Or she and the rest of the department for that matter. For some reason crystallography seems to be a hotbed of left-wing agitation apart from young Margaret."

Harrison re-lit his pipe. "The problem with Dorfmann as a suspect," he said, "is that according to you he couldn't possibly have done it except by magic. You've said all along he was in the Master's Lodge with you and we know the murder was committed in Clark's rooms. How do you get round that?"

"The very question I'd been asking myself," said Forrester. "And in fact this evening I intend to go into it, if I can persuade the Master to let me. If he's agreeable to us doing a walk-through, are you available?"

"You bet," said Harrison. "There's nothing like a chance to visit the scene of the crime."

15

A WALK IN THE LODGE

Winters looked at Forrester in some surprise when he broached the subject at High Table that night. "I hate to say this, Forrester," he said, "but this feels to me like clutching at straws."

"It feels a bit like that to me too," said Forrester, "but I feel I have to."

"Tell me what you've found out so far," said Winters, and Forrester told him.

"An Old Norse manuscript?" he exclaimed, when that part of the story emerged. "But why on earth didn't Lyall come to me if he'd found a manuscript? Why go asking engineering students for help with translations? Why go calling in Arne Haraldson? I'd have been delighted to help him."

"He may have been embarrassed by the fact that there was an occult aspect to the manuscript."

"Occult?"

"He told Haraldson there were certain incantations encrypted in the text."

"I don't believe it. What nonsense!"

"Can we be certain of that? Can we be sure the Vikings never tried to use runes or incantations to summon their gods? Or demons?"

Winters stared at him. "That is very different," he said, "from claiming a Norse saga contained text that could have any supernatural power today, which is patently nonsense. But set that aside, my dear chap. If David had found a lost manuscript and wanted to publish it, we'd have been glad to help, whatever it contained. All the more grist to our mill – whether me or Tolkien. It's the sort of thing we can all make use of."

"And with your particular expertise in lost manuscripts, it's particularly odd he never came to you," said Forrester. "Professor Tolkien reminded me that you made your name with your reconstruction of the lost books of the *Heimskringla*. He said he often recites passages to his students."

"How flattering," said Winters.

"How were you able to reconstruct it?" asked Forrester. Winters rubbed his chin modestly.

"What happened was this: I found myself coming across references to the *Heimskringla* in other sagas, and I began to see a pattern. Then I collated all those references and went through dozens of hitherto unidentified scraps and remnants of manuscripts. Gradually I realised that if I put them all together and interpolated what we know of actual events, I could recreate the lost volume. To my great good fortune, in an academic sense, people accepted my interpretation and I gained what little reputation I have today."

"The *considerable* reputation you have today," said Forrester.

"*Assentatio nimia semper est acceptabilissimum*," said Winters, passing the port. "Excessive flattery is always entirely acceptable."

Forrester smiled. "So, to return to the question of whether I could have another look at the Lodge, Master, in order to pace things out a bit, get a feel of what might have happened. Is there a possibility of that?"

"But of course," said Winters. "As I said, I'm happy to do anything I can do to help poor Dr. Clark."

"Thank you, I very much appreciate that. There's an undergraduate called Ken Harrison who's been helping me; would you mind if I brought him along?"

"By all means. In fact, my wife and I are due at Magdalen this evening, and that might be a good time. I don't want to upset her by dragging the whole thing up again while she's at home. Would tonight suit you?"

"Perfectly," said Forrester. "It's very kind of you."

"Not at all. Now tell me about this gossip you've picked up about Peter Dorfmann. I've always regarded him as a perfectly respectable academic. What exactly does this MacLean fellow have against him?"

Winters had promised to leave the door to the Lodge unlocked for Forrester when he and Lady Hilary left, and he was as good as his word. The house was dark and silent;

so silent that when Harrison and Forrester had closed the door behind them and paused in the hall, they could hear the ticking of a clock somewhere on an upper landing. When they entered the sitting room there was the pleasant, lingering smell of wood smoke from the fireplace. Harrison reached to turn on the light but Forrester stopped him.

"No, the lights were off that night," he said. "Most of the illumination came from the fire."

"Do you want me to light it?" asked Harrison.

"I think that would be over-exploiting the Master's hospitality. Let's open the curtains and see what illumination we get through the windows."

Indeed there was quite a lot of light from outside: the moon had risen behind the Lady Tower with its ungainly crown of scaffolding. As their eyes grew accustomed to the dimness the shapes in the room became clear. "The furniture was arranged differently," said Forrester. "Lady Hilary got the Icelanders to swing the sofas round so we had our backs to the fire and were looking up at the minstrels' gallery."

"Where's that?" asked Harrison, and Forrester pointed up into the darkness of the upper part of the room.

"Of course it was lit differently on the night," he said. "They had reading lights up there."

"So you could see their faces?" said Harrison.

"Not so much; they were a bit obscured by the balcony, and of course the light fell on the books. But let's concentrate on the people down here first."

"How many were there?"

"About a dozen in all, I think," said Forrester.

"Bitteridge, Calthrop, Dorfmann, Lady Hilary, a few dons from other colleges and their wives."

"I wonder if Lyall had had his way with any of the wives?" asked Harrison.

"Oh, God," said Forrester. "That way madness lies. Let's focus on Calthrop and Dorfmann. Let me think where they were sitting."

"Where were *you* sitting?" asked Harrison. "That should help."

"Good point." Forrester looked around the room. "I think it was there. That armchair was a bit more to the right."

Without further ado Harrison moved the armchair into position and Forrester sat down in it.

Suddenly he could hear the voices from that night as if the readers were still up there.

I saw there wading through rivers wild
Treacherous men and murderers too,
And workers of ill with the wives of men;
There Nithhogg sucked the blood of the slain,
And the wolf tore men; would you know yet more?

"So where was Dorfmann sitting?" asked Harrison. "In relation to you?"

"To my left. Calthrop was there, a little in front of me, Dorfmann was somewhere off over here."

"I'll be Dorfmann," said Harrison, who pulled up a chair and sat down. "Does that seem about right?"

Forrester considered. "I think so," he said. "The truth

is of course I wasn't taking much notice. Good dinner, plenty of port, hypnotic voices. Let's take it as a working hypothesis that's where he was."

"Perfect conditions for an illusion," said Harrison.

"What?"

"You've just described the kind of conditions a magician longs for when he has to perform a complicated trick."

Forrester chuckled. "You think there was a trick?" he asked.

"Well, if Gordon Clark is innocent there had to have been," said Harrison. "Because somebody very effectively created the illusion that he killed David Lyall, didn't they? So keep your eye on the minstrels' gallery. Can you remember what they were saying?"

"Vividly," said Forrester.

"Think about it, imagine it happening again."

Reluctantly, Forrester obeyed, listening in his head to the voices.

The giantess old in Ironwood sat,
In the east, and bore the brood of Fenrir;
Among these one in monster's guise
Was soon to steal the sun from the sky.

There feeds he full on the flesh of the dead,
And the home of the gods he reddens with gore;
Dark grows the sun, and in summer soon
Come mighty storms: would you know yet more?

On a hill there sat, and smote on his harp,
Eggther the joyous, the giants' warder;
Above him the cock in the bird-wood crowed,
Fair and red did Fjalar stand.

"Boo," said a voice, next to his right ear, and Forrester sprang to his feet, ready for action.

"Good God," he said instead. "You frightened the life out of me."

"Sorry about that," said Harrison, "but if I could move out of the chair where I was sitting without you noticing, Peter Dorfmann could have done the same thing, couldn't he?"

"He could," said Forrester. He needed to do something, to express himself in action. Powered by the adrenalin Harrison had inadvertently triggered, his mind was racing. He looked around the room and saw a small cupboard-like entrance. "There's a door he could have used. Let's see where it takes us."

They went through the door into a hallway; at the end of the hallway was a narrow set of stairs. There were two doors at the head of the stairs; Harrison opened the one on the right and stepped into the minstrels' gallery.

"Well, he didn't go that way," he said, though for a moment both men stood looking down into the sitting room from this new perspective. The chairs, sofas and occasional tables seemed somehow to be waiting for the human observers to go away and leave them to their own devices.

They left the gallery and opened the left-hand door. Behind it was a corridor, which ended in a second set of stairs going down to the foyer through which they had entered the house.

"Hmmm," said Forrester, feeling that this did not take them very far – but Harrison was opening one of the doors, revealing a bedroom beyond. Harrison went to the window and slid up the sash. Cold night air flooded in, and Forrester joined him as he stuck his head out.

They were looking down on the lesser quadrangle, with Clark's rooms opposite across the lawn and the Lady Tower to their immediate right. "Well, even if Dorfmann or anybody else got up here from the main room, it still doesn't get them anywhere near Clark's rooms," said Forrester. "They're on the far side of the quad and even if you climbed down you'd have to climb up to them, which becomes impractical in the time. Also, there were no footsteps in the snow when we came out of the Lodge."

"You're sure about that?"

"Yes, because that's what proves Lyall must have fallen from Gordon Clark's window: there was no other way for him to get there. And he was surrounded by broken glass."

Harrison leant out, twisting himself so he could peer upwards at the roof. "You know I think you could get up onto the roof from here," he said.

"Don't be a bloody fool," said Forrester. "There's ice everywhere." But Harrison was grasping the gutter and hauling himself up.

"Harrison!" said Forrester. But Harrison was already disappearing onto the roof. Moments later Forrester heard his voice.

"There are possibilities up here," he said. "Come and look."

Grimacing, Forrester swung himself out of the window, turned around so his feet were firmly on the sill and swung himself up over the gutter; it was surprisingly easy. As he reached the roof Harrison was already across the sloping tiles of the Lodge and scrambling over the parapet which ran around the edge of the Lady Tower.

Forrester caught up with him on the tower, amid the debris left by the builders. Norton had complained bitterly about the idleness and unreliability of the British worker, views he would have condemned as reactionary in others but which, in his desire to get the tower repaired before the winter, had become more and more fervent. But in spite of many furious rows with foremen and bricklayers, the work had not been completed before it became too cold to mix mortar, and so now the Tower stood in a tangle of scaffolding, ropes and frozen tarpaulins.

But the view over the snowbound, moonlit city was heart-stoppingly beautiful. The spires and domes of the colleges, libraries and churches rose from the pure whiteness of the rooftops into a night sky packed with ice-white stars. Beyond the city the woods of the Thames Valley seemed to be filled with a darkness stretching back into the Ice Ages.

"Marvellous place, Oxford, isn't it?" said Harrison. "Like being in someone's dream."

"Literally true, in one sense," said Forrester. "Every college, every library, every chapel was a dream before it was a reality."

"And I suppose will be a dream again long after it's gone," said Harrison.

Both of them knew that this discussion was what behaviour experts would call "displacement activity", because without saying anything they both knew that their wild idea that the rooftop route might have allowed a murderer to get from the Lodge to Clark's rooms was clearly a bust.

It was true that as they looked across the quadrangle at Clark's rooms, they were no more than thirty feet away in a direct line, but two or three hundred feet if one went around the quadrangle along the rooftops. There was no need to undertake the experiment of making their way around the rectangle for it to be clear that if this had been their route, nobody could have committed a murder and made their way back before the body was discovered; the roofs were simply at too many different levels – climbing from one to another would have been immensely time consuming.

"Well," said Harrison, "it was worth a try."

They stood there for a moment longer, looking down into the quadrangle, and then Forrester said, "Let's have a look from the other side of the tower, to see what would have happened if somebody had gone out of the front door."

"Let's try it at ground level," said Harrison. "In principle someone could have slipped out of the Lodge, turned left and gone around the outside of the college buildings to get to Clark's set. Then he could have come back the same way. Let's see how long it takes."

Instead of returning to the Lodge by the way they'd

come they opened the trap door that led into the Tower and found themselves on the spiral stone staircase that wound down to the outer door. The steps were worn concave, and slippery with frost, and with no source of light once the trap door was closed behind them, Forrester found himself treading with unnatural care.

The door opened easily from the inside, though it locked behind them when they went out and Harrison used the second hand on his watch to time them as they set off around the outside of the college. The ground was thick with frozen and re-frozen snow on which their shoes threatened to slip at any moment, obliging them to go slowly and carefully.

At last they reached the door in the outer wall giving onto the stairs that led to the hallway for Clark's room. They stopped at the door, which was sealed with a notice from the Oxfordshire Constabulary. The journey from the Lodge had taken eight minutes.

"Add say three minutes for the encounter with Lyall," said Harrison, "and with the return journey that makes nearly twenty minutes."

Forrester thought about it.

"What if he'd run, at least on the way back? In fact he'd have had to if he wanted to come back into the Master's Lodge as the rest of us were going out to the body."

"So the rest of you wouldn't notice him coming back in."

"Exactly," said Forrester.

"You don't remember Dorfmann or anybody else being particularly out of breath, do you?" asked Harrison hopefully. "When you were looking at the body?"

"'Fraid not," said Forrester. "Lyall rather took our attention. And then we were all looking up at Clark's window, assuming at that point that whoever had done it was still in there. But Dorfmann and indeed Calthrop were definitely there with me when we were under the window – I remember them talking."

"Getting back from here in time to join you would have been the tricky part," said Harrison. "The killer couldn't afford not to be among those present when the body was discovered, and almost by definition it was going to be discovered straight away – the crash of breaking glass ensured that."

Forrester looked at the re-frozen snow. "How could anyone run on that?" he said. "Look how careful we had to be. He'd have had to walk or risk breaking an ankle. And he didn't have time to walk." But even as he said these words his mind was processing something Harrison had said: "the crash of breaking glass".

Harrison looked at the locked door and the police notice. "I wish we could have a look at the window from the inside," he said. There was a pause. Forrester sighed.

"In for a penny, in for a pound," he said, remembering the training course near Birmingham in picking locks and forcible entry given by a former burglar.

He knelt down and slid his fingernails under the police document, loosened the glue and pried it off without damaging it.

"I'd like to borrow a pipe cleaner off you," he said to Harrison, "but then you might want to slip away. I'm committing an offence here and I wouldn't like you to be charged as an accessory."

"I wouldn't miss this for the world," said Harrison, handing him a pipe cleaner. "I've never watched an expert at work before."

"I've only actually done it twice," said Forrester, stripping off the cotton and inserting the wire into the lock. "Most of my wartime forced entries involved a number-twelve boot slamming into a doorframe." There was a satisfying click. "But the skill doesn't entirely seem to have deserted me."

It was dark in Clark's rooms, the moonlight prevented from coming through the broken window by a sheet of tar paper held in place with three or four wooden laths.

"I'd like to take this off," said Forrester, "but try to avoid breaking the laths – I want to put them back where they were if I can." They levered the window covering off, the nails squeaking in protest, their shoes crunching on the broken glass scattered around the floor.

"Forgive me for being dim," said Harrison, "but what are we looking for?"

"I'm not entirely sure," said Forrester as they lowered the frozen tar paper to the floor, "but when you mentioned the crash of breaking glass I was trying to visualise the scene. You know, X stabbing Lyall, Lyall staggering back and crashing through the window."

He bent down to examine the smashed woodwork that had once held the broken panes.

"Lyall wasn't a heavy man," he said. "It would have taken quite a bit of force to break this window frame."

"Perhaps whoever did it threw him across the room?" suggested Harrison.

"After stabbing him? Seems a bit unlikely. I mean – imagine I'm Lyall and you're X. Mime stabbing me. We know the knife went in here." He indicated his heart.

Harrison raised his hand with his pipe clenched in his fingers and brought it down on Forrester's chest. Forrester staggered back and felt the broken frame of the window digging into his back.

"It's possible," he conceded.

"He might have been trying to avoid a second blow," said Harrison.

Forrester examined the broken frame more closely. He tugged at one of the jagged ends and it came away in his hand, the unbroken end pulling out of the socket in the main frame. "Damn," he said. "Tampering with evidence. Not what I'd intended."

"If you drop it on the floor it could have just fallen out," said Harrison.

"Yes," said Forrester. "Alright, let's get this tar paper back up before somebody sees us through the window."

Harrison turned to him as they worked. "There's a surprising amount of glass in here," he said.

"Surprising in what way?"

"Well, if Lyall went backwards out of the window, wouldn't most of the glass have gone down with him into the quad?"

"There *was* a lot of glass in the quad," said Forrester.

With some difficulty they slid the laths into position and

hammered the nails back into the holes so they held the tar paper in place once more. Before they left Harrison glanced around the room.

"No sign of a struggle," he said. Even in the semi-darkness it was clear that all Clark's books and papers were in place.

"There may not have been one," said Forrester. "If Lyall wasn't expecting the attack."

"I say," said Harrison. "Something's just occurred to me: if it wasn't Dr. Clark who killed him, why would Lyall have come here at all? I mean – what was he doing in Clark's rooms in the first place?"

Forrester considered this. "Somebody could have given him a message," he said at last. "Asked him to meet them here. Presumably he thought he was coming to see Clark."

"But hadn't there been an almighty row between him and Clark less than an hour before?" objected Harrison. "Wouldn't it have seemed odd to him to have Clark asking him to come and see him in his rooms?"

"Yes, it would," said Forrester.

"Unless the note said that Clark wanted to apologise or something?"

"Even if the note had said that, Lyall wouldn't have believed it. Clark would never have apologised to Lyall in a million years."

"You seem very certain of that."

Forrester met his eye, remembering that he had never told Harrison the real reason why Clark hated Lyall. He felt like a cheat, but he had promised Margaret, and if the police didn't know that Lyall had been having an affair with Clark's wife, Forrester certainly wasn't going to tell anybody else. Instead he gave a short smile.

"I am very certain, knowing both men," he said with finality, and they closed Clark's door behind them, carefully replaced the police notice and went back to shut up the Lodge.

16

THE PHILOSOPHER OF BERLIN

The next day, just before midnight, MacLean having been as good as his word, Forrester found himself at Northolt Aerodrome, boarding an RAF C5 loaded with engine parts destined for Berlin. He found himself sitting in a canvas seat between the crates beside a young army captain in a de-Nazification unit and a cheerful Irishman named Lynch who announced he was going to Germany to take charge of "the opera". Forrester looked at him with some surprise. "Opera?" he asked. "I didn't know that was part of army operations."

The Irishman laughed. "Oh, culture's a big deal over there these days," he said. "The Russians and the Yanks and us are all competing to take Jerry's mind off the fact that he hasn't got anything to eat. Your Hun loves opera, you see. 'Ride of the Valkyries' and all that kind of thing."

"Were you an opera administrator before the war?" asked Forrester.

"Not a bit of it," answered Lynch cheerfully. "My entire

experience consists of being in the chorus of the County Cork Amateur Operatic Society."

"You're kidding," said the captain.

"Not at all," said Lynch. "I put down opera as one of my interests on some form I had to fill out and I think from then on it was Chinese whispers. You know, somebody said, 'Does he know anything about opera?' And somebody else said, 'There was something about it on his application,' and a third chap remembered it as, 'Oh, yes, he's an expert.'"

Forrester couldn't help smiling: the great British amateur tradition was about to descend on German opera lovers.

"I plan to introduce a bit of Gilbert and Sullivan," said Lynch. "Do you think they'll like *The Mikado*?"

"I think they'll hate it," said the de-Nazification captain, whose name was Clare, "and a bloody good thing too. I'd like to make Goering sing 'I Am the Very Model of a Modern Major-General' with a bayonet up his arse."

Clare had not formed a favourable impression of the Germans coming to his office trying to prove they had no connection with the Nazis. "If you believe them it would be very hard to understand how Hitler was ever elected," he said. "According to the people who come to see me everybody in Germany in 1933 was a Social Democrat, most of them had Jewish fiancées, and their favourite politician was Winston Churchill."

Forrester laughed.

"What gets my goat is their self pity," said Clare. "They blame Hitler for getting them into this mess; they never blame themselves for putting him in power."

"And I suppose they've all torn up their party membership cards," said Forrester. Clare smiled.

"Of course they have, but it doesn't do them any good. The Nazis sent their membership records off to be pulped when they realised they were losing the war, but the owner of the pulping mill handed them to the Americans. We can check every lie that comes out of the bastards' mouths."

"So I could check if a particular person had been a party member or not?" asked Forrester.

"If you can get the right clearance to visit Wasserkäfersteig," said Clare.

"Wasserkäfersteig?"

"It's this big villa in Zehlendorf, guarded like Fort Knox, as you can imagine. They say they've even got the form Hitler filled out when he joined the party."

"So de-Nazification's going reasonably well?"

"Not really. The problem is getting rid of them even when we know they were Nazis. All too often they're the only people who can keep things running: electricity stations, water plants, underground railways. And the Russians have taken over the old Nazi system of wardens wholesale: house wardens, street wardens, block wardens – all reporting anything untoward to party headquarters. Only now it's Communist Party Headquarters instead of Nazi Party Headquarters."

"What about the universities?" asked Forrester. "Presumably you're not letting Nazi professors back there?"

"Absolutely not," said Clare. "We don't want them anywhere near education, or broadcasting, or journalism.

But that doesn't stop them trying to get back in."

"If I wanted to find out about a particular professor," said Forrester, "how would I go about it?"

"Control Commission Education," said Clare. "Ask for a chap called Templar. They're near the Ku'damm on Wilmersdorfer Straße."

Forrester went to sleep after a while, and they woke him as the plane was coming in over the city because, as the flight engineer remarked, "We thought you might want to have a look."

Berlin in the first winter after the war was indeed a remarkable sight. The initial impression was that the buildings had melted, their bricks flowing down into the streets like toffee, an illusion the covering of snow only reinforced.

As they came lower, Lynch remarked that the individual buildings looked like a big collection of opened cardboard boxes, and it was true: it seemed that every roof in the city had been blown off.

Tens of thousands of gaping windows gazed sightlessly into the whirling snowflakes. There was scarcely a vehicle to be seen on the streets. As they flew over a vast empty space near the centre, Forrester was puzzled for a moment – and then he realised it must be the Tiergarten, Berlin's Hyde Park. "Last time I saw that it was covered in trees," he said.

"The Krauts cut them down this winter," said the flight engineer, "just to keep warm."

"There's the Brandenburg Gate," said Lynch with all the excitement of a child. He consulted a map. "Which means that must be the famous Unter den Linden."

But all the linden trees had gone too, and the devastated avenue now led from the shell-shocked triumphal arch to the wrecked cathedral and the tottering remains of the Hohenzollern Palace by the River Spree.

Forrester's home town of Kingston upon Hull had borne the brunt of Luftwaffe attacks from across the North Sea. But nowhere had he seen devastation like this. The Germans had sown the wind, he thought, and now they had reaped the whirlwind – or, more accurately, it had reaped them.

"Going to need a lot of Gilbert and Sullivan to cheer this place up," said Lynch, suddenly doubtful.

"I'm not sure cheering them up is really what we're here for," said Clare. "*Cleaning* them up is more like it. And it's going to take a bloody long time."

And then the plane was landing at Tempelhof Airport. Twenty minutes later they were walking through the vast, echoing halls of the airport terminal through which Hitler used to swagger after triumphal flights over conquered nations. Now it was so cold that frost covered the gigantic walls and their breath condensed in the frigid air.

MacLean had arranged for Forrester to be given a billet in a building on Fasanenstraße requisitioned for officers, and an army driver took him there. What struck him first as they entered the wrecked city were the remains of imitation Greek and Roman columns, disfigured by hundreds, indeed thousands of bullet holes and shrapnel gouges. Statues of victorious warriors, usually missing arms and sometimes heads, leant drunkenly from shattered plinths. Grandiose porticos which had once been the entrances to the corridors of power now guarded nothing more than mounds of debris. Ghostly roof-beams supported non-existent roofs. One apartment block he passed was just a triangular corner section five storeys tall; bizarrely, it was in these corners that the big European tiled stoves had been built, and there they remained, one above another, as if offering to try to heat the whole freezing, broken city.

Burnt-out tanks lay half-buried under bricks; anti-aircraft guns still pointed at the sky, waiting for attackers who had nothing left to attack. There was a seeping odour of dampness, of charred remains, of brick dust.

On the splintered remains of the few trees that still flanked the pavements were hundreds of scraps of paper: messages asking for news of lost loved ones; offers to swap crystal chandeliers and Turkish rugs for things that could be eaten or worn; pleas for work or marriage or suggestions of the availability of other pleasures. And around each tree were little crowds of people making notes; thin people, their faces gaunt, their clothes ragged.

Around them, ignoring them, worked the *Trümmerfrauen*, the rubble women, their hair tightly bound in scarves against the dust, steadily picking up the bricks from the fallen buildings, knocking off the mortar with rusty hammers in their frost-reddened fists and stacking the bricks into neat piles. With millions of German men still in Russian prison camps and millions more dead, wounded and in hiding, it was the women who had to literally dig Germany out of the abyss into which it had plunged itself.

"If you've got the right chits you can get 200 cigarettes a

week from the Naafi," said the driver, a Geordie called Flint with a cheerful, ugly face, "and twenty of those'll buy you pretty much any woman in Berlin. If you run out of ciggies a can of Spam's a very acceptable substitute, so it's not hard to have a good time in this place, whatever it looks like."

"I'll bear that in mind," said Forrester, as they drew up outside the elegant turn of the century villa on Fasanenstraße – exactly the sort of place Forrester had seen as a child in the illustrations for *Emil and the Detectives*.

There was a large, elegant hall with parquet floors, across which it was easy to imagine respectable German bourgeoisie bowing and clicking their heels to each other at the turn of the century. Now the wood was scuffed and scratched by hobnail boots, and a dark-haired captain in a British Army greatcoat boomed into the field telephone. The man looked familiar to Forrester, but he couldn't remember from where.

"I need seventy gallons of printer's ink by Thursday," he was insisting. "And I can let you have half a ton of coal in exchange." He listened for a moment and then said, outrageously, "No, I can't, I'm in Hamburg. Sorry. But my chaps'll be round to pick up the ink Wednesday night. Bye." The captain hung up, meeting Forrester's eye and grinning to include him in the barefaced lie.

"Well, Berlin isn't too far from Hamburg, is it?" he said, and strolled out.

Forrester found his room, deposited his kit, washed up and sat on his bed looking down into the garden, which seemed, under its carpet of snow, to have remained miraculously untouched. Where to start? With Templar at the Control Commission as Clare had suggested? The offices of the Social Democrats, the party for which he was planning to stand for election? But he could hardly stroll into party headquarters and begin asking questions without alerting Dorfmann to his presence. Besides, would people in his own party be likely to say anything against him? As he asked this question Forrester realised what he should be doing. The Social Democrats might not have a word to say against Dorfmann, but what about his likely opponents in the election? The Christian Democrats? The Workers' Party?

An hour later Flint had driven him to the headquarters of the Democratic Workers Party in a wrecked building in Kreuzberg, in a street where women were operating a rusty hand pump to fill buckets and jugs with icy water to lug back to their ruined apartments. The smoke from cooking fires rose from piles of rubble where families without apartments were making their homes, their children playing on burned-out tanks. Forrester made his way gingerly down a flight of broken stairs into a basement room where a tired-looking man was turning the handle of a Gestetner duplicating machine. The room was freezing, the green linoleum was pitted with cigarette burns and there were broken chairs propped in forlorn rows against the walls where makeshift political posters had been pinned. An old woman sat typing furiously at a desk propped up on bricks.

The man pulled a sheet out of the Gestetner and examined the blotchy mess on the cheap, yellowing paper. "No-one will be able to read this," he said. "I think the ink has frozen." He turned as he heard Forrester come in and straightened automatically as he saw the uniform.

"Your name?" said Forrester, steering his German into the Prussian accent he knew would be most effective here.

"Gellsen, sir," said the man, cringing slightly. "I have a licence for the Gestetner."

"I dare say," said Forrester. "But I'm not interested in that. I'm looking into the background of Peter Dorfmann, who'll be standing on behalf of your opponents in this district."

Gellsen's watery eyes flickered with wary interest. "You want to know if he was a Nazi?" he said.

"I want to know everything about him," replied Forrester. He had been about to say "anything" but he realised it was the wrong approach. Authority was supposed to be uncompromising. Anything else would look like weakness.

"Well he kept his job at the university under the Nazis," said Gellsen. "So he must have been one of them."

"You know perfectly well that not everyone who helped the party was a member," said Forrester sharply. "There were plenty of significant figures who avoided joining. But he may have spoken at gatherings, spouted government propaganda, that kind of thing. I imagine you'll have been looking into that for the election." But even as he made this assertion Forrester doubted it. Apart from the typist there was no-one else there. This was not exactly a centre of humming political activity.

"Naturally," said Gellsen. "For myself I never trusted the man, though as for hard evidence—" The woman at the typewriter coughed discreetly, and when Gellsen glanced at her she inclined her head. He went over and listened as she whispered. He looked at Forrester doubtfully.

"Fräulein Mundt has some information," he said. Forrester turned to her. Her face was pinched and pale, hair tightly wound into a meagre bun. He realised she wasn't an old woman at all: hunger and strain had made her look twenty years beyond her real age.

"He was unjustly promoted during the war," she said. "Over the head of a better qualified professor." Forrester nodded without enthusiasm. This sounded like the kind of academic rivalry that went on all the time, everywhere.

"I see," he said. "For political reasons?"

Fräulein Mundt's eyes glinted behind her glasses, clearly fearful she was about to lose the chance of doing someone down. "Everything was political," she said. "Who you knew was political. Who your friends were was political. Dorfmann can only have got that job because he had friends in high places. He was not the best man."

"Who was?" said Forrester.

"Professor Schopen, of course," said Fräulein Mundt, as though Forrester should have had this information at his fingertips. "He was my professor. He was the best. But he had no friends at party headquarters."

"Write his name down," said Forrester, as much to give himself time to think as anything. "Write down where I can find him."

"He is still at the university," Fräulein Mundt replied, writing something on a scrap of paper. "But not the head of his department, which he should be." As she gave the paper to Forrester she said bitterly, "Professor Schopen knows more about *The Sorrows of Young Werther* than a dozen Dorfmanns!"

As he walked up the basement steps back to the car, Forrester had the sinking feeling that his efforts to save Clark were descending into an academic quagmire about who knew the most about Goethe. But it was his first lead.

"Berlin University," he said to Flint. "On Unter den Linden."

At the junction of Kommandantenstraße they had to wait while a long line of trucks, each marked with a red star, lumbered past, laden with machinery that looked as if it had been torn up by the roots.

"Lathes and stuff from German factories," said Flint. "On their way to Russia. Doesn't look like they'll be much use when they get there, does it?" Forrester was inclined to agree: whoever had removed the machinery had clearly preferred the sledgehammer to the oxy-acetylene cutter, and nobody had bothered to wrap the equipment to protect it against the snow. By the time the war-booty had travelled a thousand miles to the east it would be so much scrap.

Beside them, as they waited, was a group of children carrying sacks full of scavenged firewood; on the other side of the road a woman was pulling a cart with a long cardboard box on it. "Berlin hearse," said Flint drily. "Whoever that is in the box, she'll have to leave him at the cemetery till the ground thaws up a bit – it's too hard to dig graves now."

The children came over to the car. "*Was hast du für mich?*" asked a small boy, and Forrester remembered the signs in England exhorting him to save any chocolate he came across "for the children".

"Bugger off," said Flint, but he also reached into the glove-box and pulled out half a dozen boiled sweets, which he threw to the children as the Russian convoy finally cleared and they were able to move again.

"Poor little bastards," said Flint as he changed gears. "No place for a kid, this." Then they were driving down Unter den Linden, with the Brandenburg Gate at one end and the wreckage of the Palace at the other.

At the university, students were lined up in the courtyard, each, bizarrely, carrying a piece of torn cardboard. As Forrester left the car he couldn't resist asking the girl at the head of the line what the cardboard was for. "For the windows," she said. "Without the cardboard, the wind blows through where the glass used to be. The professors have asked each of us to find a piece of cardboard and bring it. That is not so easy."

Beside the line a man was selling textbooks from a barrow; or at least the remains of textbooks – many were charred, and most were missing their covers. And yet the students were examining them eagerly, exclaiming over finds, turning the pages with as much enthusiasm as if they had been pristine copies, fresh off the press.

"Can you tell me where I can find Professor Schopen?" Forrester asked, and soon he was making his way through the wrecked corridors, where lectures went on in bombed-out halls and students listened more attentively than they did at Oxford, while the wind moaned through the cardboard window-coverings.

Professor Schopen didn't even have a building. He was lecturing in a wooden hut in a rubble-filled courtyard when Forrester finally found him. He was wearing a tattered overcoat and a scarf that looked as if it had been knitted out of sacking, and the spectacles perched on his nose had been broken and mended with dirty string. He also wore a hat against the cold, and had Forrester seen him crouched in a doorway he would have been tempted to throw him a *pfennig*.

"All intelligent thoughts have already been thought," Schopen was saying as Forrester entered. "What is necessary is only to try to think them again." Beneath the professor's overcoat Forrester could see layers of newspapers wrapped around his thin body. But his students were hanging on his every word.

"You see, a person hears only what they understand," the old scholar went on, "and age merely shows what children we remain. Goethe taught us that daring ideas are like chessmen moving forward. They may be beaten, but also they may start a winning game. Every day we should hear at least one little song, read one good poem, see one exquisite picture, and, if possible, speak a few sensible words – that is our goal."

The students wrote assiduously, stubs of pencils filling sheets of old bills, torn magazine pages, account books they must have found among the ruins. Their faces were haggard; some of them still bore the marks of wounds. But none of them, at that moment, seemed to care. As their professor spoke they were in a world of artists and philosophers; a world their country had for twelve long years turned its back on. Schopen was coming to the end.

"And now I think we have done our duty to great thoughts for today," he said, "and I am beginning not to be able to feel my feet, let alone the tips of my fingers, so I will end this lecture and thank you very much for your kind attention." As he gathered up his papers, the class applauded.

As Schopen came abreast of him Forrester said quietly, "When ideas fail, sometimes a word comes in to save the situation," and held up his army pass. To his surprise Schopen took it from him and examined the photograph closely, then looked at Forrester's face.

"I love those who yearn for the impossible," said the old man.

"I'm assuming Goethe wrote that," said Forrester. Schopen smiled.

"Very little comes from my lips that did not once emerge from Goethe's. For example, have you ever thought that 'an overly sensitive heart is an unhappy possession on this shaky earth'?" Schopen's wise old eyes met Forrester's, and suddenly, quite without warning, he felt a strong desire to tell this ragged old man everything that was in *his* heart: his guilt over Barbara, his secret desire for Margaret Clark and how his efforts to save Gordon Clark were partly to make amends for it, his desperation to return to Crete and find his real purpose in life.

But he did not. Instead he found himself saying, as if he were a policeman, "I'm investigating Dr. Peter Dorfmann. I understand he was unfairly promoted over your head by the Nazis."

Schopen smiled. "They say sixty million people have

been killed in this war. Almost every city in Europe has been bombed and shelled; many have been razed to the ground. Six million Jews have died. And you expect me to complain about not getting a promotion?"

"What I want to find out is how close Dorfmann was to the Nazi hierarchy," said Forrester.

"I have no idea," said Schopen. "How could I know?" He looked at Forrester innocently, but Forrester sensed he was holding something back.

"You could know because he was a close colleague," he said. "You could know because you are an intelligent man. You would have heard him in casual conversation. You would have seen people he associated with."

Schopen rubbed his fingers together – the tips were indeed blue with cold. "It has been said of the Germans that they love to denounce one another. It's true. I saw it when Hitler ruled us; I see it now the Russians and the Americans and the French and the British are here. I am determined not to be such a German."

Forrester was silent for a moment.

"I respect that," he said. "But you know this man is being groomed for power. If he was part of the Nazi regime, in whatever capacity, he should not be given power."

"We were all part of the Nazi regime, in whatever capacity we worked, if we were not in the resistance," said Schopen.

Suddenly Forrester was gripped by a seething impatience. Here was a good man, behaving as he thought was right – and in doing so denying him the help he needed. He wanted to shake him, to shout at him, to make him answer, and he felt in his bones how power corrupts. Instead he said, "I understand what you say, Professor. It makes perfect sense. May I tell you why I want information about this man? I may have given you the impression it's for official reasons. But it's not."

And he proceeded to tell Schopen the whole story, almost as if he was speaking to some sort of father confessor. When he had finished Schopen shook his head, smiling to himself.

"We are in the midst of great historical forces," he said, "and yet it is our own dramas which dominate our lives. Age merely shows what children we remain. We are never deceived; we deceive ourselves." Forrester held himself in check, waited.

"The truth is," said Schopen, "that in the midst of all the carnage I *was* outraged at Dorfmann's advance within the university, and consoled myself by saying it must be because of his Nazi connections – for which pettiness I despised myself. Now he is the coming man, and again I despise myself for resenting his success. And you want to know if my suspicions of him during the era of the Third Reich were correct, so that you can save your friend. The truth is I don't know; I looked the other way, as we all did, and immersed myself in the past. It seems petty to bring it up now."

Again, Forrester wanted to argue with him, to convince him to give way to denounce his enemy. But he knew his only means of getting at the truth was to let this man reach that decision himself.

"Thinking is easy, acting is difficult," said Schopen, "and to put one's thoughts into action is the most difficult thing in the world. The truth is I saw Peter Dorfmann with certain people who seemed to me to be people of importance in the government. I formed the impression he was valued by them, cosseted by them, but that was only an impression, and no basis on which to denounce him."

"Can you give me any names?" asked Forrester.

Schopen shook his head. "As I say, I looked the other way," he said. "Perhaps I should not have done so, but I did." He smiled sadly at Forrester. "Believe me," he said, "I would tell you more if I knew more, but I do not."

Forrester believed him, and ground his teeth. Here was the tantalising scrap, the hint that something about Dorfmann was not what it seemed – and it looked as if, thanks to this man's determination not to give way to envy, a tantalising scrap was all it would remain. Schopen saw the disappointment in Forrester's face. "I'm sorry," he said. "This must be very frustrating for you."

"Yes," said Forrester, simply – and then a woman came up to them and spoke softly to the old academic.

"A Goethe evening?" he asked her, surprised.

"Yes," said the woman. "The invitation comes from Colonel Tulpanov."

"Then I had better respond," said the old man. To Forrester he said, "Our Russian occupiers place a great deal of emphasis on culture. I think they are trying to make us forget their behaviour when they first arrived." Behind him, Forrester felt the girl stiffen. He had heard something of what the Soviet troops had done when they reached the city. But as he looked at her, something clicked in his mind.

"Is this lady your secretary?" he asked.

Schopen smiled. "Frau Kruger looks after all of us professors in the Literature Department," he said. "Without her we would be like so many lost children."

"Were you secretary to the department during the war, Frau Kruger?" Forrester asked, but she shook her head.

"I was working at Siemens during the war," she said, "making radio equipment."

Forrester turned back to Schopen.

"Do you know who Dorfmann's secretary was?" he said. "Is she still here?"

A shadow crossed Schopen's face.

"No," he said. "Greta has left academic life."

Almost automatically, Forrester glanced at Frau Kruger for corroboration, but she avoided his eyes; however a few minutes later, as he was getting back into the jeep, she came running after him.

"If you go to the Blue Cat Club around nine or ten, Greta Rilke will be there. She knows what happened." And before Forrester could ask anything further, she had vanished into the crowds of students, each carrying his or her piece of cardboard, each searching for the wisdom that had eluded their nation for a generation.

17

THE BLUE CAT

Forrester spent the rest of the day at the Control Commission and visiting the headquarters of the other political parties to see what else he could discover about Dorfmann's activities, but came away with precious little: as far as the records revealed, he'd simply been an ordinary academic who'd been lucky enough to keep his head down and survive.

In the early evening he returned to the villa on Fasanenstraße and fell sound asleep. At 8.00 p.m. Flint came in and woke him as instructed, and they set off through the ruins to find the Blue Cat Club.

They heard the band first, clear in the frozen air, and Forrester was reminded of Noël Coward's remark about the extraordinary potency of cheap music, especially when heard at a distance. Here, as it echoed down the wrecked street, it seemed to mock the devastation. The two men walked down cellar steps slick with melted snow, the walls dripping with moisture, but as the door at the bottom opened, a blast of warmth rushed up to envelop them.

The cellar was packed solid with servicemen of all nations – French, Brits, Russians and Americans; the air was solid with cigarette smoke and down here the noise of chatter almost drowned out the music. Waiters carrying trays loaded with beers hurried through the room as customers yelled out their orders; there seemed to be a woman at every table, sometimes several, their carefully hoarded make-up doing its best to hide faces pinched by hunger.

Flint went off to join a group of other drivers in the far corner and Forrester found himself a seat at a table being vacated by an American airman, who was leaving with a sloe-eyed blonde. As he ordered a beer from a passing waiter he heard a voice he recognised at the table behind him.

"I can give you a hundred and twenty yards of copper wiring," boomed the speaker, "in return for ten rolls of newsprint." Forrester glanced around: it was the dark-haired captain from the villa on Fasanenstraße. The other man at the table said something in reply, and the captain said, "Alright, seventy yards for seven rolls. Done?" There was the sound of wine behind poured into a glass.

When the waiter came back with his beer Forrester asked him if he knew a woman called Greta Rilke. "You're listening to her," said the waiter, and Forrester swung around to look at the singer.

She was a slight brunette, with a face that reminded Forrester of a monkey. At first it was off-putting, but as she sang he was reminded of the French phrase "*jolie laide*". There was a hint of savagery in that face, a hint of the primitive that held its own erotic charge. Her silvery dress hugged her thin figure, clinging tightly to her small breasts. She sang in German, English and Russian about love, betrayal, loss and longing. Her voice was low and husky, seemingly too deep for that fragile body. By the time her set was over Forrester had almost forgotten why he was there.

There was applause for her act, but not wild applause; she was soon replaced by a big-bosomed blonde who to the crowd's delight shook her ample body and ladled innuendo over every phrase. As Forrester was about to leave his table to find Greta, she sat down beside him, smiling at his surprise.

"The waiter," she said. "He will expect a good tip." And as if in confirmation the man brought an ice bucket with wine and two glasses, winking as he did so. As Forrester poured out the wine, he introduced himself, explaining his mission and his meeting with Professor Schopen. Greta smiled sadly.

"How I wish I was with him now," she said.

"Why did you leave?" asked Forrester.

She looked him in the eyes. "The university couldn't afford to pay me, I could not afford to eat, and they offered me a job here. Then the Russians came. You know what happened then."

Forrester did know. As Russian troops pursued the retreating German Army across Eastern Europe, there had been an almost systematic campaign of mass rape, often gang rape, if possible carried out in front of the husbands, fathers or children of the victims. It was part of the Soviet revenge for the horrors the Germans had inflicted on them in their years of victory. It had reached its climax when Berlin fell, when an estimated hundred thousand women were violated. Of these, several thousand had committed suicide. Whole families sometimes hanged themselves after a daughter was raped.

Knowing what would befall them if they were seen by the Russians, women had hidden in attics, cupboards, laundry baskets, coal cellars; they appeared on the streets only when the Soviet troops were sleeping off their previous night's drunkenness, and they stopped going to work.

"I hid too, of course," said Greta, "but they found the daughters of the woman in the apartment below. She thought it would save them if she betrayed me, and they dragged me out of my hiding place. There were six of them, and I knew at least one of them was a killer. The others would use me; afterwards that soldier would kill me – I could see it in his eyes. So I threw myself out of the window."

Forrester blinked. He could see the scene all too clearly. Greta smiled grimly. "The rubble saved me," she said. "The fallen bricks came halfway up the wall of the house. I slid down to the bottom as the first soldier came after me, and then he stopped and saluted." She let Forrester puzzle on that for a moment. "It was an officer, a captain. He had only slowed down because his car had to manoeuvre through the rubble. He glanced at me and saw something – I don't know what, it was certainly not my beauty – but he motioned me to get into the car. And that was all there was to it. He took me to the house he had requisitioned and I became his." She saw the expression on Forrester's face. "Many women here in Berlin have done the same," she said. "Better to belong to *one* of the invaders than be at the mercy of them all."

"And you're still with him?" asked Forrester, and when she nodded went on, "He doesn't mind you singing here?"

"He likes it," said Greta. "He likes to show me off, to say he has a famous singer as his mistress. I'm not a famous singer, of course, but that's what he tells his friends." She gave him a sharp glance. "He'll be here in an hour," she said. "Tell me what you want to know."

Forrester explained his mission, and watched a wary expression come into Greta's eyes. "I know nothing definite against Peter Dorfmann," she said, "but I think the reason he was favoured over Professor Schopen was that he was close to the Nazis."

"And you know that because…"

"They used to collect him from the university. Several times I saw a big car arrive and he would go off in it." She saw his scepticism and added, "The kind of car only the top Nazis used."

"Did you see anyone in the car?"

"Only the driver. They were taking him somewhere, but he was not afraid. He always came back. This I saw several times."

Forrester contemplated this information – it was tantalising.

"And there was nothing to suggest what he was going to do, where he was going?"

"Nothing. Except the Viking book."

Forrester felt an almost visceral jolt. "What Viking book?"

"I don't know *what* Viking book, but it was his big secret. I came across it one day when I was bringing him a message. It was open on his desk and I looked at it. He was very angry when he found me."

"Tell me more about this book. What did it look like? Was it a printed book, or a manuscript?"

"A manuscript, the kind that monks used to write. There were pictures of men in ships in it, dragons and such. The letters at the beginning of each sentence covered in leaves, and little heads and things. He had been tracing one of the drawings."

"Tracing?"

"There was tracing paper in the book. He snatched it away when he saw me looking at it. After that I only saw it when he was carrying it to that car."

"And this big car was the only link with the Nazis? That you can be sure of?" said Forrester. "Did you ever see him outside the context of the university, for example? A party rally, a government meeting, something like that?"

"The Press Club Ball, maybe you have heard of it, early in the war, before such things were stopped." She smiled, reminiscing. "It was held at the Funkturm, very glamorous; all the film stars were there, and the professors in their best evening dress, and army officers in their dress uniforms, and diplomats with gold embroidery."

"And party big-wigs," prompted Forrester.

"That was the only time I actually saw him with them," said Greta. "Or one of them, anyway."

"His name?" asked Forrester.

"Walter Schellenberg," said Greta.

Forrester blinked. "The intelligence man?"

"I don't know," said Greta. "He was in the uniform of the SS. A *Standartenführer*, I think. There was an admiral with them too."

"Not Canaris?"

Greta shrugged. "It could have been," she said. "I did not recognise him, but Walter Schellenberg was handsome and not easy to forget."

"And Dorfmann was clearly familiar with them both?"

"So it seemed to me," said Greta. "So I was not surprised when he was promoted. You see—" she broke off, as a Russian officer appeared behind Forrester.

"Darling," said Greta, and stood up to embrace him. He was quite young, his blond hair shaved close to his scalp. Greta made the introductions; his name was Captain Sergei Bolkonsky and he worked for a man named Tulpanov, who was the Russian Commissar for Culture in Berlin. Forrester remembered the invitation to the Goethe evening Professor Schopen had received from Tulpanov during their meeting. He had seen pictures of the Russian, a man with a brutal reputation who was competing furiously with the British and the Americans to make the Germans think well of the Russians, despite their atrocities, by keeping them entertained with opera, film and drama.

Forrester made to leave, but Bolkonsky insisted he share a bottle with them, and quizzed him about Oxford. Despite the fact that Greta was, in effect, his concubine, he seemed inordinately proud of her, waxing lyrical about her talent as a singer, her knowledge and sophistication. Even the fact that she had been talking to Forrester did not appear to concern him; he was just proud of the fact she could hold her own in a conversation with such a distinguished man as he took Forrester to be. Gradually Forrester realised the young man was quite out of his depth here; he'd grown up on a collective farm and couldn't quite believe he was in the almost mythical city of Berlin as one of the victors.

When Greta performed her second set he watched with wide-eyed admiration, and confided to Forrester that he found it hard to believe a woman like Greta had consented to be his mistress. "She has taught me so much," he said. Later he insisted they both accompany him to an artists' club called the Seagull the next day, which his boss, Tulpanov, had set up to provide important German artists with perks they could not get elsewhere.

"Some bad things were done when we first arrived," he said, "but Colonel Tulpanov believes that if the significant people can be persuaded the Soviet Union is their friend, those things will be forgotten. Already, do you know, we have begun opera again, at both the national and the city theatre?"

Forrester tried to look impressed, but the idea of these starved, desperate, degraded people who had tortured Europe for six years performing Mozart and Rossini amidst the ruins seemed grotesque.

As they walked through the rubble-filled streets, shadowy figures slipped past, pushing prams laden with absurd items – ornate clocks, huge gilt mirrors and aspidistras in brass pots – which they were prepared to barter in return for anything they could eat. Gaunt women hovered in wrecked doorways, offering themselves for a pack of cigarettes. A tram lurched past, sending out a shower of blue sparks, and then stopped in the middle of the road as the power gave out.

It was one in the morning before Forrester finally got back to Fasanenstraße, and the minute he lay on the bed he immediately fell into a deep sleep.

18

THE BOUNCING CZECH

Forrester awoke with a headache and a sense of being overcrowded with possibilities. He followed the smell of bacon and sausages down to a room full of officers tucking into plates brimming with beans, egg and fried bread all liberally garnished with tomato ketchup, took out a notebook, swallowed a mugful of tea strong enough to stand a spoon up in, and wrote down, almost at random, everything he'd heard about Dorfmann since he'd arrived in Berlin.

Then he went through the list and circled several of the words. Among those highlighted were "Viking book" and "Schellenberg". As he was doing this a voice said, "You don't happen to know where I could get hold of twenty typewriters, do you?" and he turned to see the dark-haired officer whose conversations he kept overhearing all over Berlin. This time he introduced himself. "Captain Robert Maxwell," he said. "They've put me in charge of one of the newspapers here, and I'm trying to get it up and running.

I've got the coal for heating, I've got the electricity for the presses, I've got the paper and I've got the ink. But the bloody reporters are having to write their copy in longhand." Forrester stared at him. Suddenly he realised why the man seemed familiar.

"We've met," he said. "Back in England." A shadow passed over Maxwell's face.

"Sorry, old man," he said. "Can't recall."

"But you had a different name," said Forrester, trying to bring it back. Then it came to him: the man had been called Private Ivan du Maurier, and he'd been part of a labour battalion digging latrines at one of the country houses where Forrester had been on a training course. His name had stuck in Forrester's mind because it sounded so upper crust, and the young private had announced it with a thick Czech accent – and indeed looked like a Czech peasant.

"Du Maurier didn't suit me," said Maxwell, who now sounded as if he'd been to Eton. "I tried 'Jones' for a while, but that wasn't right either. My commanding officer suggested Maxwell because it sounded Scottish."

"Ah," said Forrester. "But your real name is…?"

"Hoch, Ján Hoch," said Maxwell, shaking hands. "Penniless Czech refugee in 1940, now an officer in the British Army, husband to the beautiful daughter of a French industrialist, and proud holder of the Military Cross." Forrester registered that he was duly impressed, which he was. It was quite a transformation. "So," said Maxwell without missing a beat, "about those typewriters?"

With some difficulty Forrester managed to disabuse

Captain Maxwell of the notion that he could provide him with anything for *Der Telegraf*, the paper he'd been assigned to oversee, but by the time he'd managed it he'd realised two things: that Maxwell was a force of nature who was going to come out of the ruins of Berlin considerably better off than when he'd entered them, and that he himself was now on the young ex-Czech's list of people who would at some point be useful to him, if not now, then later.

He decided, therefore, to get in first, and as they demolished their full English breakfasts and swilled down several more mugs of tea, he got Maxwell to tell him what he knew about Walter Schellenberg, the man whom Greta Rilke had seen with Dorfmann at that distant Press Club Ball.

"Schellenberg's a real operator," said Maxwell, with what was clearly the respect of a fellow operator. "Came out of law school in the middle of the Depression, couldn't get a job for love or money and joined the SS. Heydrich put him in their counter-intelligence department."

"The *Sicherheitsdienst*," said Forrester, automatically.

"Exactly," said Maxwell. "Then Himmler spotted him and made him not just his personal aide but a *Sonderbevollmächtigter*. What's the translation?"

"Special Plenipotentiary," said Forrester.

"It was Schellenberg who dreamt up the Venlo Affair," said Maxwell. In 1939, a certain "Captain Schämmel" had contacted British spies in Holland, claiming to be disaffected with Hitler. He arranged a meeting with the British near the border at a Dutch town called Venlo. But instead of revealing German secrets, Schämmel dragged the British agents over the border into Germany. With the information the Gestapo got out of them the Nazis were able to roll up spy networks all over Europe, particularly in Czechoslovakia.

"Captain Schämmel's real name was Walter Schellenberg," said Maxwell. "Later on he tried to kidnap the Duke of Windsor so he could set him up as the King of England."

"I see what you mean about him being an operator," said Forrester.

"He set up a brothel with a recording studio in the basement," Maxwell went on enthusiastically, "and then had the girls entertain all the top Nazis so he could blackmail them. He had a machine gun built into his desk so he could cut people in two at the touch of a button."

Schellenberg had clearly caught Maxwell's imagination.

"Where is he now?" asked Forrester.

"Spandau," said Maxwell briefly. "He was arrested in Denmark trying to negotiate a separate peace with Churchill. He isn't a man for half measures."

"I wonder if there's any chance I might be able to get in to see him," said Forrester.

"What for?" asked Maxwell. Forrester hesitated.

"This is confidential," he said.

"Of course," said Maxwell, but was unable to suppress the glint in his eyes, which suggested that he would make whatever use of the information suited him. Forrester, however, did not really care.

"It's about a man named Peter Dorfmann," he said. "He's being groomed for power in the new democratic Germany and as far as the Control Commission is concerned he was no more than a conscientious Professor of Literature while the Nazis were in power. I've found someone who claims to have seen him with Walter Schellenberg."

"Schellenberg was a cultured man," said Maxwell. "He could have been discussing literature."

"He was also one of the most powerful figures in German intelligence," said Forrester. "Could Dorfmann have been one of his informants?"

"Informants on what?" asked Maxwell. "Tittle-tattle about university politics? Not likely. Schellenberg was involved in bigger things than that."

"My informant said there was an admiral with them. I'm wondering if it could have been Canaris." Admiral Canaris had been the head of the Abwehr, the intelligence service of the German Army, but, appalled by German atrocities in Poland, had begun to work secretly for the downfall of Hitler. Ultimately he'd been found out and hanged.

"I'm afraid if you're looking for something damaging against Dorfmann a connection with Canaris isn't going to get you far," said Maxwell. "He was practically on our side."

"But Schellenberg's a different matter," said Forrester.

"Well, it's worth a try," Maxwell said, "but getting to him will mean you have to cut enough red tape to wrap round all Berlin. And I don't see why Schellenberg should help you. He's got his own neck to think of, when they start trying the big Nazis."

"That might just make him co-operative," said Forrester.

"Possibly," said Maxwell, wiping the last vestiges of egg and ketchup from his plate with a slice of bread. "But if

I hear anything that might help, I'll let you know."

"Thanks," said Forrester. "And I'll keep my eyes open for spare typewriters."

Forrester spent the rest of the morning driving from office to office trying to get clearance to visit Walter Schellenberg at Spandau. In the afternoon he gained admittance to the former boiler factory where the surviving records of the Gestapo, the *Sicherheitsdienst* and the Abwehr were being slowly put in order by teams of young soldiers under the command of a sardonic American major named Elliot, who looked as if he would be more at home on a football field, and prowled the towering aisles of his paper kingdom muttering to himself as if searching for a way out.

But the soldier-clerks who, surrounded by so much paper, had already taken on the demeanour of medieval librarians, moved slowly and methodically around the vast shell of a building, typing up labels, sliding paperclips carefully into place, sighing before they pressed down on a staple gun to reattach stacks of often violently separated papers.

Most of them had been too young to take part in the fighting, and now the enemy was defeated, all their country required them to do was plough through this paperwork. Forrester himself felt a sinking of his spirits at the sheer scale of what lay before him, but remembering Gordon in the prison cell in Oxford, and Margaret waiting for whatever news he could bring, he began, with the aid of one of the clerks, to search for any reference to Peter Dorfmann.

Three hours later he had achieved nothing except a thundering headache and the conviction he was getting nowhere. Even if Dorfmann had worked with the *Sicherheitsdienst* or indeed the Abwehr, he'd almost inevitably been referred to by a code name. He was about to give up and return to his efforts to arrange the interview with Schellenberg when a single phrase caught his eye: "with the aid of the saga".

The document was an internal report from one department of the German intelligence services to another; which one wasn't clear because the first page was missing. But the second ended with a paragraph beginning:

```
with the aid of the saga Erik has been
able to maintain a constant flow of coded
contact with Saint, whose position appears
unassailable. Saint's information on the
Murmansk convoys has been proved accurate
time and time again, and what he has been
able to glean about Soviet intentions has
been invaluable, particularly as regards
Stalingrad. And though he refuses, citing
security concerns, to recruit any sub-agents,
he also refuses any payment, insisting
his commitment to our cause is purely
ideological, and based on his loathing of the
Bolshevik threat. I therefore recommend
```

Forrester turned the page eagerly – and found himself

reading about an intelligence operation in Rumania. He looked at the page number: it was a hundred pages on from the page with the saga reference. He called the clerk over.

"There's something missing," he said.

The clerk, a slow-talking youth from Ohio, shifted the gum in his mouth and examined the pages. "It's not even the same file," he said. "Some dope's smooshed a whole bunch of pages together. Again."

Forrester restrained his impatience. "So I wonder where the page would be that follows this?"

"Yeah," said the clerk. "I wonder about that too." He looked around the boiler factory: the shelves of files seemed to go on for ever, disappearing into the gloom. "One of these days somebody'll find 'em. But you know something, Dr. Forrester? I bet we'll both be long gone by then."

Forrester knew he was right, but he looked anyway, drafting an impatient Major Elliot into the search and refusing to give up. But by the time it was dark and the place was about to close for the night, he'd found nothing, despite the best efforts of the youth from Ohio.

"Sorry about that, Dr. Forrester," said the clerk as he prepared to leave. "Looked kind of interesting, too."

Interesting, thought Forrester. Interesting indeed if he could prove that "Erik" was Dorfmann, and even more interesting if he could discover the identity of "Saint" and what role the "saga" had played in their communications. He was certain the saga was the manuscript Greta Rilke had described, the one that Dorfmann had been so protective of. But where had Saint been based? Russia, by the sound of it. Somewhere, certainly, he had been in a position to know about both the Murmansk convoys and Soviet plans for Stalingrad.

Suddenly he remembered his conversation with Haraldson about secrets encrypted in the saga. What if the encrypted secrets had not been about the dark arts, but about the Murmansk convoys?

He called the Control Commission, but there was no news on his request to see Schellenberg. "I wouldn't get your hopes up, either," said the official. "There's a long queue ahead of you wanting to talk to that gentleman."

19

UP THE DOWN STAIRCASE

That night Forrester went to Colonel Tulpanov's Goethe evening and stood at the back of a ruined hall near the Gendarmenmarkt to hear Professor Schopen talk to a packed house. It was freezing cold; every member of the audience was bundled up in overcoats. Most of them – apart from the Russians – were patched and ragged; their breath condensed in the freezing air. But they listened intently.

"There is nothing so terrible as activity without insight," said Schopen. "But to the person with a firm purpose all things are servants."

Forrester recognised Colonel Tulpanov up on the platform, nodding sagely. He looked like a military Sydney Greenstreet, as hard as nails. Forrester was convinced the Russian had singled him out among the audience, and was fixing him with the kind of stare he would normally have given people he was interrogating. Even across a crowded hall, and without being held down in a chair by a couple of NKVD thugs, it was intimidating.

"Be generous with kindly words, especially about those who are absent," said the professor. "What is uttered from the heart alone will win the hearts of others, and as soon as you trust yourself, you will know how to live." The audience nodded thoughtfully, as if this was a question they had been pondering for years.

There was a reception afterwards, with the Russians taking pride in the professor as if he were a performing bear, and the audience devouring the sandwiches and tea as if they hadn't eaten for days, which quite a lot of them, Forrester thought, probably hadn't.

"*We* should be doing this," said an American voice beside him. Forrester looked around to see Major Elliot surveying the scene gloomily.

"Winning hearts and minds with Goethe?" said Forrester. "Or sandwiches?"

"Doesn't matter," said the major, who seemed even more disaffected than he had at the records office. "We can't let these bastards win them. And they will, unless we stop them."

"They *are* still our allies," said Forrester.

"For how long?" said Elliot. "We have to start fighting the next war now. We have to get in the first lick before those bastards do."

"A bit soon, surely?" said Forrester. "Isn't everybody rather sick of fighting?"

The big American didn't seem to hear him. "Hitler had some things right," he said. "He knew the communists were the real enemy. Now he's been cleared out of the way we're going to see how right he was."

"The Russians are as exhausted as we are," said Forrester. "Twenty million dead. Most of their industry wrecked."

"Hasn't stopped them taking over half of Europe already, has it?" said Elliot. "And if you don't think they also want the other half, you're suffering from terminal naivety."

"Sounds like a terrible condition," said Forrester, seeing a gap around Professor Schopen. "But I suppose chaps like you are the cure." And he darted away before Elliot could reply.

"A wonderful lecture, Herr Professor," he said, and then, before the kindly old man could unleash another swarm of Goethe quotes, got to the point. "There've been several references to Peter Dorfmann having an important book, a Norse manuscript I believe, that he often carried with him to important meetings. I know it must seem an absurd enquiry, but were you ever aware of a particular manuscript, perhaps a Nordic saga, that seemed particularly important to him?"

Light glinted off Schopen's ravaged spectacles as he turned towards Forrester, and Forrester was certain he detected in the old man's eyes a sudden wariness he hadn't seen before. "As you say, Herr Forrester, I could hardly be expected to take particular notice of a book held by a colleague. Especially in a literature department." And he began to turn away. Forrester was about to follow him when he felt a heavy hand on his arm, and found himself looking into the blank, pebble-like eyes of Colonel Tulpanov.

"The professor is tired, my friend. Perhaps you could continue your conversation when the British organise a literary evening of their own?"

And by the time Forrester had disengaged himself, Schopen was gone. He buttoned his coat and left the hall, his mind racing.

He'd given Flint the evening off and his footsteps rang on the frosted pavements as he walked back towards Fasanenstraße, the moonlight pale on the ruins. He remembered Tolkien's words: "During the thirties your own Master made his name with his brilliant reconstruction of the lost books of the *Heimskringla*... Stories of the Norwegian kings. There's a particularly dramatic passage about the sacking of Konungahella, which has survived. I often recite it to my students."

But there was nothing to suggest that the Norse manuscript on which Dorfmann had placed such value was the *Heimskringla*, let alone that it had had anything to do with the manuscript that Lyall had brought back from Norway. And even if it had, in what way would it help Gordon Clark escape the hangman?

After a while Forrester realised he was making no progress in solving these questions and was merely repeating them like a mantra. The second thing he realised was that he hadn't been taking any notice of where he was walking: when he looked around he had no idea where he was. And the third thing he realised was that someone was following him.

Unlike his, their shoes made no noise on the pavement, and they kept well back – but he was now aware of long shadows appearing and then disappearing on the fallen bricks and pitted roadway, and felt a sudden shiver of disquiet. He acted on it instantly, as he had learnt to do, stepping sideways into the darkness, and as he did so a brick in the wall beside which he stood exploded. Instinctively he reached for his gun – and realised he had no gun, no weapon of any kind. He had put those days behind him when peace was declared – or so he thought.

His enemy fired again, and Forrester melted into the ruins, but he couldn't run. Fallen bricks lay everywhere, and there were potholes at every turn; with nothing but the moonlight to guide him he was almost certain to either twist an ankle or break a leg.

He heard his assailant coming after him, stepping quietly, and heard too, the crunch of glass off to his left as a second person closed in. Of course there would be a second: whoever they were, they weren't amateurs. And then with a sharp crack his foot went through a broken board and as he pulled it free he knew he had no option: he had to run, regardless of the risks.

There was liberation in flight, exhilaration even, despite the dangers, and suddenly, bizarrely, he was running up a carpeted staircase with a wallpapered wall on his left and wooden banisters on his right – and he was halfway up before he realised he'd run right into one of the houses that had been blasted open by the bombing. "House" was putting it too strongly: all that remained of the building was the angled corner of two walls – and the staircase that ran up them.

How far up the staircase went he had no idea; the

remaining walls blocked out the moonlight. The stairs themselves could end at any second, and he'd be plunging down into the darkness like a puppet whose strings had been cut.

On the other hand, if he stopped he was dead, because one of his pursuers was coming up the stairs after him, firing as he came, the bullets splintering the banisters and sending puffs of plaster out of the walls. Dorfmann, he thought, dispassionately. Dorfmann was behind this and Dorfmann wanted him dead because of the manuscript. Suddenly he knew there was no point hanging around in Berlin, being shot at, while he waited for permission to see Walter Schellenberg – he had to go much farther north, to where the manuscript had come from. As he swung himself around the corner of the next flight of stairs he dropped flat against the treads, and his pursuer ran blindly over him, stumbled at the unexpected obstacle and then cried out in pain as Forrester took the gunman's arm and used it as a lever to tip him over the banisters into the blackness below.

There was an almost plaintive cry as the man fell, and then a snapping sound as he hit the bricks below. And then another shot, from farther back as the second killer stepped into the breach.

Going back down the stairs was not an option. Ahead was pitch darkness. Forrester dropped back onto his belly against the rain-soaked stair carpet and crawled upwards. There was a window on the next landing. Or its frame, at least; the glass was long gone. He grasped the woodwork and hauled himself over the edge.

As he went through the second man's shots would have hit him but for the fact that the entire window crumbled away the moment Forrester put his weight on it and he found himself slithering downwards in a sort of urban avalanche of broken bricks. Several of the bricks hit him – in the ribs, on the skull, in the back – but he'd slid to a halt and risen to his feet again before the pain registered and then he was running zigzag with more shots whistling around him, and there was no time to feel pain.

He remembered Churchill's remark, after his time in the Spanish–American War in Cuba, to the effect that there were few things more delightful than the sound of bullets missing you. Then he was in the middle of a street with a British Army jeep coming towards him, and by the time his pursuer had reached the street, he was on his way to Tempelhof.

20

NORTHERN LIGHTS

At Tempelhof Airport Forrester sent a cable to MacLean telling him what had happened and suggesting that he follow up the Schellenberg/Erik/Saint/saga lead. Then he was able to talk his way aboard an RAF flight for Copenhagen.

He got a lift into the city, found his way to the picturesque old Nyhavn district docks, had a breakfast of pickled herrings, and caught a ferry to Norway.

A century ago Oslo had burned down and the Norwegians, then poor and lacking in self-confidence, had unwisely hired the most pompous architects in Germany to mastermind the rebuilding of their capital. The result was street after street of heavy-browed Victorian edifices which would have justified the title of the ugliest capital in northern Europe had it not been for a backdrop of fir-covered hills and a fjord full of little islands that reminded Forrester irresistibly – as he walked along the Rådhusgata from the ferry terminal – of Christmas shop-window displays.

Not surprisingly, the inhabitants left the city whenever

they had the chance, packed up their skis and headed off into the forests, leaving the streets deserted.

To his right, on a rocky outcrop overlooking the fjord, he could see the copper spires of the Akershus, the sturdy castle that had been the headquarters of the Wehrmacht during the occupation. From there he turned onto Karl Johans gate, the busiest street in Norway, with the royal palace – until recently the home of the Nazi governor – behind him, and the national theatre to his right, all looking much the worse for wear after years of neglect under the occupiers.

And then there was the university, with its magnificent Greek portico and row upon row of windows – behind one of which lurked Arne Haraldson.

Forrester contemplated it for a long moment, and wondered whether to confront him in his lair. But he was almost certain by now that Haraldson had not killed David Lyall; that he had been his dupe, lured to London by promises of occult revelations Lyall may or may not have been able to sustain. Haraldson had returned, Forrester was certain, to find the knowledge he had been promised, but Forrester knew in his gut he had not found it – that the answer to the mystery lay elsewhere.

And now he thought he knew where. He turned away from the university and asked directions to the Central Post Office.

The Post Office proved to be as battered and forlorn as the rest of Oslo, and when he asked for the telephone number he was seeking he was told that services to that part of the country had not yet been restored.

This was much as he had expected, so he left the building and returned to Karl Johans gate in search of a bookshop. He was not surprised that so many were doing business; the Norwegians were the most avid readers in Europe, and he soon found the map and guidebook he was looking for – though they had been published well before the war.

So equipped, he walked to Oslo Central Station and sat down in a nearby café to study the books he had bought, piecing together what Ollie Sepalla had told him of Lyall's movements after his abortive wartime mission, to identify first the home of the aristocrat with whom Lyall had taken shelter – the Grevinne Sophie Arnfeldt-Laurvig of Bjornsfjord and then the nearest railway station.

With the aid of a man in the ticket office he found the train he needed, and an hour later he was seated in a railway carriage breathing in the distinctive smell of Norwegian coal as the train headed north through a landscape of endless pine trees.

Sitting opposite him was a man he knew he'd seen before somewhere. A stranger who took covert glances at him during the first half hour of their journey, and then suddenly shook his fist under his nose. "False!" he said in English. "False fist!"

Forrester gaped for a moment, and then remembered. "You were rotten," he said. "And your name was Thor... something. I remember because I sometimes thought you were using Thor's hammer on the keys."

The man laughed. "I was bored," he said, "bored out of my mind – but it was not your fault: you were a good teacher."

Forrester could smell the peculiar ozone odour of the little shed in Hertfordshire where, for several months in 1942, he had taught would-be commandos how to disguise the signature of their radio transmissions for when they were parachuted into occupied Europe. Among them, a group of tall, lanky Norwegian exiles; including, it seemed, this man.

"They forgot us, you know," said the Norwegian. "Promised to send us back to fight, managed to lose us in the system. I spent three *years* training and three *months* actually fighting."

"I wouldn't complain about that *too* bitterly if I were you," said Forrester.

"You know, when I wanted to get into the army they didn't need me," said Thor. "But the minute I wanted to get out I was suddenly indispensable. Couldn't get permission to go home. You know what I did? I walked into army headquarters, found an empty office and typed out my own discharge papers."

Forrester grinned. He remembered how the passionate young Norwegian had brought a sense of vast possibilities with him to that cramped, uncomfortable little communications hut, a sense of wonder about the world most people never experienced.

"I'm beginning to remember," he said. "Didn't you live on a desert island before the war, in the Pacific or somewhere?"

"Good memory. Yes, I did. It was paradise. My wife and I made a hut out of plaited bamboo and ate breadfruit and coconuts and bananas. Every day we swam in a rock pool. It was like the Garden of Eden."

"You felt as if you were part of nature," said Forrester. "That was how you described it."

"Exactly," said the Norwegian. "If people fight their environment, they can win every battle except the last, and then there will be an end to them. On that island nature wasn't there for us, it *was* us."

"You plan to go back," asked Forrester, "now the madness is over?"

The man glanced into the train's corridor, as if making sure they weren't being overheard. "I discovered a great mystery on that island," he said. "And I must solve it."

"What kind of mystery?"

"It concerned a stone fish. You see, one day a native, a good friend of mine, took us far inland, to a rocky promontory, and there it was: over six feet long, head, tail, fins and all, outlined in the rock. The first petroglyph ever discovered on that island. It was covered in little hollows like cups, and sun symbols. I cut away the vegetation and as more and more of these petroglyphs appeared, the man who had brought us there said '*Tiki, Menui Tiki*'."

Thor grinned triumphantly at him and Forrester knew his cue. "Which meant?"

"Gods, many gods. Those carvings seemed to stare at us, with huge eyes."

"Must have been quite a moment."

"It was – and then I saw a petroglyph that sent a shiver down my spine. It was a ship shaped like a crescent moon. Curved hull, high bow and stern, a double mast and rows of oars, completely different from the rafts these people used. You know what it reminded me of? The vessels used in ancient Peru."

"Most people think Polynesia was settled from Asia."

"I think most people are wrong. I believe it was South America, and I intend to prove it."

"How?"

Thor leant forward and spoke softly, but his eyes glittered as he spoke. "I intend to build a raft out of Peruvian balsa wood and sail it across the Pacific to Polynesia."

Forrester looked at him with respect. "Quite an undertaking," he said.

Thor smiled conspiratorially. "I think you and I have both become accustomed to risky operations, Captain Forrester. It is Captain Forrester, isn't it?"

"It is," said Forrester. "Remind me of your second name, so I can say 'I knew him when you're famous."

"Heyerdahl," said the Norwegian. "Thor Heyerdahl."

They sat in silence for a while, listening to the comforting clatter of the train on the tracks, and then Heyerdahl asked him what he was doing in Norway, and Forrester told him. Heyerdahl raised an eyebrow when Forrester mentioned the countess. "I met her once, before the war."

"And?"

"She was a fine-looking woman," said Heyerdahl. "But very haughty. Her husband the count was then a senior army officer."

"And now?"

"Now he is dead," said Heyerdahl, "but I imagine the countess is still haughty."

Forrester laughed. "Can you tell me anything else about them?"

Heyerdahl's face darkened. "Only gossip," he said.

"Gossip will do," said Forrester. "I'm clutching at straws here."

Heyerdahl considered. "The rumour was that the count drank heavily," he said at last. "And did not keep good company."

"What does that mean?"

"There was a man called Alistair."

"Alistair?"

"He was some kind of magician. He had a sinister name: Crawling or something."

"Do you mean Crowley, Aleister Crowley?"

"Yes! That's it."

"The wickedest man in the world. Or so he claimed."

"I believe he dabbled in the occult."

"More than dabbled – he swam in it. He was accused of the most appalling depravities, including human sacrifice. He called himself the Great Beast. And the count associated with *him*?"

"So they said. I don't know if it's true."

Suddenly all Haraldson's hints and prevarications came back to him. Had Lyall's claims about the secrets contained in the manuscript been based on something that had taken place while he was hiding on the count's estate?

"Was the countess part of these goings on?"

"I can't tell you," said Heyerdahl. "Though they say she is a very strong-minded woman."

Forrester stared at him as the train lurched over a high bridge crossing an abyss. He looked down into its snowy depths, and felt a shiver of unease.

They were winding west through Telemark, where the Norwegian and Allied commandos, some time after Lyall's aborted mission, had skied in to blow up the German heavy water plant. They had succeeded, at great cost, and effectively prevented Hitler from getting the atomic bomb: one of the major victories of the war. Forrester looked at the slate-grey river winding through the snow, seeing that night in his mind's eye as the flames devouring the plant reflected off the snow and the commandos sped away into the darkness.

He dozed then, and when he awoke Heyerdahl had gone and the train was pulling into a tiny railway station with elaborately carved wooden canopies like something out of Tolstoy's Russia. He disembarked hurriedly, and as the train vanished around a bend in the track and the noise of the engine died away, the silence enveloped him like a blanket.

He took a long breath of chilled, clean air and raised his head to look around the valley. Thick pine forests, broken only by tiny farm clearings, marched up into the mountains. It was mid afternoon, and already the sun cast a dusty rose-coloured light on the peaks.

From the station he took an ancient, hearse-like taxi up the road towards the head of the valley, which finally turned into a private drive leading into deep forest. Snow slipped from the pine trees on either side, falling in clumps as the vehicle finally approached not the castle of Forrester's imaginings but a collection of log buildings clustered around a sloping lawn. There was a flagpole in the middle of the lawn and a barn on either side, and it was a moment before Forrester took in their sheer size: each must have been more than a hundred feet long.

The taxi pulled up in front of the main house, a simple three-storey wooden building with two wings joined by a balcony and steeply pitched roofs. Forrester got out, paid his fare and indicated that the cab driver was dismissed. The man looked at him doubtfully, but Forrester was firm. Without any obvious means of transport back to the station, it would be harder for Countess Arnfeldt-Laurvig to send him on his way.

As the taxi vanished down the drive, Forrester pulled at a wrought-iron chain in the massive weathered door. After a long moment a bell tolled somewhere far off in the house, and when the door opened he found himself facing a dignified old woman dressed in traditional costume. Guessing she was the housekeeper, he read out his carefully rehearsed Norwegian words of introduction. She stared at him for a long moment before vanishing into the house. As Forrester stood on the massive stone steps he felt the silence again, stretching away to eternity.

Finally the housekeeper came back and beckoned him to follow her through a tall panelled hall with a vast Turkish rug covering the floorboards and medieval images of angels and demons on the massive roof beams. In the middle of the hall there was an ancient sleigh. Everything was spotless, and smelt strongly of furniture polish.

The housekeeper said something he did not catch before leaving him at the door to a small dimly lit drawing room where the walls were hung with dark landscape paintings. In the far corner of the room was an armchair and it was a moment or two before Forrester realised there was someone in it. Then the occupant raised her head. Her hair was blonde, but faded a little; she was about five years older than Forrester.

"Grevinne Arnfeldt-Laurvig? My name is Duncan Forrester. From Oxford."

"Oxford?" she said, puzzled, as if he'd said Zanzibar.

"Yes. I hope you'll forgive me for arriving unannounced. I tried to telephone from Oslo but they said there was no service."

She looked at him steadily, as if the pieces of a jigsaw were falling into place.

"You are a friend of Captain Lyall," she said, and it was a statement, not a question. Her English was formal, as if remembered from a long-ago governess, and lightly accented. Before he could reply, she rose to her feet. "Something has happened to him. You have come to tell me."

"Yes," said Forrester. He came towards her. "I'm afraid he's been killed." Her eyes did not leave his. "I'm sorry," he said. "I'm very sorry to have to tell you this."

She reached for the tall chair-back to steady herself, and then turned and walked through a door on the far side of the room. Her back was very straight; she held her head high. Forrester hesitated for a second, and then followed her. The afternoon light was already leaking away and for a moment it seemed as if she had vanished.

But when he followed her into the next room he stopped, astonished. The front of the manor house had been hemmed in by trees beyond the lawn. But the windows of this room gave onto the fjord that dropped away behind, a deep, dramatic fissure in the earth where a vast arm of the sea reached up into the land. Bjornsfjord. Of course, this must be Bjornsfjord.

The water was immensely far below, the few fishing boats on its surface like children's toys. There were pine trees clinging to rock walls so steep that even the snow could not find a purchase. It was one of the most extraordinary landscapes Forrester had ever seen. Then he became aware of Sophie Arnfeldt-Laurvig staring blankly out into the grandeur and went over to the massive carved sideboard, poured two whiskies. She drank hers without seeming to notice it. "Tell me what happened," she said. And he told her, and hid nothing. When he had finished she sat down in the chair.

"It seems very strange that David should have escaped from so many Germans who wanted to kill him, and then found death in the quiet places of Oxford University. What do you call them? It is to do with monks."

"Cloisters," said Forrester.

"Cloisters, yes. He always thought of the cloisters of Oxford as his place to be safe."

"And he should have been safe there," said Forrester. "That is one reason I am determined to find out who killed him."

"What if the murderer was your friend?" said Sophie Arnfeldt-Laurvig.

"I am as certain as I can be that my friend did not kill David Lyall," said Forrester.

She looked at him thoughtfully, as someone might stare into a mountain stream, wondering, Forrester thought, from what spring its waters flowed. He met her gaze without reserve, allowing her to draw from him whatever truth she sought – but it took all his willpower to resist the almost overwhelming urge to reach up and touch her face. She wore no make-up. There were grey smudges of weariness below her eyes, but her lips were full. He imagined how they would feel against his.

"What help do you want from me?" she asked. "I think you have come to me for that, and not just to tell me that David is dead."

Forrester tried to pull himself together – what the hell was he thinking?

"You're right, Grevinne; I do hope you'll help me solve the mystery. But the truth is I don't know how. I suspect the murder had something to do with a manuscript David may have seen when he was with you during the war."

"A manuscript?"

"An Old Norse manuscript. He was showing such a manuscript around Oxford before he died, and I wondered if he'd taken it from here."

Countess Arnfeldt-Laurvig smiled sadly. "I know exactly what David took from here when he left me, Mr. Forrester," she said. "I packed his bag myself, and a Norse manuscript was the last thing he would have added to his load: he had to ski two hundred miles to the Swedish border with the German Army hunting for him. The only things in that pack were what he needed to stay alive."

Forrester was silent; it looked as if he had reached a dead end. And yet he did not want the conversation to be over.

He did not want the conversation *ever* to be over.

The countess looked at him. "I'm sorry," she said. "It looks as if you are having a wasted journey." She paused for a moment. "But at least I can offer you some hospitality. There will be no train to Oslo tonight, and there is plenty of room in this house."

"That's very kind of you."

"Also I would like you to tell me more about David. About his life in those Oxford… cloisters. It's very hard for me to think of him as…"

And suddenly her composure cracked and she was weeping silently against his chest and Forrester held her as she sobbed, not saying anything, just letting her grief pour out. He felt her body against him, her tears dampening his shirt, her delicate shoulders shaking. Then her outburst subsided and she gently disengaged herself, took a deep breath and picked up a small bell from the sideboard.

"Helga will show you to your room," she said. "You will want to clean up after your journey. There are some of my late husband's clothes in the wardrobe and if you find any that fit you, please borrow them. We dine at eight."

* * *

The dining room had clearly been designed for large parties, if not the crew of a Viking longship. The table was a massive slab of oak, and the chandelier that hung over it was the size of a cartwheel. Even the candle-holders were huge, and the candles that burned in them were massive cylinders of beeswax. Duncan and the Grevinne Sophie Arnfeldt-Laurvig sat at one corner across from one other, with Helga and an ancient manservant called Josef silently laying the dishes and refilling their glasses.

"This place must have seen some festivities," said Forrester.

"We had many parties before the war," said the countess. "My husband loved to bring people here. There was always hunting and hiking and music in the woods."

"It sounds idyllic."

"Sometimes there were English people. They talked about Henley and Ascot and polo matches. Did you play polo?"

"No," said Forrester. "Polo wasn't big in Hull."

"Kingston upon Hull? Some of the timber from our estates went through that port."

"A lot of things come through Hull. Fish. Copra. Seed oil. All very glamorous."

She smiled, a little hesitantly. "I think that is the opposite of what you mean."

He inclined his head. "Yes, it is. Hull's a very working-class city. And even if there had been people playing polo there before the war, which is a very unlikely thought, our family wouldn't have been among them. My father worked on the fishing trawlers."

She looked into his eyes. "Why are these things so important to English people? And to you?" she asked, gently.

"What makes you think they are?"

"Your eyes are – I don't know the right word in English – hot."

"Hot?"

"Angry. Not at me – at something. Perhaps a little hurt too, as if this subject is giving you pain. And your speech is not like someone from a poor background. You speak as if your father was a gentleman."

"My father *was* a gentleman. He was honest, hard-working and intelligent. But no-one in England would think of him like that, because he was a trawlerman."

"Ah… class," said the countess.

"Yes, class. That's what rules England."

"And yet you, the son of a poor man in a poor city, have risen to become a professor."

"A lecturer."

"At Oxford."

"True."

"You should be proud of yourself."

This time he smiled, a little shame-facedly. "I should be, shouldn't I? And not go about with a big chip on my shoulder."

"A big ship?"

He laughed. "Not ship, *chip*. It means feeling resentful. I'm not, really. I don't envy people who grew up in big houses with servants and garden parties. It's just not the world I knew, and I don't want to pretend it was."

"No, you do not seem to be a man who likes to pretend,"

she said. A shadow crossed her face. "And I know such men from experience." She took a drink from her wine glass, and Forrester remained silent, waiting until she was ready.

"My husband was such a person: a weak man who pretended to be strong. He fooled many people, but he did not fool himself."

"Weak in what way?"

"He drank and he did not have a good head for drink. He made wagers when he could not judge the odds. He took risks to make people think he was brave. I believe that was what led to his death in the war."

"I'm sorry," said Forrester.

"There is a strange quality to the death of a husband you no longer love. You tell yourself you should be feeling more than you do. You ask yourself whether you could have made him a better man if you had tried harder." She met his eyes again. "And you, Dr. Forrester, have you been happy in love?"

He tried to look away, and could not. "I have known great love," he said, "and what it is to lose it." Suddenly, to his fury, he felt his eyes pricking. "She was killed by the Gestapo. I feel I bear some of the blame." Then unshed tears blurred his vision and her hand was closing over his.

Later, he had no idea how, they were in the library and she was pouring brandy into a heavy glass. Firelight flickered gently over the polished spines of the leather-bound books that lined the walls. The mood was easier now, like the air after a storm; as if, worn out with the tempest of his long-suppressed emotions, he was easier with himself than he had been for a long time.

"There is one other thing you should know about my husband," said Sophie Arnfeldt-Laurvig. "Something about the reputation of this place."

"What is that?" asked Forrester, though he was already certain he knew.

"There was a time, during the thirties, when my husband was interested in... how do you say it? Dark magic."

"I have heard that," said Forrester. "In fact I'd heard that an Englishman named Aleister Crowley came here."

"He did," said the countess. "He was a disgusting man; powerful, and horrible. I want you to know that I had nothing to do with these things; in fact my husband and I parted for a time when those men were here, and I went to Oslo. But the things continued while I was away."

"What things?"

"They tried to raise the Devil," she said softly.

"In this house?"

She nodded. "In this house. When I came back, there were pentagrams carved into the beams of the hall. And out in the woods – things had happened out in the woods. Things I am glad I know nothing about."

"What happened when you returned?"

"I confronted the man Crowley and drove him from this house."

"That must have taken some doing."

"I have never encountered such strength. I thought I was going to die. I felt as if I was wrestling with... a great serpent."

"But you prevailed."

"I prevailed."

Forrester moved slightly so that he could look at her face. He knew now what it reminded him of: one of the angels carved into the beams in the entrance hall. If anyone could have overcome the evil that was Aleister Crowley, it was she. And then a thought occurred to him.

"Do you think Norse incantations played any role in what they did?"

"Incantations?"

"Runes, rituals. Sacrifices to Odin, that kind of thing."

"I do not know; it would not surprise me. Some of our Old Norse books were damaged when I came back. Engravings torn out, pages removed." Forrester glanced at the shelves: there were many gaps.

"And later some manuscripts were lost entirely," she said.

"Lost?"

"I think it was partly in revenge for me coming between him and his magic that my husband began to gamble. When my back was turned he used the most valuable manuscripts in this library as his stake."

"He gambled them away? To whom?"

"It could have been anyone. As I said, people came here from all over Norway, all over Europe; there were times when the fjord was full of yachts. Famous people. Distinguished people. Not all of them beasts." She looked him in the eye. "It may be hard to believe, but there were times when this was a good place. When the magic in the air was good magic."

"So you were happy here, sometimes?" said Forrester.

"I sometimes used to dream about what it would have been like to be here with a man I truly loved."

Her face was turned towards him, and this time he could not stop himself. Gently, he took her face in his hands and kissed her. The kiss went on for a long time, and it felt to Forrester as if he had been waiting to feel those lips on his since the world began. After a moment they opened their eyes and looked at each other.

"We have met before," said Sophie.

Forrester nodded. "But not in this life."

"And now we have found each other again," said Sophie Arnfeldt-Laurvig.

They sat there on the worn leather sofa so long the blaze of the burning log became a dull glow, lost in the realisation that whatever tides of time and space had torn them apart in some other age, those same tides had, finally, brought them back together.

As the fire died, she rose to her feet. "My room is directly above yours," she said. "Come to me before you sleep."

21

NIGHT IN THE FOREST

Forrester sat for some time after she had gone, staring into the embers. Then he stood up and wandered around the room, picking up photographs of long-lost social gatherings in heavy silver frames. There were photograph albums, too, showing picnic parties on the shore, games on the lawn, expeditions in the forest. He turned to a page where two photographs had once been – and saw that the lower one of them had gone. Beneath the place it had occupied were the words: "Who were these two? One was English, I think, and one German. But anyway, here they are playing cards with Ernst, June 1937."

The remaining photograph – presumably a precursor to the missing picture – showed a yacht anchored in the fjord in the background. In the foreground two men rowed towards the shore in a dinghy. The Englishman and the German of the missing image? The man on the oars had his back to the camera, and the other was sitting in the prow facing the shore, and though the image was so small

Forrester was convinced that it was Dorfmann. Something about the shape of the head and light hair – as he had seen him that night at High Table. He pulled the photograph out of its mount to see if he could read the name of the yacht and then, when he could not, slipped it into his pocket.

He heard the servants going to bed, and waited a little longer before walking into the entrance hall, kneeling down beside the rug and lifting the edge.

There, incised deeply in the ancient pine, were the outer markings of what could only be a vast pentagram. The image of Haraldson lying on the floor of Lyall's set flashed into his mind, and he knew what had drawn the Norwegian to Oxford when Lyall had summoned him. He listened. Silence. Everyone was asleep except for the one person who suddenly mattered more to him than anyone else in the world.

Silently, he made his way up the stairs. Her door was ajar and after a pause he pushed it gently open. When she saw him, she smiled.

"Close the door behind you," she said.

Afterwards she slept, and the moon rose, and silvered their bodies. Forrester opened the window onto a little balcony, letting the night air flow over him, breathing in the elusive scent of the snow. As he stood there he heard the crunch of a boot, cutting through the frozen crust. Just one, and nothing more, but it was enough. He closed the window quietly, went back to the bed, breathed into her ear. "Wake up, Sophie."

Instantly her eyes opened and seconds later they were dressing. She asked no questions, revealed no surprises, simply did what had to be done. They did not hear either window or door being forced below them in the house: they did not need to. Neither of them was surprised as they heard the first creak on the stairs.

Forrester glanced towards the bedroom door: no lock. There was a chair, folk-painted with flowers. Would it delay them if he jammed it under the door handle? No, too flimsy. Sophie was already thrusting bolsters under the bedcovers. Pillows where the heads would have been. As the door handle turned, they flattened themselves against the wall on either side of the door.

The door swung open and as the silenced gun fired twice into the figures in the bed Forrester brought the painted chair down hard on the extended forearm. The chair disintegrated, but the impact was enough. There was a cry of pain and the gun went flying. Before the man had time to react Forrester was on him, grasping the gun-arm and wrenching it sideways.

But the man was strong, fit and trained. His free hand rabbit-chopped Forrester's neck and his left foot entwined itself with Forrester's, bringing him down through the open door onto the landing – as the second and third men came up.

But Forrester had not released his grip on the man's arm and with a sudden jerk he sent him careering backwards down the stairs into the other two, darted back inside the room and slammed the door. Sophie was ready, pushing a heavy wooden chest towards the door even as he returned – and she had the fallen gun.

But the chest would only delay them for a moment, and whatever the first man's injuries, there were still two more of them. "Window," said Forrester, and seconds later they were climbing out. Already the door was shuddering under the blows of the men trying to get in, and the chest was beginning to move.

Forrester was out on the balcony and about to jump when her hand grasped his shoulder and the moon came out from behind a cloud, illuminating the old ploughshare lying in wait. Behind them, the chest screamed against the wooden floor as the men forced the door. "Up," said Sophie, and then they were heaving themselves up from the balcony ledge and onto the roof, clawing their way over the snow-covered shingles, chunks of snow falling away behind them. The first of the intruders appeared on the balcony before they had reached the roof crest. Sophie swivelled round, pointed the gun and fired.

The shot went wide, but the man ducked back out of sight as Forrester and Sophie slithered down the far side of the roof, sending more snow avalanching before them. This time, as they reached the edge, the ground below them was clear, and without hesitation they jumped, landing thigh deep in the thick crystalline covering of the lawn.

Perfect targets, both of them, as soon as their pursuers saw them. Ahead, the lawn stretched level and unencumbered: a moonlit killing ground. "The trees," said Forrester. "Make for the trees."

And then they were running towards the darkness of the forest, as the first of the intruders reached the roof crest. Bullets hissed into the snow around them and sent splinters flying out of the trunk of birch trees as they ran on, their feet sinking into the snow, plunging blindly into the blackness. Forrester swerved to avoid a fallen log, hit an unseen dip, and as he crashed down into the snow slammed his face into a fallen branch. Suppressing a cry of pain, pressing one hand against his nose to stem the flow of blood, he rose to his feet with the branch in his hand and smashed it into the man pursuing him; his gun went flying.

And then he saw her, a hundred yards off, running hard up some kind of promontory, and the moon came out from behind the clouds and there was a shot from somewhere ahead and she cried out and fell. Sick with shock, Forrester began to run diagonally across the slope towards her.

But the killer was faster: he sprinted straight up the promontory towards the fallen body, gun held out before him, ready to fire again if she stirred. *No*, said Forrester, *no*, and then the man was gone, vanished as if plucked from the surface of the earth and Sophie was rising from the snow, unhurt, gesturing him away from the snowhole.

"They didn't know the terrain," she said. "I did." Forrester looked down into the darkness and heard a splash as the man hit the water a thousand feet below.

Then they went looking for the man he had felled with the branch, but when they came to the bloody patch of snow where he had fallen he was gone and far away. Down the drive, they heard the sound of a car engine starting.

It was over, and Helga and Josef were coming out of the house to look for them, and Forrester allowed himself to be led back inside.

22

PRINCE OF DENMARK

The hours after Sophie and Forrester returned to the house were unrelenting. He kept guard while the two old servants helped Sophie pack; only then did he allow them to deal with the damage to his nose. Even while they dabbed at him with antiseptic and various pine-scented herbs he kept the loaded gun at his side and his eye on the expanse of lawn that led down to the drive. During the war he had several times used the euphoria that often overcame defenders after they had repelled an attack to return when they were least ready for it – he was determined that was not going to happen now. But even if the killers did not come back tonight that did not mean they had given up. Even after Forrester himself left, this place would not be safe. Sophie must leave too – and Josef and Helga with her, because they too would be vulnerable. He cursed himself for assuming that whoever had been sent to attack him in Berlin would give up when they failed there.

At the same time he realised that this was exactly what

had happened, time and time again during the war, when MacLean had sent him on some expedition and assured him it was just to gather a few facts he was almost certain of anyway, and that the whole thing would be a doddle. It never was then, it certainly wasn't now.

His next task was to persuade Sophie of this, but to his relief, it didn't take long. The Grevinne Arnfeldt-Laurvig had also spent the last five years in occupied Europe, much of it outwitting the occupying power – she knew when there was time to argue and when there was not. And despite her slightly formal, accented English, their communication was lightning fast. Each knew what the other meant almost before anything was said, and if there was any uncertainty, when their eyes met, it was gone.

He had guessed Sophie would have a car, and indeed she did, in one of the barns, but the tank was empty and so were the petrol cans. Instead, they hauled the big sleigh out of the front hall while Josef harnessed the horses. Helga brought fur coats from the cupboards and when they were all aboard, the old man cracked the whip and the horses began to move. Helga sat beside Josef and Forrester and Sophie sat bundled in furs behind them, while the horses' breath crystallised in the freezing night air and the runners slid smoothly over the moonlit snow. Forrester kept his eyes on the dark verges of the road: if their attackers were going to try again, that's where they'd be.

But no shots came from the darkness and after a mile or so he saw the tracks of the assassins' car swing away onto the main road. He tapped Josef on the shoulder and gestured for him to bring the sleigh to a halt. Then he got out and knelt down to examine the tyre tracks. Worn, of course, as all tyres would be in Norway after the war years, but with a distinctive chunk out of the one that had been on the right rear wheel.

With numb fingers he drew out his notebook and made a sketch of the tyre track. "How will that help?" asked Sophie, not taking her eyes off the trees.

"I think they followed me from Germany," said Forrester, "so they must have come by air and hired a car here. If we give this to the police they may be able to use it to trace the hire."

"It's possible," said Sophie, "there are not so many cars back on the roads here yet."

As he got back into the sleigh Forrester said, "They might still pull off the road and wait in ambush. Is there another route?"

"Yes."

"Might it take us past a police station?"

"It will pass through a small town where I am known to the authorities."

"Then we should go there," said Forrester, and when they reached the next junction the sleigh hissed off to the left, away from the road bearing the tracks of their attackers.

"What should we tell the police?" asked Sophie.

"Everything," said Forrester. "If only for your protection later on. At least one man is dead, but your house was invaded; you have nothing to hide. Josef and Helga should feel free to tell the truth too."

"What about you?"

"I can't stay," said Forrester, and he felt rather than saw the expression on Sophie's face. "As long as I'm with you, you're in danger. And I have to get back to England as soon as possible. Is there a station somewhere along our route where you could drop me, so I can catch a train back to Oslo?"

There was a beat before she answered, "Yes."

He took her hand. "I'll come back," he said.

She turned to look at him, and he wanted to look into those eyes for ever. "I'll be waiting," she said, simply.

Then they were racing along the edge of another fjord, the moonlight glittering on the distant waters and the sky above them jammed with stars. Forrester held Sophie's hand until they paused beside a little log-built station beneath an icy mountain peak, glittering as if it was made of silver. He opened his mouth to speak, but she shook her head.

"We will talk again when you are safe," she said, and moments later they saw the plume of white steam of an approaching train rising in the distance, and the sleigh slid back up to the road, turned a bend and disappeared.

He stood there for a long moment after it had gone and then walked onto the snow-covered platform and waited until the train pulled in.

Forrester sat in the carriage, looking into the darkness of the forest, fighting off sleep. He could not afford to sleep. Besides, his nose hurt too much, which was good: the pain would keep him awake.

The train rattled along the edge of a long lake and Forrester saw, or imagined he saw, the sleigh racing along the road that ran along the far side and a tide of longing swept over him. Love had died in him long ago, and now, out of nowhere, it had returned, and he felt like a sleeper in a tomb when the stone is lifted from the entrance and the world opens up to him again.

The coffee in the station at Oslo scalded his mouth, and he drank it scanning the crowd, ready for the slightest thing that seemed out of place, but there was nothing. He needed to get out of Norway, back to Denmark at the very least. He would take the ferry. As he walked through the city to the terminal he watched warily, but no-one took any interest in him.

Little notice was taken of him on the ferry either, although he took the precaution of seating himself with his back to a metal bulkhead and a good view of the arriving passengers. With every minute that passed it was harder to fight off sleep, but he was determined to, and determined to think through what had happened and what he had learned.

But he managed neither. Instead he found his eyes closing and his thoughts filling with Sophie and then sleep came and when he woke the ferry was bumping against the jetty in Copenhagen and he was being bundled off with the others.

He drank more coffee at a restaurant on the Nyhavn, the dockside red-light district where Hans Christian Andersen had once lived and where Forrester had eaten before he crossed to Norway – a lifetime ago, it seemed, now – and then made his way to a phone box and called the RAF base at Lindquist.

The sergeant who answered was matter-of-fact and helpful. There was a flight leaving for Blighty at midnight, and if he was there, they could get him aboard. He looked at his watch: it was not yet noon. He had no desire to wander around Copenhagen until midnight, wondering if anyone was going to take a potshot at him, and even less desire to sit in a Nissen hut at the RAF base listening to bored squaddies make predictions about the Cup Final. And as one of the things Forrester had learned during the last five years had been that if any downtime became available you should seize it, he decided to visit the home of a man with whom, at times, he felt a certain spiritual affinity. He had lived in Kronborg Castle in the town of Helsingør and his Danish name had been Amleth.

Helsingør was just an hour or so up the coast from Copenhagen, and Forrester took a bus there, gazing idly out of the window at the deserted beaches as the road wound along the coast. At one point he passed a group of men removing the iron plating from what had clearly been an improvised armoured car, presumably used by the Danish resistance.

The resistance in Denmark had been slow to gather momentum, but they had kept crucial German reinforcements from heading to France after D-Day by sabotaging the railway network and to their everlasting credit they had steadfastly refused to persecute the Jews. Directive after directive from Berlin was sidestepped or prevaricated, and when German patience finally ran out and Hitler decided to send all Danish Jews to the concentration camps anyway, the Danes packed every Jew they could find aboard motor boats and fishing smacks and ferried them across the Baltic to the safety of Sweden. It was, Forrester thought, a typically Danish combination of decency and pragmatism.

Finally the bus reached Helsingør and he got out to stroll through the winding streets into the medieval Carmelite Priory, whose cloisters Hans Christian Andersen had insisted were the most beautiful in Denmark.

As he walked he let what he had learned during the last few days float down through his mind like sand drifting down through water. The first was that his attempts in Berlin to uncover the true nature of Peter Dorfmann's activities during the war had clearly stirred up a hornets' nest. A team had been assembled in Berlin to kill him, and when they had failed a second attempt had been made in Norway. Considerable resources had been devoted to this effort: this was clearly more than a personal matter.

What had he found out in Berlin? Essentially, that although Dorfmann had indeed been a relatively obscure academic during the Nazi years, he had enjoyed good relations with senior members of the party, including its intelligence apparatus. That he had been in possession of some kind of Old Norse manuscript, and that such a manuscript had been used by German intelligence, involving two figures codenamed Erik and Saint, the latter having been in a position to give information on the intentions of the Soviet High Command and the Murmansk convoys.

Which reinforced the idea that Dorfmann might be

behind Lyall's death, because there was no doubt Lyall had been talking up his possession of an ancient Norse manuscript when he was killed. Both Haraldson and his conversation with the Scandinavian students confirmed that.

On the other hand, there was the fact that Dorfmann had been in the room with Forrester when Lyall was killed – and Forrester now knew that, contrary to what he had supposed, Lyall had not taken a manuscript from the Arnfeldt-Laurvig estate when he had been there during the war.

But he might have taken the knowledge of the manuscript's existence. Knowledge gained in that depleted library with its sinister history.

And suddenly Forrester was certain that Lyall had used both the manuscript and the occult associations of the house from which it came to draw Haraldson to Oxford.

But why? Why had he wanted the Norwegian in England in the first place? What had he got to gain by it?

Forrester walked out of the cloisters into a shadowy quarter full of half-timbered medieval merchants' houses and emerged into the Axeltorv, where a farmer's market was going on under the watchful eye of Erik of Pomerania. Erik, after being dethroned as King of Denmark, had set up as a pirate and piled up vast quantities of treasure, now reputedly hidden in a castle in Pomerania. But treasure or no treasure, the eyes of Erik's statue seemed to be fixed wistfully on a large ball of Gouda on the stall below him. Perhaps even pirate kings longed, in the afterlife, for a bit of cheese.

Even as he contemplated Erik's statue, Forrester thought

of Lyall eyeing the photographs in Sophie's albums – and slipping into his pocket the photograph revealing the identity of the visitors who had come to Bjornsfjord in 1937.

But if he *had* taken the photograph Lyall had never spoken about it to anyone in Oxford; he had just talked about a manuscript. And he had taken no manuscript from Sophie's house. Forrester's thoughts were beginning to march in a circle, and he had to stop. He began to walk towards Hamlet's Castle.

It wasn't really Hamlet's medieval Elsinore, of course, but a handsome renaissance building complete with pitched roofs and elaborate towers around a central courtyard. The story that had inspired Shakespeare had originated long before his time in a document known as *The Saga of Hrolf Kraki*. In that version the murdered king had two sons, who instead of pretending to be mad, while trying to solve the mystery, went about in disguise. There was also a tantalisingly elusive Icelandic hero called Amlóði, who accidentally killed the king's advisor in his mother's bedroom before dispatching the usurper himself. Whether any of those events had taken place here at Elsinore was another matter, but Forrester was prepared to believe they might have, and enjoy the sensation of being, for a while, in the heart of a legend.

He approached the castle across the star-shaped expanse of grassy fortifications, crossed the bridge over the moat and gazed up at the green copper spheres of the Trumpeter's Tower. Beneath the tower was the statue of Ogier the Dane, the Viking chieftain who was supposed to wake and save his country if it was ever in peril, but who never had.

Inside the castle, he walked under huge seventeenth-century chandeliers along the length of the Great Hall and through the Royal Chambers. In the Royal Library a gnome-like librarian, looking like a character in a Hans Christian Andersen fairy tale, was perched on a tall wheeled ladder, pulling out one leather-bound book after another, examining it and writing in a large notebook before putting it back. As Forrester watched, the librarian leaned out too far and the ladder began to tilt dangerously. Forrester darted in and steadied it until the man could climb down. "*Tag,*" he said, and when Forrester replied in English, immediately switched languages.

"Thank you," he said. "Very quick you were."

"Very high were you," said Forrester, and then realised there was a reason why the man had been leaning out instead of wheeling the ladder along: the castors on which it ran were jammed. He took out his penknife and bent down to free them. "Wonderful library," said Forrester, as much as anything to make polite conversation while the man calmed down. "Any early editions of *Hamlet*?"

"If we had them," said the librarian, "they would have been stolen by the Germans."

Forrester processed this. "Of course. I imagine they took a fair bit."

"Anything they thought they could get away with."

"Including sagas?"

"Probably. That is what I am trying to find out. Nordic they believed they were, though they really just as gangsters should be described in my opinion."

Suddenly Forrester's mind was racing. "Listen," he said, "I wonder if I could ask a favour." And he wrote down his name and address. "If you do find out that the Germans removed any Old Norse manuscripts during the occupation, would you let me know?"

"Certainly," said the librarian. "May I be asking why?"

Forrester smiled. "It's a long story," he said.

23

CONVERSATION WITH A WIFE

Forrester landed at Northolt in the early hours of the morning and hitched a ride on an army lorry going to the Kensington Barracks. From there he called MacLean's office at the War Ministry and was told he wasn't in yet. He took the tube to Whitehall, had a cup of tea and a bun at a cabman's stand and called again. This time MacLean's secretary told him to go to the bridge in St. James's Park and wait there. By the time MacLean finally arrived Forrester was feeling unwashed, unshaved and exhausted; all he really wanted to do was go to bed.

"So you dropped me in it again," he said as MacLean appeared. "Why do I never learn?"

MacLean took out a cigarette, lit it judiciously, and offered one to Forrester, who declined.

"You seem to have survived very well," he said. "Although your nose is looking a bit bent."

"I would have had a better chance of surviving if I'd been told what I was up against."

"My dear chap, if I'd known, I'd have told you," said MacLean, "but I'm all ears now," and he listened intently as Forrester gave a short précis of what had happened to him since landing in Berlin.

"You really seem to have put the wind up somebody, don't you?" said MacLean, when Forrester had finished. "Good for you. So, let's have a look at the snap you pinched."

He examined the photograph Forrester had taken from the album in Sophie's drawing room, and said he'd keep it to see if the boys in photo analysis could glean anything more. Forrester said he wanted to show it to the police first as part of the evidence about Lyall's murder, and MacLean looked reluctant. "Tell you what," he said, "let's go back to the Ministry and see if we can get it copied."

Forrester agreed, and they walked back through the park to Whitehall along paths covered in ice, which had melted and refrozen so often it was like a range of miniature mountains. The snow on the grass was grey now, and miserable-looking ducks watched them suspiciously from the bleak surface of the lake.

"But whatever we get out of the photograph, you did very well, you know," said MacLean. "Your hand seems to have lost none of its cunning." Forrester suppressed a wry smile at his old boss's continued use of judicious flattery. He remembered all too vividly how MacLean had been able to deploy a little understated flattery to calm his agents after the most disastrous and ill-planned missions, as though the whole point had really been to allow them to demonstrate their remarkable abilities to stay alive. Before Forrester could point this out Maclean said: "And it was worth it, of course. What you've found out could prevent a very bad apple from rising to the top of the barrel. I think I'm mixing a couple of metaphors there, but you know what I mean."

"It'll only mean something if the Americans take it seriously," said Forrester. "I haven't exactly got definitive proof that Dorfmann is a bad apple."

"Circumstantial evidence may well be good enough in a case like this," said MacLean. "And if we can track down the rest of the files referring to 'Erik' and 'Saint' and identify them, we may have something actionable."

"The problem is," said Forrester, "I'm not sure any of this is going to help save Gordon Clark. Dorfmann may have been part of the Nazi intelligence apparatus, but that doesn't prove he killed David Lyall."

"Unless Lyall thought what he'd found out about Dorfmann in Norway gave him some sort of leverage. Something to do with Satanism?"

"You think he might have tried to blackmail Dorfmann?"

"What do you think?"

Forrester considered. "He was perfectly capable of it," he said, and then added, "The problem is Dorfmann has an alibi: me."

"Because you were with him when Lyall was killed?"

"Exactly."

"Perhaps he had an accomplice. After all, he didn't come after you himself, did he, in Berlin or Norway? He sent professionals. Perhaps one of them did it."

"Good point," said Forrester. "Let's hope we can

persuade the police to consider that possibility."

"Anyway," said MacLean. "I very much appreciate what you've done. We need good Germans in power when we hand the place back to them, not people like Dorfmann."

Forrester telephoned Inspector Barber from Oxford Station as soon as the train pulled in, and made an appointment at a time that allowed him to return to the college, bathe, shave and change before walking down to the police station. There was a message waiting for him from Margaret Clark, but he decided not to respond until he'd spoken to Barber – he might, after all, be able to bring her some good news.

He began to suspect he was wrong about this about two minutes into the meeting. Forrester could always sense when his words were having the effect he was looking for – and this time he was certain they weren't. Barber listened attentively and politely. He even made notes, but he also drew pictures of sheep on his blotter, and when Forrester had finished he said, "This is all very interesting, but it doesn't get us very far, does it, sir?"

He paused, and Forrester bit back the impulse to object, and waited.

"You've got no proof Mr. Dorfmann did work for German intelligence," said Barber, "just a very obscure reference in some mis-filed dossier and a lot of academic tittle-tattle. And as he was a German national in a time of war, provided he didn't commit war crimes he was perfectly entitled to lend his services to the German government. In fact he probably had little option. So if Lyall was trying to blackmail him by threatening to reveal his intelligence connections, that wasn't much of a threat, was it? Certainly not enough, in my view, for Dorfmann to respond by taking the risk of murdering the man."

"Unless Lyall also had evidence Dorfmann had been in Norway in the 1930s and taken part in Satanic rites."

"What evidence? You've got no proof David Lyall had anything to blackmail Dorfmann with."

"Except the photograph I've given you."

"Of two blokes rowing a dinghy? That proves nothing at all. And you couldn't blackmail anybody with that anyway, because you can't identify anybody in it."

"But I'm sure the missing photograph *did* have an identifiable face. And that's the one Lyall took."

"The one you *say* Lyall took. But anybody could have taken it. It could have just fallen out of the photograph album. You can't tell me what was in the picture and you can't show me any proof Lyall ever had it."

"What about the fact that Dorfmann tried to have me killed in Berlin and Norway?"

"It's not a 'fact' that Dorfmann tried to have you killed in either place," said Barber. "It's your supposition. You stirred up a hornets' nest there, that's obvious, with all this amateur detective work, and God knows who you annoyed. But the fact that you nearly got yourself killed doesn't necessarily implicate Dorfmann and doesn't do a ha'porth of good to Gordon Clark either, as far as I'm concerned." He stood up.

"Look, I fully respect your determination to help your friend, and I see you've taken a lot of risks for him, which I can only admire. But nothing you've found out materially alters the case against him, does it?"

There was a pause. Forrester stood up too. "Not yet," he said. "But it should give you pause, Inspector Barber. If nothing else, what I've found out in Germany and Norway shows this case is a lot more complicated than it seems. All I ask of you is this: don't shut your eyes to the possibility that Gordon Clark is innocent. Because if you do you could be perpetrating a terrible injustice."

And he left the room. If his words sounded confident, it was an illusion. Inside, he was certain he had achieved nothing at all.

He was glad he had spoken to Barber before he met Margaret Clark: he had no false hope to hold out. They met in the churchyard of St. Mary's, where Forrester had last fought his demons before the night of Lyall's murder. It seemed a lifetime ago, and when Margaret Clark came through the archway it seemed even longer. He stared at her in astonishment as she approached, suddenly aware of an enormous change within himself.

His secret infatuation with her had utterly vanished. After Sophie Arnfeldt-Laurvig, Margaret Clark looked as cheap and artificial as a ring on a Woolworths counter. Still beautiful, still intelligent, still exuding a powerful sensual appeal; but not, any longer, for him.

It was, in truth, a profound relief to be freed of his fascination with her. It felt as if a weight had been lifted from his heart. And the change in his feelings made him more determined than ever to save Gordon Clark – if only to stop his friend from being destroyed for the sake of this shallow woman.

So he was blunt when he told her what had happened to him while he was abroad, what he had found out, and how the police had reacted. She didn't seem to take that in – instead she seemed to be excited by his adventures, by the danger he had encountered.

"You could have been killed," she said.

"Yes," said Forrester. "I was very lucky."

"Very *strong*," said Margaret Clark, and Forrester knew those words would once have made his heart turn over. She took his hand. "Thank you," she said.

Forrester let his hand remain in hers (how he would once have thrilled to that touch) just long enough not to offend her, and then withdrew it.

"We have to see if we can build on what I've found out," he said. "We have to find proof that David Lyall *was* trying to blackmail Dorfmann."

"Of course," said Margaret.

"For example, that photograph I believe he took from Norway. Have you any idea where he might have hidden it?"

"No," she said, "but I'll think about it."

"We also have to find out if someone killed Lyall on Dorfmann's behalf. It can't have been Dorfmann himself because he was beside me in the Master's Lodge when it happened. But he may have hired someone, or perhaps brought some bodyguard with him that we don't know about. I don't expect there's much you can contribute there, but keep your ears open; keep thinking whether there's anything David told you that might provide a clue."

"And then there's the manuscript."

"Exactly. If there's anything you can do to help track it down, it could be crucial; anything David might have said, a hint he might have dropped."

"I'll do everything I can," said Margaret Clark, and looked into his eyes to emphasise the intensity of her determination.

And as he returned her gaze Forrester realised he did not believe a word of what she was saying. That she would have been perfectly capable of killing David Lyall herself, if he had crossed her. And to the best of Forrester's knowledge, of course, David Lyall had crossed and double-crossed just about everyone he had ever encountered in life.

24

THE ENTHUSIASM OF KENNETH HARRISON

Forrester had two more visits to make before his first tutorial; the first was to Gordon Clark's solicitor, who undertook to do everything in his power to follow up Forrester's suggestions, and who in Forrester's opinion seemed terminally unlikely to do anything that would upset the Oxfordshire Constabulary.

The second was to His Majesty's Prison Oxford, to visit Gordon himself.

He was shocked by what he saw. It was not just that Clark was pale, his eyes hollow and his cheeks sunken, but that he seemed to have given up. He showed polite interest in Forrester's adventures in Berlin and Norway, and expressed the appropriate gratitude for the risks he had run, but it was as if he was looking back on his old life like a man at the stern of a ship heading out into a darkening sea. As if Barber had convinced him of his guilt, and his only task now was to resign himself to the consequences.

"I'm sorry I haven't got anything more concrete for

you, Gordon," said Forrester, "but I'm certain Dorfmann was behind Lyall's murder, and your lawyer ought to be able to make good use of that in court."

"Thank you, Duncan," said Gordon Clark, but there was no conviction in his voice – none at all.

As Forrester walked away from the visitors' room along the narrow stone corridors of the prison, he felt his own hope draining away, and by the time he was being let out of the prison, all his remaining energy had drained out too, all the mental force that had been sustaining him since he caught the RAF plane to Berlin, and as he hauled himself up onto a bus towards Barnard College he was so tired he could barely stand.

He was not some super-brained sleuth who could take a couple of clues and work them into a brilliant theory. He was not even a methodical detective, with all Barber's resources at his disposal. He was a historian, for God's sake, an exhausted ex-serviceman who had seen too much service and no longer had the strength for a task like this. As he took his leave from Gordon Clark he had smiled reassuringly, but he knew his smile was as false as sin; that all his confident words about making this all come out right were no more than that: just words.

He went back to his room, fell into bed and slept long and dreamlessly, and when he woke the next morning and answered the knocking on his door there was his student and loyal assistant, looking at him, concerned. "I'll come back another time," said Harrison, but Forrester, not yet coherent enough for speech, gestured him towards the armchair while he went to the sink and splashed cold water on his face.

"I'm sorry, old chap," he said as he dried himself off. "I'm not quite together yet."

"Totally understood," said Harrison. "Let's reconvene when you're back on your feet."

"No," said Forrester. "You have a tutorial. I'm your tutor. Let's just do it. Do you have an essay to read to me?"

"Solon," said Harrison.

"Solon, very good," said Forrester. "You read it, I'll come back to consciousness while you do."

So Harrison read it, and as he read, Forrester returned to the land of the living.

The essay dealt with Solon's effort to legislate against the political and moral decline of Athens in the sixth century BC. His reforms, proclaimed Harrison stoutly, may have failed in the short term, but they also laid the foundations for the whole great experiment of Athenian democracy.

Forrester was inclined to agree, but felt obliged to point out that the archaeological evidence for Solon's greatness consisted of little more than a few carved stone inscriptions, that what fragments of his writings survived were probably full of interpolations by other writers, and that those later orators who claimed to be championing his beliefs were actually using Solon's name to give their own ideas credence. "There are some scholars," he said, "who claim that the whole Solonic achievement is no more than a fictive construct based on insufficient evidence. How do you respond to that?"

Harrison grinned.

"The same critique applies to all history," he said. "How much evidence is 'sufficient'? Even if we had all Solon's writings, what about the writings of the people who opposed him? The graffiti by the people his laws affected? The treasury rolls showing whether his reforms actually worked? Not available, any of them. The same applies to Sumer, to Assyria, Rome, your beloved Crete. We always have to construct coherent narratives based on the evidence that *is* available, however much or little of it there is. That's what being a historian is all about."

"Very good," said Forrester. "I'll accept that."

"Thank you," said Harrison. "And now I absolutely refuse to leave the room until you've told me what you uncovered among the wretched Huns."

And so Forrester told his story – fairly streamlined by this time – and Harrison listened, lighting and relighting his pipe judiciously throughout the narrative. When Forrester had finished he said, "You've had quite a time of it, haven't you?"

"It hasn't been boring," said Forrester.

"By all rights you should be dead by now under a pile of bricks in Berlin."

"I was lucky."

"You were bloody good. And even better in Norway, I suspect. I hope I've got you on my side if I'm ever in trouble."

Forrester was obscurely gratified by Harrison's praise,

because the feeling was entirely mutual. "Well, let's hope you're never in this kind of trouble," said Forrester. "Because all these efforts of mine, however valiant, don't seem to have been of much help to the Senior Tutor, do they?"

"I'm not sure about that," said Harrison. "Let's focus on the Norse saga part for a minute. What's our starting point for thinking that's an element?"

Forrester considered – and this time found it a relief to talk, as if Harrison's question had released the jammed cogwheels of his mind. "The starting point is the fact that Lyall told Arne Haraldson he had a Norse manuscript to show him, hinted it might contain some encryption of occult significance, and then discussed it with various Scandinavian students in Oxford."

"And conspicuously did not discuss it with, or show it to Tolkien or Winters, whose field it is," added Harrison.

"Exactly. Then in Berlin I found witnesses who testified that Dorfmann had been seen carrying something that sounded remarkably like a Norse manuscript when he went off to consult with Nazi intelligence."

"Plus the reference in German intelligence files to a saga having been used in some sort of espionage operation involving the Russians."

"Exactly."

"Then when you went to Norway to see the woman who sheltered Lyall during the war – this countess of yours – the Norse manuscript came up again."

"Yes; her husband, who had in fact been involved in black magic, had apparently sold off or gambled away several of these manuscripts before the war."

"And among the possible recipients was at least one German, who you believe, from the photograph you saw, to have been Dorfmann."

"Yes. Although I can't be certain of that."

"And you think David Lyall stole a second photograph, which *proves* it was Dorfmann."

"Yes."

"We have to find that photograph," said Harrison.

"I assume the police have long since searched Lyall's rooms."

"They may well have done," said Harrison. "But that doesn't mean we shouldn't search them again ourselves, does it?"

And Forrester knew he was right. Suddenly all his weariness was gone. He had a goal: to find the photograph Lyall had taken from the Arnfeldt-Laurvig estate.

"You know, Harrison," he said, "you are a tonic."

That evening Forrester found himself once again in the Lodge, talking to the Master. Winters listened with total concentration to everything he said, and then congratulated him on his persistence and fortitude.

"Although I have to agree with Inspector Barber," he said, "about the real significance of any intelligence activities Peter Dorfmann may have engaged in during the late hostilities. I'm not surprised the Abwehr or the S.D. called him in: he was a distinguished professor. They had codes to break. He was a German citizen in wartime – he would have had no option but to comply. I myself worked for British Intelligence, as you know. I can't see that Lyall, even assuming he'd found out that Dorfmann assisted German intelligence, had much to blackmail the man with."

"What about this Norse manuscript?" said Forrester. "We do know Lyall was hawking it around, and conspicuously avoided showing it to you or Tolkien or anybody else who might really have been able to evaluate it."

"Except Haraldson," said Winters.

"Well, he told Haraldson about it," said Forrester. "Haraldson never actually saw it."

"In fact nobody ever actually saw it," said Winters, "including the students Lyall consulted. We don't even know what it was."

"I'm certain it came from the Arnfeldt-Laurvig library in Norway," said Forrester, "and that Dorfmann was there before the war, in 1937."

"Because of the photograph?"

"Exactly."

"Do you have the photograph?"

"I gave it to the police."

"Ah, of course. No copy?"

"A contact of mine at the War Ministry made one, but I don't have it."

"Who was that? It may have been someone I worked with."

"Archibald MacLean."

"MacLean… No, doesn't ring any bells. And you say

it showed Dorfmann and another man on the fjord below the estate?"

"I think so. One man was rowing and had his back to camera; the photo was too small to be certain that the other man was Dorfmann – but that's what MacLean is looking at."

"Well let's hope he finds something out," said the Master. "What's your next move?"

"I'd like to search Lyall's rooms to see if the photograph he took – the photograph I think he took – is hidden there somewhere."

"You don't think the police would have already found it if it was there?"

"They weren't looking for it."

"Well, that's true, I suppose."

"I'm not sure about the legality of it. Is it technically a crime scene?"

"I don't think so," said Winters. "They asked me to keep it locked, but they didn't ask me not to let anyone in there."

"You wouldn't mind if I took a look?"

"Not at all," said Winters. "In fact, I'll come myself to give the enterprise an air of legitimacy if anyone questions it."

"That's very good of you."

"It's the least I can do," said the Master. "I've lost one of my scholars to a murderer, I've no desire to see another succumb unnecessarily to the hangman's rope. When do you want to undertake this expedition?"

"As soon as possible."

"Shall we do it after High Table?"

"That would be perfect. I'd like to bring Ken Harrison along? The chap who's been helping me."

"By all means," said the Master. "He sounds like a useful fellow."

And so it was agreed.

25

THE SECRETS OF DAVID LYALL

High Table was thinly populated that night, which left Bitteridge and Norton free to get into a rebarbative discussion about the new Labour government's efforts to set up a National Health Service, which Norton championed fiercely and Bitteridge denounced as creeping communism, with the Master gamely trying to create a middle ground. Norton told them about people who hadn't eaten properly for years because they couldn't afford false teeth, and children who didn't learn to read because they couldn't afford glasses, and Bitteridge talked about doctors who had devoted their lives to medicine suddenly finding themselves being ordered about by ignorant bureaucrats with the power of the state behind them. Forrester thought a National Health Service was what every decent society should provide, but he was too preoccupied to give Norton the backing he needed, and the issue remained unresolved by the time the Master announced – with a meaningful look at Forrester – that he had some reading to do.

Forrester waited a few moments – Norton and Bitteridge were now arguing about whether it had been wise to raise the school leaving age to fifteen – and then slipped away himself. He glanced down into the body of the hall to make sure Harrison was aware he was going, and then headed out into the quiet darkness of the quad.

Lyall's rooms were on the other side of the quadrangle from Forrester's, and it took only a few moments to reach them. Although the presence of the Master made their visit legitimate, there was still a conspiratorial air as the three of them met in the corridor in front of Lyall's door and Winters unlocked it.

Harrison reached for the light switch but the Master put a restraining hand on his arm. "I don't particularly want to advertise our visit here tonight," he said. "Would you mind if we used torches? I brought one." And he produced a hefty air raid warden's torch.

"Me too," said Harrison, bringing out something even bigger. And in they went.

Their first search was deliberately superficial: desktop, bookshelves, bedside cabinet, open drawers – all the obvious places – as they familiarised themselves with Lyall's mode of living.

Then they rolled up the carpets, examined the nails in every floorboard for signs of tampering, and in one case where the nails seemed new, pulled up the floorboard and peered into the space below.

Nothing.

They took each picture off the wall, checked behind it

and examined the paper backing to see if anything had been slipped behind it. They picked the locks on the desk drawers and examined the contents; then they removed all the drawers and felt around beneath them and inside the framework of the desk. They did the same with the bedside cabinet, and then took the bedding off the bed and removed the mattress.

Nothing. Well, not nothing: there was a letter in the bedside cabinet from Lyall's father, telling him of his mother's illness, and without warning, for all his dislike of the man, Forrester was reminded that he had been a fellow human being, with parents, a home to which he would never return, hopes and aspirations which had forever been consigned to oblivion by whoever had killed him.

However much of a shit he had been, he had not deserved that.

They checked the wardrobe, the top of the wardrobe, the clothes in the wardrobe.

They checked the light fittings.

Nothing. And then Harrison walked back to the light switch, took out a penknife, and unscrewed it.

"I don't like to be a naysayer," said the Master, "but I'd be very reluctant to see you electrocuted, Mr. Harrison."

"Me too, Master," said Harrison, "so I'll be very careful," and he kept on removing screws. The plate came away. Forrester shone his torch into the little cavity, mostly filled with red and black insulated electric wires.

And there, right at the back, peeping out from the lath behind which it had been tucked, was the edge of a photographic print. Forrester recognised it at once: the scalloped edges were identical to the photograph he himself had taken from the album on the Arnfeldt-Laurvig estate.

"Oh, my goodness," said the Master. "Well done."

Harrison was about to reach in to ease it out, but Winters stopped him.

"Not until the power has been turned off," he said. "I'm afraid I absolutely insist on that, for your own safety. Do you know where the junction box is?"

"Yes," said Harrison. "It's on the other side of the quad, next to the Porter's Lodge, and it's really not necessary."

"I'm sorry, but as Master of this college I am charged with ensuring your safety, and I think that includes making sure you are not electrocuted. Would you agree, Dr. Forrester?"

Reluctantly, Forrester nodded. Winters might be being an old fusspot, but it would be his responsibility if anything went wrong. "Let's play it safe, Harrison," he said.

"Thank you," said Winters. "I believe this corridor is controlled by the fuses on the upper half of the board; there's no need to rob the entire building of power." Harrison shrugged and went off down the corridor.

Winters sat down and Forrester perched on the edge of the desk.

"Well, we seem to be on the verge of a discovery," Winters said with satisfaction.

"It is looking hopeful," said Forrester.

"I have to confess to a certain excitement," said the Master. "Who will the photograph reveal? What will it tell us about events in the Bjornsfjord in 1937? I feel as if I'm in a detective novel."

"Except with real lives at stake," said Forrester.

"Very much so," said the Master, and at that moment the lights all over the college went out.

"Oh good Lord," said Winters. "What has that young man done now?"

Forrester pushed up the window and looked out: Harrison was emerging from the door next to the Porter's Lodge as other windows shot up around the quad and angry voices sounded in the night.

"What the hell are you playing at, Harrison?" shouted somebody, and then the porter himself appeared, bleary-eyed, and began remonstrating.

"What a nuisance," said Winters. "Your young friend does seem to have been a little ham-fisted."

In the end Forrester and the Master had to go down to sort out the row, and by the time power was restored Winters was quite adamant: they had discovered what was almost certainly an important piece of evidence, and it was their duty to inform the police. They phoned Oxford Police Station and explained what had happened, but the sergeant on duty resolutely refused to give them Barber's home telephone number. He agreed, after some argument, to contact the inspector himself, and Forrester and Harrison waited impatiently by the phone in the Master's Lodge until Barber called back, in not very good temper.

It did not take him long to make up his mind when he had heard the Master out. "I will come by tomorrow," he said. "Lock the room, do not permit anyone to enter it, and be ready to accompany me to inspect it at nine o'clock tomorrow morning."

The Master began to protest that the matter was urgent, but Barber overrode him. "I think I've made myself quite clear, Professor Winters," Forrester heard him say, "and I will take a very dim view of it if anybody else goes anywhere near that room tonight. Is that understood?"

"Yes, Inspector," said Winters resignedly. "Perfectly understood."

He put the phone down and turned to Forrester and Harrison.

"And there, I'm afraid, gentlemen, matters must remain for the next—" he glanced at his watch "—eleven hours." Harrison opened his mouth to say something, but Winters held up a hand.

"I don't blame you for your mistake, Mr. Harrison," he said, "those junction boxes are in urgent need of updating. In fact, I blame myself for giving you such sketchy instructions. But no harm has been done, and if we can contain our impatience, we will find out tomorrow what we have discovered. Whether Inspector Barber wants you to be there or not, I insist, of course, that you both be present when the photograph is removed. If it had not been for you, it might never have been discovered."

And with this, he bade them goodnight.

* * *

Barber was as good as his word: he appeared promptly at 9.00 a.m. the next morning, and though he looked askance at both Forrester and Harrison, he raised no objection to their presence.

This time the power was turned off formally, with the porter present, and it turned out the fuses controlling Lyall's corridor were on the lower part of the box, not the upper. They fell into step as they went up the stairs to Lyall's rooms, and Forrester felt oddly as if he was in a Gilbert and Sullivan operetta, and that at any moment they might all be expected to burst into song about a policeman's lot not being a happy one. The Master opened Lyall's door with all due ceremony and they trooped inside. The room was still in the dishevelled state in which their search had left it, and the light switch plate was still suspended in the air in front of the cavity, held up by the rigid red and black insulated wires.

Barber looked disapprovingly around the room. "I see you did yourselves proud last night," he remarked laconically.

"Just trying to assist the police with their enquiries, Inspector," said the Master, unruffled.

"So where is it?" said Barber, peering into the cavity.

"On the left," said Forrester. "It's stuck behind a piece of lath, but you can see the edges quite easily."

"I brought some long-handled pliers," said Harrison, and gave them to Barber, who pulled a face but accepted them graciously enough. He reached into the cavity and carefully gripped the distinctively scalloped edge of the photograph with the pliers.

Then, with painstaking slowness, he pulled it out, and

held it so that only he could see it. Forrester glanced at the Master; his eyes were glittering with excitement.

"Well," said Barber. "This is interesting."

"What does it show?" said Winters.

"I haven't seen anything like this for years," said Barber. "I can see why it was hidden so carefully." And he turned the photograph so they could see it.

The image was of a plump woman wearing only a large Edwardian hat and a pair of high-heeled shoes. She was holding a parasol and the caption beneath read, "I think it's going to be wet today."

Winters gaped. "I don't understand," he said.

"I think it's perfectly clear," said Barber. "This was hidden by some sex-starved don when Edward the Seventh was on the throne, or possibly Queen Victoria. He couldn't risk it being found, he couldn't bear to throw it away, so he tucked it into what was then, doubtless, the newfangled lighting system." He handed the photograph to Winters. "I don't think this is of any interest to us, sir. You may want to add it to your collection."

And Barber took his leave. Forrester saw no smirk on his face as he turned away, but he knew perfectly well there was one there.

And who could blame him?

26

SNOWBALL ON A GREY AFTERNOON

As they came down the stairs from Lyall's rooms Alan Norton stepped out of the shadows and fell into step with them.

"It's about the Lady Tower, Master," he said. "I wonder if I could have a word."

"This is not a good moment, Norton," said Winters.

"It's just that I believe I've come up with a way we could speed up the repairs."

"I look forward to hearing it," said the Master smoothly. "Perhaps you could come to the Lodge tomorrow?"

"Certainly," said Norton, now walking with them as though they had all decided to take a stroll together. "When would be a good time?" And Forrester had the odd sensation that Norton – on the surface the least devious of men – was determined at all costs to insinuate himself into the conversation, or at the very least prevent Forrester from speaking to the Master alone for another minute. Before he could work out why, the porter hurried up and addressed Forrester.

"Young lady come to see you while you was with the

inspector, sir," he said. Forrester felt the Master's eye on him, and it did not feel like an approving glance. Normally, of course, the porter would have made no such effort to bring him such a trivial piece of information, but he was plainly agog to find out what had happened in Lyall's rooms – in fact the whole college must have been agog after the events of the night before.

"Yes?" said Forrester without enthusiasm.

"I told her you was busy with the police, sir," said the porter, and Forrester felt the Master's eye grow colder. "So she left a note." And he handed Forrester an envelope. Alice Hayley's name was written in bold script on the upper left corner, but eager though Forrester was to read it, this was not the time. "Thank you, Piggot," he said, and thrust the envelope into a pocket.

"Before there are any more interruptions," said the Master, "I think we should proceed to the Lodge where we can speak in private." To Norton he said, "Three o'clock tomorrow, Dr. Norton," and turned away.

At the Lodge, Winters did his best to be gracious, but he had plainly been mortified by his encounter with Barber and hugely embarrassed by the antique piece of pornography that was all their search had uncovered.

"Perhaps the lesson of all this, Dr. Forrester, is that it is best to leave the actual mechanics of detection to the professionals," he said finally. He picked up the photograph as if it was infected. "I assume you don't want this item as part of your case?" and when Forrester shook his head went on, "Then I propose we burn the wretched thing," and when neither of them objected, threw it into the fire.

Harrison had lectures to attend that morning, and Forrester a lecture to give, and by mutual consent they put aside the investigation and got on with their own activities. After the lecture came three tutorials in a row, and it was only that afternoon – when a student named Sitwell failed to turn up – that Forrester remembered the note from Alice Hayley and took it out of his pocket to read it.

Dear Dr. Forrester,

I have been thinking about our conversation about David's death, and there is something I would like to tell you. Perhaps you could let me know when would be a good time to meet?

Alice Hayley

Forrester noted the return address, sat down and began to compose a note in reply, and then changed his mind: if Sitwell had not turned up by now, it was unlikely he was going to turn up, and Forrester might as well use the unexpectedly available time. He put on his overcoat and set off to cycle over to Alice Hayley's lodgings, which turned out to be on Chalfont Road in north Oxford. As he bicycled down the street, there was a pinging noise from his front wheel as a large, hard snowball hit the spokes at considerable speed and sent the wheel – and Forrester – skidding across the street.

Fighting to regain control he saw two small shapes

diving for cover in a passageway between two houses, and an old inner tube nailed across a gap in a wooden fence.

At the end of the passage the boys were trapped against a gate, trying to scramble over it and finding it was too tall. "I'm sorry, mister," said one of them when he realised there was no way out. "We didn't mean to."

Forrester looked at the inner tube. "Ballista," he said.

"What?" said the older boy.

"You've made a ballista," said Forrester. "The ancient Romans used to build them, although they didn't have rubber bike tubes to work with."

The boys looked at each other and clearly made a collective decision that Forrester was harmless. They came closer.

"It makes snowballs go a long way," said the other boy, with a hint of pride.

"Yes," said Forrester. "Just be careful which way you fire them in future. You could have caused an accident."

"Alright, mister. Sorry," said the boy, relieved the man was going to take it no further, and Forrester got on his bike again and rode the rest of the way to Alice Hayley's lodgings. The landlady, when she opened the door, looked at him disapprovingly.

"I have a strict rule for my young ladies," she said. "No gentlemen visitors."

"I am a don at Barnard College," said Forrester, "and I'm coming in response to a note from Miss Hayley."

"I daresay you are," said the landlady. "But that doesn't make it right, does it?"

"Do you have a sitting room?" asked Forrester. "I'd be perfectly happy to talk to her there." The landlady looked at him narrowly, as if weighing up what trouble he could get up to in the sitting room, and as Forrester smiled reassuringly at her, clearly decided *Not much, I suppose*, sniffed, and went upstairs to fetch her boarder.

A minute later she came down. "She's not in," she said, with some satisfaction. Forrester was about to depart when it occurred to him to ask if the landlady had seen Alice Hayley leave.

"No, I didn't, as a matter of fact."

For no reason he understood Forrester began to feel uneasy. "I imagine you keep a fairly close eye on comings and goings here," he said carefully.

"Naturally I do," said the landlady.

"So I wonder how Miss Hayley slipped away without you seeing her?"

"I really can't say," said the landlady. "I can't be responsible for everything these young women do," and Forrester suddenly realised why he was uneasy. The faintest, the very faintest of olfactory sensations. "What's that smell?"

They both stood there for a moment, and then the landlady was running back up the stairs with Forrester close behind her.

"She tried this before," she said. "She promised she'd never do it again!"

The door was bolted on the inside but Forrester aimed a massive kick at the handle and it sprang open. Inside, Alice

Hayley was kneeling by her unlit gas fire, like a worshipper at a shrine, and the room was thick with fumes. "Oh my God," said the landlady.

"Call an ambulance," said Forrester, choking on the gas, and as the landlady retreated downstairs he took a deep breath, rushed into the room, grabbed Alice Hayley and pulled her away, half dragging, half carrying her towards the door. Her face was blue, her eyes rolled up in her head. Lifting her in his arms he staggered down the stairs, through the front door and out into the freezing evening air as curtains were pulled aside and doors opened in the neighbouring houses, letting shafts of yellow light out onto the trodden snow.

"What's happened?" said a man in carpet slippers, the evening paper still in his hand.

"Looks as if one of them girls tried to kill herself," said a woman in curlers.

"Oh, one of them," said a man in a singlet.

Forrester looked from one spectator to another, and wanted to knock the lot of them back to their frowsty little lives, but as the red tide of anger welled up in him, he felt a movement against his forearm, where it was hard against Alice Hayley's diaphragm.

A spasm.

Without thinking he grabbed a handful of snow and slathered it over her face, and as the shock of the cold hit her she drew in a torn, ragged breath, and suddenly she was retching, and the spectators were stepping back as she vomited into the snow.

And then the ambulance was coming, and the ambulance men were taking her off his hands, and in the distance he could hear the clanging of the police bells. Before they could get there Forrester darted up the stairs and back into Alice Hayley's grim little room, turned off the gas tap on the fire, flung up the window and stood there, gulping in fresh evening air, before he looked at her desk.

On which lay the note. A beat, and then he picked it up.

To Whom it May Concern,

I, Alice Hayley, wish to confess to the murder of Dr. David Lyall on 13th January this year. He had been my lover; he left me for Margaret Clark. I stabbed him in a jealous rage. I know it was wrong, and that I must atone. I'm sorry, I'm so sorry for what I did, and I hope you will forgive me.

Alice Hayley

Forrester gasped. He had been on the wrong track all along. It had not been Dorfmann, or anyone he had sent who had killed David Lyall. It had had nothing to do with Norse manuscripts, or wartime treachery.

Or Gordon Clark.

Suddenly he was exuberant, as if a current of air had caught him and wafted him upwards out of the void. His friend was innocent! Gordon was going to be released – and Forrester was going to be able to fulfil his promise to him. He was still holding the note when Barber came into the room.

"Well," he said. "What an interesting surprise."

Forrester stared at him.

"Normally I wouldn't come out for something like this," said Barber, "but I happened to be finishing up some paperwork when the call came in. And of course I recognised the young lady's name." A beat. "What's *your* excuse, Dr. Forrester?"

"Miss Hayley sent me a note, asking me to come."

"Is that the note?"

"No, I've just found this, on her desk. It's a confession." And he offered it to the inspector.

Barber raised a hand to stop him, and gestured for Forrester to put the note back down on the desk. "There are rules for dealing with evidence, Dr. Forrester," he said, "and you've just broken several of them. Which is why it's best to leave detective work to the professionals."

Only then did he step over to the desk and peer down at the note.

"Ah," he said. "Interesting."

"So Gordon Clark is innocent after all," said Forrester.

Barber turned and regarded him steadily. "Provided it's genuine."

"What do you mean?"

"I mean provided that Alice Hayley wrote it. Provided that she was the person who left it here."

"You know she did!"

"All I know, Dr. Forrester, is that I came into the room and found you holding it."

"Because I found it here!"

"So you say."

"This is ridiculous! The landlady was with me when we broke into the room. If I hadn't been here Alice Hayley might be dead."

"May already be dead," said Barber. "People have been known to die on the way to the hospital."

"I don't see what you're getting at."

"Well, look at it from my point of view, sir. You have been making valiant – not to say desperate – efforts to prove your friend's innocence. Now a young lady, previously not a suspect, is found unconscious with her head over an unlit gas fire and a note beside her admitting to the crime – and there you are, in the room. How do I know you didn't make her write the note and force her head over the gas yourself?"

Forrester gaped at him, hardly able to comprehend what he was being accused of, and then gathered his wits.

"Because five minutes ago I was outside the front door with the landlady," he said, "asking her for permission to come in."

"There is a window," said Barber. "And I see it's open."

"I opened it to let air in."

"Perhaps you did. Perhaps you opened it earlier to gain admittance to the room, attack Alice Hayley and plant your note before going back outside and knocking at the front door to speak to the landlady."

"This is pure fantasy. I saved Alice Hayley's life."

"As I say, that remains to be seen. In the meantime, Dr. Forrester, I'd like you to return to your college and remain there until I have time to interview you again."

"You are completely wrong about this," said Forrester.

"So you have been telling me, sir," said Barber, "since this whole affair began. But perhaps this time I am right."

And he turned back to the note. As he did so, a burly constable appeared in the doorway. Forrester pushed past him and went out into the darkness.

27

QUESTIONS RAISED BY A SUICIDE

Forrester was in a state of shock when he got back to his rooms. He had been within an ace of getting Gordon Clark out of prison, and by his very presence in Alice Hayley's room, now risked destroying the very exoneration the girl had been trying to provide. Damnation! Then he tried to reassure himself: as soon as Alice Hayley could speak, she'd say he had nothing to do either with her trying to commit suicide, or writing the note. Things would be back on track.

But what if she didn't regain consciousness? What if, as Barber had darkly hinted, she relapsed and died? Not only would Gordon remain in prison but he himself might well become a murder suspect.

And yet – what else could he have done?

Except, perhaps, read her first note straight away, and gone round to see her immediately, before any of this could have happened.

And then, he thought, if Sitwell hadn't failed to turn up for his tutorial, he would not have gone round there at all, and Alice Hayley would be dead. And her note admitting her guilt found by someone else, and thus exactly the piece of evidence needed to save Gordon Clark.

Forrester swore softly. In the last twenty-four hours, ever since the college lights had gone out, everything had gone wrong. He and Harrison had made themselves look like fools, he had alienated the Master and utterly destroyed his credibility with Barber.

Damn, damn, damn!

He took off his coat and flung it on the sofa, and as he did so he saw the envelope that contained Alice Hayley's first note, the one asking him to come and see her, lying where he had dropped it. He picked it up and was about to open it when there was a knock at the door and Harrison appeared.

Forrester looked at him without enthusiasm. "Hello, Harrison," he said. Harrison took his ammunition bag off his shoulder, fished inside and brought out something shrouded in brown paper.

"I thought you might need this," he said, and unwrapped a bottle of Chianti.

"I'm not sure I'm in the mood, old chap," said Forrester.

"That's why I thought you'd need it," said Harrison implacably, taking out a corkscrew. Forrester watched expressionlessly as Harrison filled two glasses and pressed one of them into his hand.

To his surprise, the wine wasn't actually too bad. In fact, as he rolled it around in his mouth, he felt as if he was tasting the warmth of the long-gone Italian summers.

"Here's to better days," said Harrison.

"Yes," said Forrester, wryly. "There have to be some, at some point."

And he told Harrison what had happened on Chalfont Road, and of Barber's accusation when he had found him there.

"That man is the biggest fool on God's earth," said Harrison, and it did Forrester's heart good to hear.

"Thank you for that," he said. "I was beginning to think I might have done it."

"No," said Harrison, grinning. "Not your style. But tell me this, do you think the confession was genuine?"

"I have no idea," said Forrester. "I'd just assumed it was."

"Well Barber may be only half wrong," said Harrison.

"What do you mean?" said Forrester.

"Well, you may not have faked the confession," he said, "but somebody might have. For example, what about the handwriting? Was that the same as on the note you got?"

"I don't know. Actually I was just about to have a look at it." And he turned back to the envelope.

But when he opened the envelope again the letter was gone. "Perhaps I put it down," he said. So he and Harrison searched the room, and all his pockets, but there was still no sign of it. "I might have dropped it," said Forrester. "On the way to Chalfont Road or when I was carrying her down the stairs or something."

"You *might* have," said Harrison, "but consider this possibility: somebody came into your rooms today, took the note, and used it to imitate Alice Hayley's handwriting when they concocted her confession."

Forrester stared at him. "Are you serious?"

"Perfectly."

"You're saying somebody tried to murder her and make it look as if she'd committed suicide?"

"I'm saying it's a possibility. After all, if you were the murderer of David Lyall and felt that the net was closing in on you, what better move than to have someone else confess to it and then conveniently kill themselves so they couldn't retract their confession?"

"You'd have to be a pretty devious sort of bastard to come up with something like that."

"Well, Dr. Forrester," said Harrison mildly, refilling their glasses, "don't all the facts suggest that we *are* dealing with a pretty devious bastard?"

"But why?" Forrester said at last. "If we assume that whoever murdered Lyall also tried to pin it on Alice Hayley – why did he do it?"

"Or she."

"Yes, alright, or she. But what had they to gain? Gordon Clark is already in prison; the case against him is, as far as we know, as solid as ever. Why would the murderer want another suspect?" He noticed a change in Harrison's expression. "Why are you looking like that?"

"That pronoun started me thinking," said Harrison.

"She?"

"What other suspect might that apply to?"

"Well, the only other woman... no, that's ridiculous. It was Margaret Clark who begged me to save Gordon."

"If Alice Hayley had died and the note had been found by someone else, that *would* have saved Dr. Clark. And ensured nobody blamed his wife."

Forrester looked at him narrowly.

"For killing Lyall?"

"Exactly."

"What motive did Margaret Clark have to kill David Lyall?" asked Forrester – but he already knew the answer.

"Perhaps he was going to ditch her," said Harrison.

"Do we have any evidence that was the case?"

"No, but it's a possibility, isn't it? You know what put it in my mind? Perhaps he'd got tired of Margaret Clark and wanted to move on. And I think it shouldn't be too difficult to find out if she visited your rooms today."

At which point the porter knocked on the door. "Telephone call for you, Dr. Forrester," he said, with a dark look at Harrison. He had clearly not yet forgiven him for blacking out the college the night before.

"Who is it?" said Forrester.

"A Major MacLean, sir," said Piggot, and Forrester got up.

"I'll come down," he said.

There was a small fire burning in Piggot's grate, and a half-drunk cup of tea beside a late edition of the *Oxford Mail*, open at the sporting pages. The receiver lay beside the visitors' book on the scarred wooden counter. Forrester picked it up.

"Forrester here," he said.

"Got something for you," said MacLean. "From that photograph."

"Excellent," said Forrester. "What is it?"

"Rather not say over the phone. Can you come up to town tomorrow?" Forrester tried to bring his academic calendar to the forefront of his mind.

"I think so," he said. "Late morning?"

"Eleven-thirty a.m. would suit me perfectly," said MacLean. "Come to the War Office and ask for me at the front desk," and hung up.

Harrison, needless to say, was fascinated to hear the details of MacLean's telephone call, and Forrester knew he would have gone to London with him at the slightest excuse; but he also knew MacLean would be much less forthcoming if an outsider was present. "I'll tell you what I've found out as soon as I get back," he said. "And perhaps in the meantime you can check on Margaret Clark's movements yesterday."

He was relieved to find the Master was not at High Table that night, and though in other circumstances he would have found it tedious to sit beside Alan Norton and hear him wax lyrical about the shortcomings of the British builder and the problems of getting the Lady Tower back to its pre-war condition when no-one seemed to feel any sense of urgency about it but himself, tonight it was vaguely soothing: the clatter of a mountain stream over rocks, monotonous and meaningless.

"You know how often the Master has bothered to come and inspect the works?" asked Norton, rhetorically. "Once. Just *once* have I been able to get him up that tower to look at the state of it, and since then I have had no help from him whatever."

"I daresay he has other things on his mind," said Forrester.

"If this was Russia," said Norton darkly, "those repairs would have been finished in a week."

"If this was Russia," said Forrester, "those builders would have been shot."

"Yes," said Norton, "and they would have bloody well deserved it."

And as he said these words Forrester suddenly looked at the man as if for the first time, and saw him not as a victim, not as a figure of fun, but as a coiled spring of resentment and anger. A coiled spring that could be released at any time.

And might, perhaps, despite his carefully constructed alibi, have been unleashed on the night David Lyall had met his death.

In fact, thought Forrester, if David Lyall had been killed on Alan Norton's beloved Lady Tower and not in Gordon Clark's rooms, he would have been certain the murderer was this man sitting beside him, spitting venom at the inefficiency of the British working class whose interests he so assiduously championed.

28

LUNCH AT THE CAFÉ ROYALE

The fog had returned to London as Forrester arrived at Paddington, and the bus that took him to Whitehall moved so slowly and uncertainly through the murk, its fog lights casting a sickly yellow sheen into the grey vapour, that all it seemed to want to do was curl up and go to sleep. Even the vast bulk of the War Ministry was almost invisible beneath the shroud of filthy air, and the sergeant at the front desk was coughing painfully as he wrote Forrester's name in a ledger so large it might have been used by St. Peter to list the souls entering the Kingdom of Heaven. He did not have Forrester escorted to MacLean's office, as he had expected, but asked him to wait, and when MacLean came down the stairs, moving with his usual brisk efficiency, he beckoned Forrester to follow him down a further set of steps, leading into the bowels of the building.

"They've got everything set up down here," said MacLean, as he guided his guest along concrete corridors devoid even of the War Ministry's beloved brown paint.

Forrester remembered his sergeant's advice when he had first joined up. "The rule for surviving in this army, sonny boy, is if it moves, salute it. If it doesn't, paint it."

The corridor turned and turned again and the ceiling became lower and lower until finally MacLean opened an unmarked door and Forrester found himself in a long room with very little overhead illumination and small, concentrated pools of light over every desk, at which sat analysts peering into curious pieces of wooden apparatus incorporating thick chunks of magnifying glass. With Forrester in his wake MacLean strode past desk after desk until he stopped beside a prematurely balding young man whose spectacles were almost as thick as the magnifier through which he was peering. "Bannister, this is Dr. Forrester, from Barnard College. I'd like you to show him the Bjornsfjord material."

"Yes, sir," said Bannister and began shuffling myopically through the piles of photos on his desk.

"It was Bannister who spotted the 9th SS Panzer Division at Arnhem," said MacLean conversationally. "Unfortunately no-one believed him. If they had, the war might have been shorter by six months." Bannister's ears went red, but he said nothing and finally came up with the photo album print Forrester had allowed MacLean to copy.

"Not much to be learnt from this as it stood, sir." Bannister glanced up at him sideways, and Forrester felt vaguely offended, until he realised this was just the theatrical preamble. Stuck down here in this windowless cave, Bannister probably seized on any opportunity for theatre that came his way. "But this is what we got when we blew it up by a factor of five." And Bannister brought out a foolscap-sized sheet of photographic paper and slid it under the magnifier.

As Forrester leaned into the lenses it was as if he was inside that day in 1937, on the cliff path leading down to the water, looking across the fjord at the two men rowing towards the shore. He could almost feel the heat of the summer sun, and the coolness of the water as the dinghy cut through it, almost hear the flap of the sails of the big yacht from which the men were rowing.

A shiver ran through him as he realised Sophie might have stood on that very spot, might indeed have taken the photograph, as she waited for her husband's guests to arrive. Sophie. Suddenly he could feel the touch of her fingers on his cheek, the softness of her flesh under his. The expression in her eyes when they had parted. And then he was concentrating again, and realising that the face of the man in the prow was now perfectly identifiable.

"Peter Dorfmann to the life," said Forrester. "Well done, Mr. Bannister."

"Thank you," said Bannister.

"He isn't finished yet," said MacLean, like a proud parent showing off the achievements of a talented toddler. Bannister slid an even greater enlargement of a small proportion of the original photo, in which the men in the dinghy filled the frame. "In this one you can make out the cut of their clothes too," said Bannister, and Forrester looked again. It was true; the enlargement even revealed that

Dorfmann was wearing a sort of canvas jacket of vaguely nautical cut. By contrast the man with his back to camera was wearing a striped blazer and a panama hat.

"Impressive," said Forrester. "I just wish the chap in the striped blazer would turn around."

"Never mind him," said MacLean, "we've got Dorfmann there in 1937, and it gets better. Show him what you did with the yacht, Bannister."

Bannister took yet another enlargement from the pile and slid it under the magnifier. This time the dinghy was out of shot, and the stern of the yacht filled the frame. It was clear that the name had been carved into a wooden plate curving around the stern – but only the first two letters, thrown into shadowed relief by the sun, were visible.

They were "G" and "I".

"Interesting," said Forrester. "Does that help much?"

"It certainly does," said MacLean. "Tell him, Bannister."

"We calculated the length of the yacht," said Bannister, "and that made it possible to calculate the size of the stern-plate. When we factored in the size of the letters we can see, we were able to work out that the name had just five letters in it."

"Very good," said Forrester.

"You can see the yacht had a motor," said MacLean, "so we got in touch with the Norwegian Ministry of Shipping and asked them for the list of motor yachts registered with them in 1937. There were three with five-letter names beginning with 'G'."

"Which presumably narrows down the candidates

considerably," said Forrester.

"They were only able to come up with pictures of one of them, which unfortunately wasn't this one. Which left two remaining possibilities: one was a yacht called *Gitta* and another called *Gimli*."

"*Gimli*," said Forrester.

"*Gimli*," repeated MacLean. "In Old Norse it means 'golden roof', and it referred to the place to which the gods retreated after the end of the world."

"Ragnarök," said Forrester automatically, remembering that night in the Master's Lodge when everything had changed. "Interesting."

"More than interesting," said MacLean. "Because we know the name of the owner of the yacht *Gimli*." He paused for a moment, clearly savouring the revelation to come. "*Gimli*," he said, "was registered to a gentleman named Vidkun Quisling."

Forrester blinked. Vidkun Quisling, the former ruler of Norway, had been executed by firing squad just months before as a traitor to his country. Indeed, for years now his very name had been synonymous with the worst type of Nazi lickspittle. Son of a country pastor, he had become part of the General Staff of the Norwegian Army before the Great War and been sent on missions to Russia just after the revolution. There he had worked with the famous Arctic explorer Fridtjof Nansen to relieve famine in the Ukraine; it was also rumoured he had acted as a spy for the British, for which he had been made a Commander of the British Empire.

And then the Norwegian Army had dispensed with his services, and he found himself back home and unemployed. Inspired by the radical politics he had seen in Russia and funded by the sale of the many valuable antiques he'd been able to pick up there from fleeing aristocrats, he set up a national paramilitary organisation in Norway dedicated to anti-Bolshevism and racial purity. This led to him being invited to join the government, where he made himself popular with the right by attacking trade unions and the communists. He then founded a party of his own, the *Nasjonal Samling*, and though it had little electoral support in Norway he was soon meeting with Italian fascists and Nazi ideologues and spouting the anti-Semitic rhetoric he picked up from them.

Not long after *Kristallnacht* he sent Hitler a fiftieth birthday greeting, thanking him for "saving Europe from Bolshevism and Jewish domination". As his party faltered in the polls he began taking secret donations from the Nazis to keep it going, and gave Nazi intelligence officials information of Norway's defences. When Hitler invaded, Quisling became head of the puppet Norwegian government, and participated in the deportation of Jews as part of Hitler's Final Solution.

The previous year, when Hitler was defeated and Norway was freed, Quisling had been arrested by his furious countrymen, and taken to the Akershus Fortress to be tried for treason. Not long after, he was executed.

"Well, if Dorfmann was travelling around Norway on Vidkun Quisling's yacht in 1937 there's a strong case for concluding he was a Nazi sympathiser from way back," said Forrester.

"Absolutely," said MacLean. "Bringing us this photograph was a considerable coup. It won't be forgotten."

"Thank you," said Forrester, still staring at the photo. Then he said, "Could I have a look at the other one again? The one of the chaps in the dinghy?"

Bannister slid it back under the magnifier. Forrester glanced at the image of Dorfmann again, but his interest was in the man with his back to camera – the man in the striped blazer.

"Would you agree with me," he said to MacLean, "that this is probably the Englishman the caption to the missing photograph referred to?"

"There's certainly something very English about the blazer and the panama hat," said MacLean. Forrester turned to Bannister.

"It's quite a distinctive pattern of stripes," he said. "Look, three thin, one thick, two thin. Is there any way you could identify the blazer?"

"Shame we can't see the colours," said MacLean.

"We could make some intelligent guesses, though, sir," said Bannister, "depending on the degree of light and dark."

"And possibly make some enquiries in Savile Row," said Forrester. "There's got to be someone in those elegant gents' outfitters who's an expert on striped blazers."

"I'll look into it," said MacLean, "but the main thing is we've got something to show the Americans. They're going to find it very hard to make Dorfmann their man now."

"Why were they so keen on him in the first place?" asked Forrester.

"Oh, you know," said MacLean. "He's sound on communism. Hates the Bolsheviks, that sort of thing."

"Yes," said Forrester. "Hitler was pretty consistent about that too."

Forrester got them to give him the copy of the photograph at its original size – they wouldn't release any of the blow-ups – and made a phone call before he left the War Ministry, which resulted in an immediate invitation for pre-lunch drinks at the Café Royal. MacLean had proposed the War Ministry canteen, but with insincere regret, Forrester explained he had another offer, and MacLean grinned, shook hands and ushered him out, promising to let him know if there were any further developments.

Forrester was heading north through the fog towards Trafalgar Square when he realised an indistinct figure had fallen in step with him. So thick was the fog that it was a moment or two before he realised it was Charles Calthrop, the man from the Foreign Office.

"Dr. Forrester, I think," said Calthrop. Forrester nodded. "To say we met under very unpleasant circumstances would be an understatement, would it not?" As always, he was the essence of urbanity. "Have matters progressed significantly since the police arrested Dr. Clark?"

"I'm not sure," said Forrester, remembering Calthrop's conversation with Dorfmann. Was it coincidence that today, when he was in London to see the final nail put in Dorfmann's coffin, Calthrop had happened to run into him? "You may have heard Gordon Clark is a friend of mine, and I've been trying to prove his innocence ever since he was charged."

"Any luck?" said Calthrop.

"Too early to say," said Forrester. Every instinct told him not to mention what MacLean had just discovered about Dorfmann.

"No new suspects?" said Calthrop.

"Nothing concrete," said Forrester.

"Pity," said Calthrop. "One always likes to help a friend in need. As long as it doesn't distract you from your studies of Linear B."

Forrester looked at him in surprise. "I wasn't aware you knew of my interest," he said.

"I didn't, until very recently. Then by the most extraordinary coincidence your name appeared on a list that came across my desk only yesterday."

"Oh, yes? What sort of list?"

"It's not really my field, but the Empire Council wanted to know if you were a suitable chap to send to Crete."

Forrester's step faltered. "Really?"

"Yes, I gathered you'd applied for a grant to excavate there."

"I had. But I'd rather given up on it, actually."

"Oh, never say die," remarked Calthrop lightly. "It's not my decision, of course, but with resources so limited for sending people overseas, they wanted to know you were a fit and proper person to represent your country in a foreign land. Especially one where the communists are making so much trouble."

"May I ask if you answered in the affirmative?"

"You may ask, old chap, but I couldn't possibly answer without breaching the Official Secrets Act. But I have to say, from everything I know about you, I'm sure you'd be a credit to the nation wherever we sent you. What is Linear B, exactly?"

"A written language used by the ancient Minoans. You know, Knossos, the Labyrinth, that sort of thing. When I was there with Leigh Fermor's lot I came across a set of inscriptions which may be the key to understanding it."

"Sounds fascinating. I'd imagine there'd be great kudos for anyone finding out what King Minos had to say for himself. Let alone the Minotaur. Let's hope your detective work doesn't get in the way of a great scholastic coup. Well, lovely to run into you. Hope the Crete trip comes off."

And he was gone, vanishing into the fog along Piccadilly, as Forrester stood, looking after him.

Ian Fleming was already holding court in the Café Royale, and the bottle in his champagne bucket was well breached by the time Forrester got there. "I'm sorry I can't invite you to an actual lunch, Forrester," he said, "but I've got to talk to a man who says he knows when the Russians are going to start World War III."

"Bit soon for a sequel, isn't it?" said Forrester.

"I agree, but it'll sell papers, and that's what counts

for me right now. Anyway, have some of Lord Kemsley's champagne and tell me what I can do for you. At Ann's party Archie MacLean was bending your ear. What did he bamboozle you into this time?"

"Berlin and points north," said Forrester, "to investigate Peter Dorfmann."

Instantly Fleming was all ears, and Forrester knew he had to swear him to silence until he gave him clearance to use the story.

"Of course, of course," said Fleming, "but this is very good stuff. It'll set the cat among the pigeons with the Yanks, you can be sure of that. Dorfmann's their blue-eyed boy; I've heard they see him as a future chancellor."

Then Forrester told him about his odd encounter in Whitehall with Calthrop, and Fleming lit another of his gold-ringed cigarettes, drew in a deep lungful of smoke, and chuckled.

"You realise you've just been offered a bribe, don't you?" he said.

"Seriously?"

"Yes. Calthrop wants you to back off exposing Dorfmann. If you do, he'll recommend you get your grant to go to Crete. If you make trouble, you'll never set foot there as long as you live."

"But why?"

"Oh, why do these Foreign Office chaps do anything? They have so many agendas they can't keep up with themselves. He'll have his own game to play with the Americans. He may hand Dorfmann over to them himself, he may let them put him in place and then put pressure on him for something we want, he may suppress the whole thing for the sake of Anglo-American relations."

"Devious bastard."

"He's in the Foreign Office. What do you expect?" Fleming drank some more champagne. "By the way, what I told you about your Master last time we met – it seems to be coming to fruition."

"Intelligence?"

"Absolutely. The word is he'll be the new 'C'. Calthrop's very much behind that too. Has Winters dropped any hints?"

"None whatsoever. Although he's clearly becoming distinctly embarrassed by my efforts to clear Gordon Clark."

"Not trying to stop you?"

"No, no, on the contrary – he's been very helpful. But we put our foot in it the other night while searching for evidence and he's gone off us a bit." And he told Fleming the story of the dirty picture in the light fitting. Fleming was delighted, and was only with difficulty persuaded to keep the yarn to himself, at least until later. As he was chuckling, and saying how much he wished Forrester had kept hold of the saucy postcard, Forrester offered him another photograph instead.

Fleming snatched it up like a hungry seagull.

"Not for publication at this stage," said Forrester, "but there's Dorfmann, facing camera, and that's Vidkun Quisling's yacht. What I want to know is who the man in the blazer is. From the caption in the original album, I suspect he was English."

Fleming examined the photograph carefully. "And

probably a member of Henley Sailing Club," he said. "If I identify the blazer correctly."

"MacLean's people are looking into that," said Forrester. "I'll pass the suggestion on. But here's the point: if this chap was English, and a pal of Quisling, and associated with Dorfmann, I wonder if their association ended when the war began."

"How do you mean?" asked Fleming.

"Whether this pro-fascist Englishman kept in touch with a German literature professor who was working with Nazi intelligence after war was declared."

"I see what you're getting at," said Fleming.

"Was there ever any suggestion during the war that there was a traitor in British intelligence?"

"There was almost certainly someone – perhaps several someones – passing information to the Russians."

"The Russians?"

"Oh, yes. They clearly knew all sorts of things they shouldn't have known. For example, when Roosevelt sprang news of the atomic bomb on Stalin at Yalta, he showed not the slightest surprise. Someone had told him, and I think that someone was in British intelligence. My personal belief is it was the Cambridge lot. They were all communists in the thirties, you know."

"Of course the Russians *were* our allies."

"That's what made it so difficult. There were people in the intelligence services who felt we weren't treating them as allies, but as potential enemies."

"Which they were."

"Exactly." Fleming emptied the last of the bottle into their glasses and signalled the waiter for another.

"But what about people passing information to the Germans?" Forrester persisted. "Was there any hint that was happening?"

"All the time," said Fleming, and leant closer. "But it was supposed to. We rounded up most of Jerry's agents as soon as the war began, and those we didn't hang, we turned. They were sending stuff back to the Abwehr and the S.D. that we wanted Jerry to believe."

"And *only* stuff we wanted them to have?"

"As far as I know," said Fleming. "Do you have any reason to think otherwise?"

"I was just wondering if the other man in the photograph was in British intelligence," said Forrester.

"Why?" said Fleming. "Because he's wearing a striped blazer?"

Forrester grinned back. "Absolutely," he said. "I mean, if he was a member of the Henley Sailing Club he was clearly a wrong 'un, wasn't he?" Fleming chuckled appreciatively.

"You chaps from the lower orders," he said. "You don't trust your betters, do you?"

"Absolutely not," said Forrester, and raised his glass across the table. "That's how we survive."

He saw a large, smooth man in a well-cut suit striding purposefully towards the table; Fleming's lunch partner, he guessed. Getting up, he retrieved the Bjornsfjord photograph and slipped it into his pocket. Fleming looked wistful, and Forrester decided to give him a consolation prize.

"While I was in Berlin I came across a misfiled page in a bunch of Abwehr documents which talked about two agents, one codenamed 'Erik' who I think may have been Dorfmann, and a second codenamed 'Saint' who was giving Jerry information on things like the timing of the Murmansk convoys and Soviet plans for Stalingrad. They seemed to be using some kind of Norse saga in their communications."

"Good God," said Fleming.

"I wondered if Saint might have been one of the German agents we didn't round up. Someone who managed to keep in touch with Berlin throughout the war."

Fleming blinked. "I'll make some enquiries," he said.

"It may not be easy," said Forrester. "I asked Archie MacLean at the War Ministry to do the same thing, and all he's got is the run-around. I get the impression this is a bit of house-cleaning which for some reason the powers that be are reluctant to undertake."

"Well it may be one of their own," said Fleming.

"Anyway," said Forrester, "if you can find out anything about bad eggs in wartime intelligence, people who might have been in touch with the Nazis, the chances of my being able to let you have the photograph for publication are that much higher." Fleming looked at him wryly.

"I see you've learned something from Brother Calthrop," he said.

"I have," said Forrester. "Like how to swim in deep waters. Thanks for the champagne." And retrieving his overcoat from the cloakroom, Forrester headed back into the real world.

Out in Regent Street, the fog was thicker than ever, and the buses moving more slowly than ever, and he decided to walk back to Paddington. But as he walked his mind was moving much, much faster than his feet.

29

A MESSAGE FROM HAMLET'S CASTLE

When his train finally reached Oxford, Margaret Clark was walking into the station as Forrester was walking out of it. As he saw her, Forrester felt a jolt, like an electric shock, of pure dislike. Dislike, and deep distrust. Whatever he had found out about the role wartime espionage might have played in the death of David Lyall, he no longer trusted Margaret Clark.

"Hello, Margaret," he said as they came abreast. She stopped, letting the crowd flow into the station around her like a rock in a stream.

"Any progress?" she asked.

Forrester gave her an edited summary of what he had learned so far.

"That sounds promising," she said, "though I'm not quite clear how it helps."

"At this stage neither am I."

"Gordon's not holding up well," she said. "He seems to have given up hope."

Forrester looked at her, and was certain that her concern for Gordon's state of mind was a performance. Once again he considered the possibility that after some lovers' quarrel, it was she who had lured David Lyall up to Gordon's rooms and stabbed him in the heart.

But with such force that he crashed backwards through the window? Not really physically possible. And as this thought came to him he had the sudden sensation of holding the broken inner tube in his hands on Chalfont Road, and the ping of the snowball as it catapulted into the wheel of his bike.

Catapulted. Yes. It was as if David Lyall had not just been stabbed, but catapulted out of the window of Gordon Clark's rooms. So vivid was this image – if impossible to conceive how it might have been achieved – that for a moment Forrester did not realise that Margaret was speaking.

"…he was sympathetic," she was saying. "But I don't feel he's going to be any use."

"I'm sorry, who are we talking about?"

"Why, the Master, of course. I thought he might be able to help, but I sensed he just wanted to distance himself from the whole thing."

"That may be my fault: we had something of a debacle the other night searching Lyall's rooms."

"No, it wasn't that. He's been against me from the start."

"I don't understand. What do you mean, from the start?"

"Of my affair with David."

"I don't understand. He knew about that?"

"I'm sure he did. Well, not exactly sure; it wasn't him who saw us."

"Saw you where? What are you talking about?"

"Lady Hilary came across us on the towpath one day. She pretended not to have seen anything, but it was perfectly obvious. And I'm sure she told the Master. I'd hoped it wouldn't matter, but I'm afraid it does. It's so unfair, though – it's Gordon I'm asking help for, not me!"

Forrester stared at her. "Just to be clear, you're saying Lady Hilary knew you were having an affair with David Lyall all along? She knew Gordon was being cuckolded?"

"Don't use that horrible word! But yes, she did. Is it important?"

Forrester was silent for a moment. "It depends who she told, doesn't it?"

There was a crackle of incomprehensible chatter from the station loudspeaker, and a guard blew a whistle.

"That's my train," said Margaret. "Do go and see Gordon soon, Duncan. He needs all the support he can get."

And she was gone. Forrester stood there for a long moment, his hands deep in the pockets of his overcoat, thinking about what she had said. Then he set off for the college, where a letter was waiting for him in the Porter's Lodge.

It was postmarked Copenhagen.

Back in his rooms, before he could open the letter – before, indeed, he had taken off his coat – Harrison was knocking at the door in a state of some excitement.

"I've had an idea," he said, without preamble, as soon as Forrester had let him in.

"Fire away," said Forrester, taking off the British Warm and hanging it up.

"What if Lyall wasn't killed during the reading?"

"What are you talking about? We know he was."

"*How* do you know?" demanded Harrison.

"Because," said Forrester patiently, "we heard the sound of him smashing through Clark's window and came out and saw the body lying in the snow."

"That's not the same thing as knowing he was killed then."

Forrester dropped into his armchair. "The police doctor said nothing about the body having been dead for some time."

"Yes, but it needn't have been dead for 'some time' – just long enough for whoever did it to put him there and get back into the reading, thus establishing an alibi."

"Hmm," said Forrester, thinking this over.

"Which greatly widens the number of potential suspects," said Harrison. "You said it couldn't be anybody in the room with you, including Dorfmann, but if he'd killed Lyall *before* the reading began, he's back on the list, and with what you've found out, he absolutely ought to be there."

"I'd love to put Dorfmann on that list, but even if we hypothesise that Lyall was killed earlier – and we've got no evidence for that – it still leaves the question of the smashed window. There's no way anyone could have smashed the window in Clark's room and got back to the Lodge while the reading was still going on. We tried that experiment ourselves: it couldn't be done."

"True," said Harrison, crestfallen.

"And there's also the fact that Lyall was lying in a patch of virgin snow: no-one could have carried the body there without leaving footprints, and there were none."

"Blast! I'm not sure I can see a way round that."

"Never mind," said Forrester. "There's still a bit of that Chianti left. Pour a couple of glasses while I read this letter." And as Harrison did as he was told, Forrester slit the envelope, took out the heavy, creamy sheet of paper with the embossed heading "*Biblioteket fra det kongelige palads i Helsingborg*".

But the spidery writing below was in English of an oddly endearing kind.

Dearest Mr. Doktor Forrester,

I am to myself wondering should you by God with the second sight have been gifted? Because I have this day, the very day we were meeting, evidence discovered that our late German occupiers indeed have taken several volumes from these historic shelves, and one of these being, as suggested by you, a saga of the Norsemen. This theft remained undetected because this volume in our catalogue was listed as *The Lay of Asgaard*, and *The Lay of Asgaard* on our shelves safely remains.

"Fascinating," said Harrison, handing Forrester a glass. "Not sure it gets us very far, though."

"Wait," said Forrester. "There's more." And he turned the sheet over.

This was puzzlement to me, as imagine you can, so back through the older catalogues went I, always dustier and dustier were my garments becoming. And there was much coughing before I was coming over a note with *spørgsmålstegn* attached, which interested me greatly. I am sorry, I do not know the English word for *spørgsmålstegn*.

"Bugger," said Harrison, "neither do I. You?"
"No," said Forrester, and read on.

Beside this *spørgsmålstegn* was just one word. "Heimskringla." It is not surprising to me that a *spørgsmålstegn* to this was amalgamated, because it is known to all that this particular saga was as long ago as the seventeenth century from sight disappeared. I am sorry this information not more conclusive can be, but as I have promised to inform you on this subject, all the particles of fact I have at this moment are by this letter now available to you, as promised on that day you were from a bad fall saving me. Oh yes, a colleague of mine has just the information provided. The English word for *spørgsmålstegn* is "question mark".

Yours, in the extremity of sincerity,
Emil Lundquist, Librarian, Kronborg Castle, Helsingør

Forrester and Harrison looked at each other.
"What on earth was all that about?" said Harrison. "Apart

from *spørgsmålstegn*? Good Lord, he sounds a rum 'un."

"He was very sweet, actually," said Forrester. "And this may be rather important."

"I'm damned if I can see how," said Harrison.

"Never mind, for the time being," said Forrester, "but there's something you can do that might be rather useful."

"Ask away," said Harrison.

"Did any of the Scandinavian students you spoke to come from Denmark?"

"I think one did. There may have been others in the group."

"Would you go and see them and ask if any of them have any Danish postage stamps they could lend you?"

"Danish stamps?"

"They can be used ones. Perhaps from letters from home."

"I'm not sure I fully understand," said Harrison.

"You don't need to at this point," said Forrester. "I'd just be grateful if you could collect the stamps. A dozen should do it, I think."

Harrison stared at him, but Forrester was already putting on his coat. "Where are you going?" he asked.

"To see Kenneth Tynan," said Forrester. "I think the moment has come to draw on his particular expertise."

The glass of slightly oxidised Chianti remained halfway to Harrison's lips as Forrester put his overcoat back on and hurried out of the room.

* * *

Tynan was alone in the darkened Borringer Theatre when Forrester arrived, building a model of a theatrical set from pieces of cardboard, and rather to Forrester's surprise, recognised him at once.

"Ah, the inquisitor," he said. "Were you responsible for robbing me of my second lead?"

"I was responsible for getting your second lead *away* from the gas tap," said Forrester. "And I have my suspicions about who might have put her in there." Tynan looked at him with fresh interest.

"Enlighten me," he said, and Forrester did.

"Well I never," said Tynan, when Forrester had finished. "But how can I help?"

"By building me a model," said Forrester. "And then perhaps we could see how we could light it." Tynan grinned like a schoolboy.

"That sounds like fun," he said. "Let's do it."

When he came back from the Borringer, Forrester went to the telephone box outside the college, called the Porter's Lodge and said he had an urgent message for Dr. Norton. As soon as Forrester saw Piggot leave to bring Norton down he slipped into the Lodge and took the key to the Lady Tower.

With any luck, he thought, Norton would not realise it had gone.

This task completed, Forrester went to Harrison's rooms and woke him for a technical discussion based on his experiences in the army signals corps, after which they drew up a list of army surplus communications equipment that might reasonably be rounded up in Oxford within the next twenty-four hours.

Only then did Forrester return to his rooms and go to bed.

30

PREPARATIONS

The next morning, when the first of Forrester's students arrived for a tutorial, they found a note on the door apologising that he would not be available that day.

The reason for this was that at 9.30 a.m. Forrester was closeted with the secretary of the committee which awarded the Rotherfield Lectureship.

As he left him, he passed Dr. Alan Norton, who looked at him suspiciously but said nothing.

At 10.00 a.m. Forrester was with Professor Roland Bitteridge, who had, it turned out, also been on that committee.

At 11.00 a.m. he was with the Reverend Robert Glastonbury, Vicar of St. Mary the Virgin in his study, going through the back issues of *Clear Skies*, the magazine he had edited in the thirties.

At 12.00 p.m. Forrester used the vicarage phone to call the War Ministry, and asked to speak urgently to Archibald MacLean.

At 12.30 p.m. Forrester telephoned the Foreign Editor

of *The Sunday Times*, catching him just before he left to take a former Czechoslovakian prime minister to lunch at the Gay Hussar.

At 12.45 p.m., insisting on leaving Reverend Glastonbury enough money to cover the cost of the two calls he had made from his study, Forrester walked across the city towards the Eagle and Child pub.

As he walked down Cornmarket Street he was certain that Margaret Clark was watching him from the doorway of a newsagent, but affected not to be aware of her presence.

Shortly after 1.00 p.m., he met with Harrison in the Eagle and Child, went over certain technical matters and took possession of a small collection of used Danish postage stamps.

At 1.15 p.m. Professor J.R.R. Tolkien came in to the Eagle and Child and Forrester had a brief, discreet conversation with him.

At 2.00 p.m. Forrester made a purchase at Blackwell's bookshop.

At 3.00 p.m. he visited the Churchill Hospital, and asked to speak to Alice Hayley. He was prevented from doing so by Detective Inspector Alec Barber.

Between 3.15 p.m. and 3.30 p.m. a short, sometimes acrimonious conversation took place between Forrester and Inspector Barber, with each retiring to consult other parties.

At 4.30 p.m., as a Post Office van was delivering the afternoon's mail to Barnard College, Piggot was drawn out of his Porter's Lodge by the sound of a firecracker being let off in the quadrangle, an activity specifically forbidden by college regulations.

At 4.45 p.m., having failed to find the culprit, but holding the spent firecracker as evidence for use in future investigations, the chagrined porter returned to his cubicle and found, to his further annoyance, an unusually large pile of mail awaiting distribution.

At 5.00 p.m. both Alan Norton and the Master visited the Porter's Lodge to collect their mail, and noted the large parcel that had come for Dr. Forrester, festooned with an impressive number of Danish stamps.

At 5.15 p.m. Piggot informed Dr. Forrester this parcel was awaiting his collection.

At 8.15 p.m., during High Table, Forrester passed a note to the Master, asking for an urgent meeting during which he promised to be able to reveal the identity of David Lyall's murderer.

The note was passed to the Master via Alan Norton, who held it in his hand for a long moment before passing it on.

When the Master read the note, somewhat to his surprise, he found that Dr. Forrester was asking him to hold this meeting that night, at the top of the Lady Tower.

31

THE SECRET OF THE BOOK

"To say you are testing the limits of my goodwill, Forrester, would be an understatement," said Winters, genially enough, as they climbed the stairs to the top of the Lady Tower. "But I must warn you that if this results in the kind of embarrassment your last investigation produced, you will not rise in my estimation."

"I quite understand, Master," said Forrester. "But I think this time you will be impressed. In fact, I think I'll finally be able to show you not just who murdered David Lyall, but how they did it."

"Then it will all have been worth it," said Winters, "and I will heartily forgive you for any inconvenience caused."

"Thank you, Master," said Forrester. "I appreciate your patience."

Winters and Forrester came out through the trap door onto the flat roof of the tower, still covered in its frozen tangle of building equipment. The night was clear and it was bitterly cold, the moonlight glittering on the frosted surfaces.

Winters looked around, as though expecting something to reveal itself. When it did not, he turned to Forrester.

"Well?" he said. "Is there something I should already have taken in?"

"Let's put it this way, Master," said Forrester, "the idea came to me when some children fired a snowball at me on Chalfont Road."

"A snowball?" said Winters, with just a hint of asperity. "I trust you weren't injured."

"No, no; but the spokes of my bicycle were slightly bent," said Forrester, "and the reason for that was because the boys had used an inner tube to create a sort of primitive ballista."

"How ingenious of them," said Winters. "Perhaps there is hope for the younger generation yet."

"Once I began thinking about ballistae, I was alerted by Mr. Harrison to the idea that Lyall might have been killed not in Dr. Clark's rooms, but elsewhere."

"Elsewhere?"

"And propelled there."

A beat.

"By a conveniently available ballista?" said Winters.

"By an improvised ballista," said Forrester.

He turned to the building debris.

"Such as might have been constructed from the materials here." There was a pause.

"With respect, Forrester, this sounds very far-fetched."

"It does, doesn't it?" said Forrester. "But let me demonstrate. Let us say, just for the sake of argument, that Dr Lyall was stabbed here. His body might well have fallen – there."

And he gestured to a frozen tarpaulin.

"You'll note," he said, "how the material has been left carelessly, not in a neat roll, but with a distinct dip in the middle, so it forms a kind of chute."

He picked up the rigid tarpaulin and propped one open end between two of the crenellations of the tower.

"You can imagine that anything sliding down this chute would fly right out from the tower into the quadrangle below," he said.

"I can," said Winters, "and I estimate it would travel perhaps twenty feet beyond the tower, ending up, at best, a third of the way across the quad. Not beneath Dr Clark's window, which was where we found David Lyall's body."

"Exactly," said Forrester. "And this is where the ballista concept comes in." He walked to the far side of the tower and picked up an ice-stiff coil of rope. "But if I attached this end of the rope to the upright scaffolding here," he said, "and the other" – he walked across the tower – "to this upright here, there would be room to pull the rope backwards until it was stretched as tight as a bowstring. Then, when the rope was released, Lyall's body would not simply slide out of the chute, but be propelled like an arrow from a bow."

"With enough force to send it right across the quad, and into Dr. Clark's rooms?" asked Winters, sceptically.

"Not into Dr Clark's rooms: just far enough to hit the window before falling to the ground beneath them. But that was all that would be needed to create the illusion he had been killed in there. We could try an experiment, if you like."

"I'd rather not, Forrester, if you don't mind," said Winters. "I can see a host of embarrassing outcomes from such a venture, however entertaining it might be for you. But I must say, I am impressed, as always, with your enthusiasm and ingenuity, and I suggest that you pass on this idea to the police. Is our business completed for the night?"

"Not entirely," said Forrester. "I did promise to tell you the identity of the killer, didn't I?"

"You did, but frankly, I didn't take you very seriously. And I have to tell you that your latest theory does not encourage me to do so."

"Well, you must admit that at the very least the ballista idea greatly widens the range of suspects, because if David Lyall was killed here and not in Dr. Clark's rooms, many people sitting in the Lodge with me during the saga reading could theoretically have done it."

"I can't argue with that," said Winters. "Even if I consider it a very far-fetched premise."

"It could mean, for example, that Peter Dorfmann might have been responsible."

"We discussed this," said Winters. "I pointed out to you that Lyall would have had little to blackmail him with if all he was able to reveal was that Dorfmann had been drafted in to help German intelligence during the war. I thought you'd understood that."

"I did, Master, I did," said Forrester. "And to further exonerate Dorfmann I had someone help me make a little cardboard model of the Lodge and the Lady Tower."

"A cardboard model? This is becoming absurd," said Winters, but Forrester ploughed relentlessly on.

"A model which made it very clear it would have been almost impossible for anybody with me in the drawing room to have reached the tower, killed Lyall, sent him flying off into space and returned to his seat by the time we all heard the crash."

"Well, that at least is something," said Winters.

"Indeed," said Forrester. "But when I examined this model – it was made for me by Kenneth Tynan, by the way, a man I think has a very bright future ahead of him in the theatre – I realised that these strictures did *not* apply to anyone sitting up in the minstrels' gallery." He paused. "The minstrels' gallery where the reading was taking place."

Winters said nothing.

"Remember that night when you kindly allowed Harrison and me to go up onto the roofs? We conclusively proved it would take at least twenty minutes to reach Dr. Clark's rooms from the Lodge and return there. But from the minstrels' gallery it would take only three minutes to reach the Lady Tower."

Winters put a hand on his arm. "But my dear fellow, everyone who saw us in that gallery can provide us with an alibi: we were all reading the saga. You heard us yourself."

"Yes, I heard you," said Forrester. "But I didn't *see* you. The gallery was in darkness apart from the reading lights over your texts. And I have no idea when one reader left off and the next began. One of you could easily have left his seat in the darkness and slipped away to the Lady Tower during the reading."

"Killing David Lyall with a single blow en route and setting up this absurd Heath Robinson contraption you ask us to imagine?" said Winters. "Really, Forrester, with all due respect, this is becoming laughable."

"I agree it would have been impossible in the time had there been no preparation," said Forrester. "But what if the contraption had been set up earlier that day? And if Dr. Lyall had been lured up to the tower and stabbed between the end of High Table and the beginning of the reading, the task would have been relatively simple. All the murderer had to do was slip out of the room under cover of the Ragnarök reading, send the body flying across the quad, and then mingle with the crowd as they left the Lodge in response to the noise of breaking glass."

Winters was silent for a moment.

"So which of the saga readers do you suggest performed this feat of malign ingenuity?" he said. "One of the young Icelandic engineers? Haraldson? Not me, I hope?"

"How could I suspect you, Master, when you've done so much to help me find the real killer?"

"I'm glad you appreciate that," said Winters.

"Of course," said Forrester. "You were the last person on my mind. And then I received something in the post today. From the librarian of Kronborg Castle in Helsingør."

"And what was that?"

"A complete manuscript of the *Heimskringla*."

For a long moment Winters did not speak. And then he

broke into a huge smile. "This is wonderful! I can't believe it. You're telling me it's been found – after all these years!" and then he paused. "Are you sure?" he said. "I find it very hard to believe any librarian would entrust something as precious as that to the post. And why did they send it to you, of all people?"

"The librarian sent it to me because I saved him from a fall. But he hasn't, of course, sent the original, just a facsimile, which had just turned up in the stacks after having been miscatalogued in the nineteenth century. The original was stolen by the Germans shortly after they occupied Denmark in 1940."

"The Germans?"

"Yes. And here's the odd thing: this was not the only manuscript of the *Heimskringla* to have experienced an odd fate. A previous version was either sold or gambled away by the Norwegian Count Ernst Arnfeldt-Laurvig some time around 1937. About the time you and Peter Dorfmann were visiting Bjornsfjord."

"I beg your pardon?"

"In Vidkun Quisling's yacht," said Forrester. Winters stared at him.

"What on earth makes you think I was ever on Vidkun Quisling's yacht?"

"The photograph taken by the Grevinne Arnfeldt-Laurvig. The one David Lyall brought to show you."

"That photograph was destroyed."

Forrester pounced.

"Which you know – how?" There was a moment of silence.

"I thought it was *you* who said the photograph you saw in Norway was missing."

"I said it was missing, not destroyed. But you know it was destroyed, don't you, Master, because you destroyed it yourself after you took it from David Lyall's rooms."

"The only photograph from Lyall's rooms that I destroyed, with your acquiescence, was a piece of Edwardian pornography."

"The photograph Barber extracted from the light fitting was certainly a piece of Edwardian pornography," said Forrester evenly, "but that wasn't the photo that was in there when we left the room that night."

"I fail to comprehend your meaning," said Winters.

"You must have been desperate, when we opened that light fitting. I'm sure you'd searched those rooms yourself, several times, and failed to find anything. You'd even taken the risk of striking Haraldson down, when he was searching them on the night of the murder – probably, I suspect, with your trusty air raid warden's torch. And in all the times you'd searched them, you'd found nothing. That's why you were prepared to seem so co-operative, letting us search them again. Then Harrison had his stroke of genius, unscrewed the switch plate and there it was, tucked just out of reach. The second we pulled it out, the game was up. Proof that you and Peter Dorfmann had been in Norway as guests of Vidkun Quisling. So you pulled a remarkable stunt."

"I don't know what you're talking about."

"In the guise of concern for our safety, you tricked Harrison into turning off all the lights in the college. You gave yourself the perfect excuse to close the room and stop the investigation for the night. And as soon as we had gone you went back to the Lodge, carefully cut the edges of an old postcard to resemble the scalloped edges of the print we'd seen, returned to Lyall's room, took the photograph that was there, and substituted your own. The pornography was a neat touch, by the way: it gave you an excuse to look shocked and embarrassed, it infuriated Barber, and it made us all look ridiculous. You even, under the cover of mild disgust at the whole incident, persuaded us to let you burn the evidence in front of our eyes, so there'd be no opportunity to confirm it was a substitute."

"Your imagination impresses me, Forrester," said Winters. "I just hope it doesn't infect your historical studies; if it became known this is how your mind works, it could seriously damage your scholarly reputation."

"Yes, scholarly reputation," said Forrester. "Let's turn to that. Because the photograph of you and Peter Dorfmann on Vidkun Quisling's yacht was only part of the problem. The other part was the manuscript you'd obtained from Count Arnfeldt-Laurvig."

"You have no evidence whatever that I obtained any manuscript from Count Arnfeldt-Laurvig," said the Master.

"I did not, Master – until I received my communication from Denmark today. The *Heimskringla* was lost, has been for centuries. And you had made your scholarly reputation by ingeniously reconstructing it from missing fragments and references in other Norse manuscripts. Then I began to realise how embarrassing it would have been if it had been revealed that you'd had the complete manuscript all along. That you'd had it, in fact, since 1937. That your reconstruction was no more than a transcription. That you had the original in front of you as you were supposedly making all your brilliant deductions. That you are an academic fraud."

"Show me it then – let me see it," said Winters, and there was a hint of desperation in his voice now. Forrester reached into the lining of his British Warm and drew out the book he had received at the Porter's Lodge that day. Winters' eyes glittered in the darkness.

"Give it to me," he said.

But Forrester held it away.

"This is what David Lyall pretended he had, but didn't. He'd learned about your visit to the Arnfeldt-Laurvig estate in the thirties, the fact that you and Dorfmann had inveigled the *Heimskringla* from the count, and he knew it was the perfect tool with which to blackmail you. So he created the illusion he had it, that he had the proof. That was why he questioned those Scandinavian students; that was why he wrote to Haraldson, luring him here with hints of encryptions and occult secrets hidden in the saga. He wanted you to be terrified that he could expose you as an academic fraud."

"This makes no sense at all."

"On the contrary, it makes complete sense. David Lyall was a meretricious second-rater who wouldn't have set foot in the door of Barnard College if he hadn't had you on his side. But you let him in because he threatened to expose you.

Then, once he was in, his demands kept escalating – right up to the Rotherfield Lectureship. You knew he didn't deserve it, you knew it should have gone to Gordon Clark, and you told him so. And that was when he brought Haraldson into the picture, threatening to show the manuscript to him.

"And it worked, didn't it? You believed his threat and strong-armed the committee into awarding the lectureship to Lyall. Because otherwise he might have robbed you of the greatest coup of your life."

"And what would that be, pray?"

"Control of MI6."

"I beg your pardon?"

"That was why Charles Calthrop was here that night, wasn't it? To discuss the prospect of you becoming the next 'C'. But what an irony that the very person he brought with him, a possible future leader of democratic Germany, was your old comrade in arms, Peter Dorfmann."

"Dorfmann and I were on different sides in the late hostilities, Forrester, or had you forgotten?"

"Ah, but were you? Or were you both working for the victory of Adolf Hitler – each using your own copy of the *Heimskringla*. Yours from the Arnfeldt-Laurvig estate, his looted from the library at Kronborg Castle."

"Using them how?"

"To construct an unbreakable code by which you and Dorfmann could communicate from the very heart of British intelligence about things like the Murmansk convoys."

Winters stared at him, saying nothing, and Forrester went on. "Think of it: you and Dorfmann, old friends from before the war, each possessed a book which the rest of the world believed did not exist. With a single word or numeral you could direct your friend in Berlin to a line or passage which meant whatever the two of you had agreed it would mean. It was the ultimate unbreakable code. It was the perfect arrangement. So perfect you were never detected. So perfect that even now the mandarins in Whitehall think you're a suitable person to be in charge of Britain's anti-Soviet spy network."

Forrester heard the sound of Winters swallowing. It sounded unnaturally loud in the silence on the tower.

"No wonder you danced to whatever tune Lyall played," said Forrester. "With what he'd discovered on the Arnfeldt-Laurvig estate it wasn't just your reputation he held in his hands – it was your life."

Winters had found his voice.

"All this rests on your assumption that I would betray my country. What on earth makes you think I would do such a thing?"

"You didn't believe you were betraying your country. You believed you were ensuring its future by ensuring what you referred to as 'the triumph of the Aryan race'."

Winters stared at him, frankly astonished. "Where on earth did you get that from?" he said.

"From certain articles in a magazine called *Clear Skies*, for which you wrote, between 1930 and 1933, under the name 'Hiberno'."

Forrester paused, but this time Winters said nothing.

"It was pure chance," said Forrester. "The day after

Lyall was killed I found myself on a train going to London with the man who used to edit the magazine. You may remember him: Roger Glastonbury. Not a political man at all, indeed a very unworldly one; I don't think he realised the significance of what you were writing at all." Winters was watching him intently now.

"But *I* did, when I went through the back issues in the vicarage yesterday. What was it you wrote? 'Nietzsche was right. Salvation lies only through the advent of the Superman. Where is he to be found? In the uplifting glow of the Nordic past; in the unsullied purity of our Aryan heritage, cleansed of all the accretions of lesser breeds.' Paraphrasing, perhaps, but not totally inaccurate. I'm sure if any of your intelligence colleagues had come across that and realised who Hiberno was, you wouldn't have been allowed within a mile of British intelligence. But they didn't, did they? And you found yourself in a perfect position to help give that Superman victory over your own country."

"The real enemy was Bolshevism," said Winters unexpectedly. "I was there, you know, not long after the revolution. Part of the British mission. I saw the Bolshevik massacres, the starvation, the destruction of culture. Do I plead guilty to wanting to protect my country from all that? Yes, I plead guilty. Do I plead guilty for wanting to save my race from the pollution of lesser breeds? Yes, I do. I risked my neck for Britain, Forrester. And I am about to be rewarded for it, by being put in charge of the fight against Bolshevism in its most dangerous form. Calthrop knows how much I hate Moscow and all it stands for; he knows

I am the perfect man to wield the sword of intelligence against our foes. And if David Lyall was endangering that, he deserved to die."

And without warning Winters seized the *Heimskringla* from Forrester's hands and struck him a crushing blow across the temple, sending him staggering backwards.

"As do you, damn you!" he said, and too late Forrester saw the blade glitter as Winters brought it down into his chest.

Where half an inch of the lapel of Forrester's British Warm slowed the knife sufficiently for his fingers to close around the Master's wrist. He pulled the older man close to him, and spoke almost in a whisper.

"I realised, by the way, why you had to hurry up to Gordon's room as soon as we found the body: *to scoop up the extra glass*. Because if Lyall had really been propelled *out* through the window, there shouldn't have been much glass on the inside, and of course there was. That was why your hand was bleeding. You were covering your tracks." And then, as his unarmed combat instructor had taught him long ago, Forrester swung himself upright again, so he and Winters were face to face – and the knife fell from Winters' paralysed fingers and skittered along the stones into the shadows.

"I saw what your pure Aryans did to men, women and children all across Europe," said Forrester. "I saw what your treachery cost this country in young lives that need never have been lost. You are a rotten, rotten man and I will make sure you hang for it." And then he heard the step behind him where the knife had fallen and knew he had miscalculated. Everything he had done and said had been on the assumption that they were alone on the tower – and suddenly he knew they were not.

"My husband is a good man," said Lady Hilary, "and you will not hurt him," and she brought Winters' knife slashing down at Forrester's unprotected neck.

Without a conscious thought, Forrester swung Winters around to take the blow.

For a moment he was looking beyond Winters' face, wide-eyed with pain and astonishment, into Lady Hilary's, as she realised what she had done.

And then Winters collapsed like a rag doll onto the chute that had brought him so close to the perfect murder, and slid out into the night, through the crenellations and over the edge of the tower, curving in a perfect arc until he thudded into the snow in the middle of the quad.

"Oh, God," said Lady Hilary. "Oh, God."

The tower door slammed back against the stonework and Barber came rushing towards Forrester, the headphones still on his head, Harrison close behind him still holding the army surplus recording equipment they had installed earlier in the day, with MacLean on his heels.

"It's alright," said Forrester. "It's all over. Everything's – sorted itself out now." And he sat down suddenly on a pile of building equipment.

Beside him, the hollowed-out book which had been masquerading as the *Heimskringla* fell open, and Harrison's microphone rolled out onto the frosted leads.

"We got everything on the wire recorder," said

Harrison. "And Barber heard it all as it came through. Well done, Dr. Forrester. Dr. Clark should be a free man by tomorrow morning." He clapped a formidable hand on Forrester's shoulder.

"Thank you, Harrison," said Forrester, "but I couldn't have done it without you."

32

THE GORGE OF ACHARIUS

The path wound through the gorge beside the stream, almost invisible in the mist. Forrester could see, at the top of the cliffs enclosing him on either side, the tortured pines clinging to the bare slopes of the mountain; but down here in the narrow coolness, immense cypress trees, luxuriating in the water far beneath their roots, rose majestically past layer after layer of the ancient rock worn away by the modest, persistent work of the tiny river that had cut the gorge.

Vetch, speedwell and asphodel had lodged themselves in the crevices, and as Forrester inhaled their scent on the morning air he felt as if he were breathing in time with the Minoan priest kings who had walked here four thousand years before, when Egypt was still young and the Tower of Babylon not yet built.

The air was thick with the murmur of bees and somewhere in the distance he heard the tinkling of goat bells and the questioning, plaintive cries of the kids. Then he turned a corner and squeezed past the gnarled and ancient pine tree and there was the cave, waiting for him since the day he had first taken shelter there.

Inside its dark recesses, he knew, was the stone, its pictograms and hieroglyphs ready at last to give up the secrets of the dawn-time of Europe, when gods were real.

He hefted the pack off his back, leant it against the entrance to the cave, and turned to the Grevinne Sophie Arnfeldt-Laurvig.

"Well," he said, "this is it."

ABOUT THE AUTHOR

Gavin Scott is a British Hollywood screenwriter, novelist and journalist, based in Santa Monica, California. He spent twenty years as a radio and television reporter for BBC and ITN, during which time he interviewed J.B. Priestley, Iris Murdoch and Christopher Isherwood, among many others. He is writer of the Emmy-winning mini-series *The Mists of Avalon*, he developed and scripted *The Young Indiana Jones Chronicles* for George Lucas, wrote the BAFTA-nominated *The Borrowers*, and worked with Stephen Spielberg on *Small Soldiers*. His film, *Absolutely Anything*, which he co-wrote with Monty Python's Terry Jones, was released in 2015.

THE BLOOD STRAND

A FAROES NOVEL

CHRIS OULD

Having left the Faroes as a child, Jan Reyna is now a British police detective, and the islands are foreign to him. But he is drawn back when his estranged father is found unconscious with a shotgun by his side and someone else's blood at the scene. Then a man's body is washed up on an isolated beach. Is Reyna's father responsible? Looking for answers, Reyna falls in with Detective Hjalti Hentze, but as the stakes get higher and Reyna learns more about his family and the truth behind his mother's flight from the Faroes, he must decide whether to stay, or to forsake the strange, windswept islands for good.

PRAISE FOR THE AUTHOR

"This is bound to be a highly successful series."
Hearthfire

AVAILABLE NOW

THE KILLING BAY
A FAROES NOVEL
CHRIS OULD

When a group of international activists arrive on the Faroe Islands, intent on stopping the traditional whale hunts, tensions between islanders and protestors run high. And when a woman is found murdered only hours after a violent confrontation at a whale drive, the circumstances seem purposely designed to create even more animosity between the two sides. For Faroese detective Hjalti Hentze and DI Jan Reyna, it becomes increasingly clear that the murder has other, more sinister aspects to it. Knowing evidence is being hidden from them and faced with deception on all sides, neither Reyna or Hentze know who to trust, or how far some people might go to defend their beliefs.

PRAISE FOR THE AUTHOR

"Unmissable and thrilling fiction."
Lancashire Evening Post

AVAILABLE FEBRUARY 2017

TITANBOOKS.COM

IMPURE BLOOD

A CAPTAIN DARAC NOVEL

PETER MORFOOT

In the heat of a French summer, Captain Paul Darac
of the Nice Brigade Criminelle is called to a highly
sensitive crime scene. A man has been found murdered
in the midst of a Muslim prayer group, but no one
saw how it was done, and it soon becomes clear
that the man was doing anything but praying. Then
the organisers of the Nice leg of the Tour de France
receive an unlikely terrorist threat. In what becomes a
frantic race against time, Darac must try and unpick a
complex knot in which racial hatred, sex and revenge
are tightly intertwined.

AVAILABLE NOW

TITANBOOKS.COM

BABAZOUK BLUES

A CAPTAIN DARAC NOVEL

PETER MORFOOT

In the heart of the old town of Nice, the Babazouk, a woman's body is found. A quarter rich with the smell of Moorish coffee and fresh fish, the Babazouk is also Captain Paul Darac's own home, and he and his officers from the Brigade Criminelle are called to the scene. Then it is discovered that the woman suffered from a heart condition and her death is put down to natural causes, but Darac becomes fascinated by the woman's life and the anomalies of the case. He must put aside allegiances past and present to disentangle a story of greed and murder – and become a target himself.

AVAILABLE APRIL 2017

TITANBOOKS.COM

For more fantastic fiction, author events, competitions,
limited editions and more

Visit our website
titanbooks.com

Like us on Facebook
facebook.com/titanbooks

Follow us on Twitter
@TitanBooks

Email us
readerfeedback@titanemail.com